The Blue F

James

© 2025 James E Arnold

All rights reserved. No part of this publication may be reproduced, stored in a retrieval system, or transmitted in any form or by any means without the prior written permission of the author.

To my wife Susan, thanks for your support.

Chapter One

He dragged his feet toward a lamppost that didn't smell of dog piss, unusual for this street. Pulling his grey hood low, he leaned against the post.

Careful, he scanned the quiet street. No one around. Dark clouds rolled in. Typical London. No flashy cars.

A battered sign hung loosely on the lamppost: Resident Parking Only. Permit Must Be Displayed. Peeling paint. Front doors opened straight onto cracked pavement. He was glad he didn't live here, but it was perfect for tonight.

Footsteps approached. He tucked his head lower.

"Oi, what you doing here, you scruffy bastard? Go on, fuck off."

He smiled. He'd thought long and hard about this, his clothes, his look. Plenty of homeless about. He fit right in.

"Oi! You fucking listening? I said fuck off."

He said nothing. Turned, walked away.

"And don't come back, you dirty bastard," the man shouted.

No glance back.

Three minutes' walk. Timed exactly. Tonight was the night.

From his spot, he could see three ways: left to the Underground, right to the offices, and behind him, a shithole.

The street was getting busy. He'd parked his black Ford van four and a half minutes from the coffee shop, which was three minutes from the station. Now all he had to do was wait.

He'd watched her leave the offices many times, laughing, turning right past the Underground, calling into the coffee shop, then heading home past his van.

He'd even followed her once to be sure.

He glanced at his watch. A cheap eBay special. No one would notice. People only saw what they wanted.

Then she appeared. Right on time.

He loved how she dressed, always different.

Tonight: long black boots, short red skirt, a long-sleeved top, like a summer jumper for chilly nights.

She passed, no glance his way.

Thirty seconds later, he moved out behind her.

He crossed the road, eyes on his watch. Almost three minutes. A flicker of worry.

Then, the bell on the coffee shop door.

He quickened his pace, readying himself.

This was it.

As she neared, he stepped into her path.

"Careful, nearly had my coffee all over you."

"Sorry, miss. I didn't see you."

For the first time, he looked at her. Short, styled black hair. Red lipstick. A red choker.

He stepped aside but pretended to stumble, reaching out to steady himself.

She reached to catch him and never saw the needle until it plunged into her arm.

Shock flashed across her face. Her gaze darted between him, her hand, and the coffee spilling on the ground.

He grabbed her, pushed her into his van's side door. Lifting her legs in, he shut the door and was driving away in under ninety seconds.

Perfect.

His route was flawless. First stop: supermarket car park, four minutes away. Fifteen seconds early.

He parked far from the store, scanned the area, then climbed into the van's rear.

She was out cold. Would be for at least ten minutes.

He gave her another injection. Quiet until we get home.

Grey duct tape wrapped tightly around her mouth. Hands tied and secured to a support bar.

He removed her boots, running his hands over smooth legs.

Paused above her knees.

One last step: legs and ankles tied, then hogtied. Black ski mask over her head.

Settling behind the wheel, he glanced back.

"Soon, babe. Soon, you and I will have some fun."

Chapter Two

The drive took just over an hour. Back roads mostly. He knew every camera, every turn. Daylight, rain, dark, it was all instinct now.

The van slowed on a gravel path veering from the main road. Trees closed in on both sides, blocking views. Old farmland. Derelict sheds no one cared about.

Outside a rusted corrugated steel building, paint long peeled, he stopped. A handmade padlock secured a heavy bolt.

Inside, cool, damp air smelled of oil and old wood.

His place.

No cameras. No neighbours. No chance.

He locked the van and slid open the side door.

Tools lined the walls: old vices, chains, hooks. Nothing suspicious. Just a forgotten workshop.

Behind a hidden wall was his true project.

Unlocking the concealed door, he stepped into a second room.

Clean. Cold. Tiled floor.

A steel frame bed bolted to the floor. Shackles at each corner.

A chair. A small fridge. Buckets. A drain in the floor's centre.

One bright overhead light.

She stirred as he carried her inside, twitching, murmuring behind the tape.

He laid her on the bed, locked her ankles.

"Welcome home," he said softly.

She groaned, dazed.

He smiled, brushing hair from her face. "We've got time to get to know each other."

Another syringe slid into her arm.

"You'll wake soon. Not yet."

She went limp.

Helpless. Bound. Utterly his.

He licked his lips.

There would be rules. Pain.

And when bored, his mark.

He already had the tattoo gun.

Something permanent.

The walls were soundproofed with thick plaster, chipboard, insulation boards, all painted in old gloss for easy cleaning. Nothing fancy, just effective. He'd thought of everything.

The bulb above the bed buzzed faintly. He liked the hum.

No window. No clock.

Time didn't exist here. Not for her.

He watched her chest rise and fall.

A ceiling camera fed to a monitor in the other room. He'd spent months wiring it. She'd never be alone, even when he wasn't watching.

A diary lay on the bench. He flipped through dog-eared pages, noting names, dates, and brief descriptions.

Some lasted two weeks. Others less than five days.

It depended on how they played.

How long they kept him interested.

He pulled on latex gloves and unzipped a heavy canvas bag.

Inside were restraints, wipes, painkillers, scissors, lube, gloves, cloth, and the tattoo gun.

He held it up, admiring its smooth shape.

She would wear his mark.

They all did.

Every woman bore a tattoo below her right ribcage. His signature. A delicate, unique design, personal to their time together.

His hands moved gently over her body.

Not for pleasure. Control.

Her breathing shifted. She was close to waking.

He kissed her forehead.

"Sleep for now, pretty thing. We've got lots to talk about when you wake."

He turned off the light and left her in darkness.

Chapter Three

The dream faded like smoke.
Her hand slipping from his. The warmth leaving the bed.
That same soft whisper just out of reach before silence.
He always woke too soon.
Always alone.

Detective David Owen stared at the ceiling, unmoving.
The bedroom smelled stale. An empty bottle on the nightstand. An ashtray filled with burnt-out cigarettes from sleepless nights. The curtains hadn't been opened in weeks. Light crept through in dull, filtered grey.
He sat up, throat dry.
Pain throbbed behind his eyes, always there, but sharper this morning.

His flat was barely a home now. One cramped bedroom, a kitchen he never used, and a living room stacked with unopened boxes. He wasn't meant to stay here so long. After she died, time froze. He left their old flat behind. Too many memories. Too many things that smelled like her.
But here, in this place, she haunted him worse.

His phone buzzed again.
DCI Patterson: "Owen. Call me. Now."
He didn't answer. Tossed the phone on the bed and shuffled into the shower.

Cold water hit him like a shock. Enough to pretend he was still functioning.
Twenty minutes passed in silence.

He grabbed his wallet, keys, badge. Paused at the door. On the wall was the only photo he kept. Her wind-tousled hair. Smiling as she pressed into his neck by the coast. His fingers lingered on the frame. Just a second longer. Then he left.

The London morning was grey and wet. Of course.
He parked outside the station and lit a cigarette before going in. It tasted like shit but gave his hands something to do.

DCI Patterson waited at the top of the stairs, arms folded.
"You look like hell."
Owen exhaled smoke. "Feel worse."
"You're not going to like this one."
"I never do."

Patterson handed him a tablet.
"CCTV stills. Woman taken outside a coffee shop. Broad daylight. Busy street. Less than two minutes from first contact to van doors shut."

Owen scrolled. The image showed a young woman. Red skirt. Short black hair. Coffee in hand mid-step as a hooded man blocked her path.
"She fit a type?"
"No witnesses?"
"One. Useless. Thought it was a domestic spat. We only got a partial plate match."

"Of course."
"We've got an analyst pulling traffic camera footage between here and the A23. But she's gone, Owen. Like smoke."
"Show me the scene."

"One more thing." Patterson led him to the car.
"What now?"
"I'm assigning you a partner. New blood. Transfer from Essex."
Owen stopped.
"I don't need a partner."
"You do. She's good. Calm. Sharp. No nonsense. Try not to scare her off in the first hour."
Owen sighed.
"Great. Just what I need. A babysitter."

Chapter Four

The rain hadn't let up.
When Owen and Patterson pulled into the narrow, cordoned-off street near the coffee shop, a light mist hovered. Yellow tape fluttered weakly, tied to bollards and lampposts. A forensic tech stood by the curb, camera hanging from his neck like dead weight. Nothing left to find.

The spot where the abduction happened was just damp pavement and a half-crushed paper coffee cup. No blood. No screams. No sign of a struggle.
That was the worst kind of scene. The clean ones.

"Here she is," Patterson said quietly, nodding ahead.

A woman stood beside a marked car at the tape's edge. Tall. Late twenties or early thirties. Dark shoulder-length hair tied back. Black trousers, boots, and coat. No umbrella. She didn't flinch at the rain.

Seeing them approach, she straightened and nodded.
"Detective Constable Brooke Daniels."
Her voice was steady. No nerves.

Owen gave her a once-over. Clean-cut. Smart eyes. No badge on her belt. Didn't like drawing attention to it. Good sign.
"Detective Inspector Owen." He offered a curt handshake, his fingers cold and damp. "You know why you're here?"
"I read the file. Watched the footage on the drive."
He raised an eyebrow. "Fast."
"Worth getting ahead."

Patterson smirked but said nothing.
Owen gestured to the scene. "Van pulled in here. Picked up on CCTV and was parked here for a total of sixteen and a half minutes. She came out of the shop. He cut her off, injected her, pushed her into the van. Ninety seconds flat."
"And with all that CCTV we only got a partial reg of the van?"
"Yes. Lima, Oscar. It drove off. No plate on the rear at least," Brooke said.

Brooke knelt beside the cup. Looked up at buildings, angles, camera placements, reflections. Quiet. Thorough.
"No one helped?"

"One man shouted at the guy earlier. Thought he was homeless. Ignored him after. Didn't even register the woman."

Brooke's brow furrowed but she said nothing. Owen caught it.
"You see something?"
"Indifference," she said. "Worse than fear. People see a man in a hoodie near a van, assume the worst, then keep walking."

He was about to respond when her phone buzzed. She read a message, then looked at Owen.
"Traffic analyst flagged an ANPR hit on a black Ford Transit. Partial plate match. Northbound on A23. Disappeared five miles out."
Owen nodded. "Could be him. Or someone with a similar van. Doesn't mean she's alive."
Brooke gave him a level stare. "Also doesn't mean she's dead."

The words hung between them. Owen said nothing. Patterson glanced between them.
"You two keep digging. Owen, give her the floor. She knows timelines."
Owen flicked ash from his cigarette, looking at Brooke. "Show me what you've got, Daniels."

They spent the afternoon walking routes, checking angles, reviewing footage frame by frame.
Brooke worked methodically, asking the right questions. She didn't try to impress. She just did the job.
Owen wasn't sure if he respected that or resented it.

As dusk crept in, Brooke turned to him quietly.
"You don't sleep much, do you?"
Surprised, he said, "What gave it away?"
"You've lit five cigarettes in two hours, haven't finished one. Keep rubbing your left hand. Old injury? Something you can't stop remembering? And you haven't checked your phone once. Usually means no one's waiting at home."

He said nothing.
She added, "I'm not here to babysit you, sir. But if we're working together, I need to know you won't self-destruct halfway through."

He stared at her a long moment. Then laughed shortly.
"You remind me of someone."
"Good or bad?"
He stubbed out his cigarette. "Haven't decided yet."

Chapter 5

He had disposed of the van as planned, and just to be certain, set it ablaze. The fire would burn long after he was gone. The spot was fifty-five minutes away, remote enough to avoid attention. His backup vehicle waited five minutes from there, ready for a quick escape.

At last. Home.
He thought it quietly, but the day wasn't over yet.

A soft noise caught his ear. He glanced at the CCTV feed.

"Ah, you're awake, my little beauty. Time for us to get to know each other."

She held her breath, heart pounding as the key turned in the lock. Blindfolded, the darkness was total. Her senses sharpened with every scrape, every creak. The door's hinges protested. The faintest whisper of movement filled the air. Then, the weight of a presence beside her.

She struggled. Every muscle tensed. But her limbs were tied, stretched taut to the four corners of the bed. No escape.

"Now, now, darling... or should I call you April? Such a lovely name." His fingers brushed her cheek. She flinched, but her scream was swallowed, muffled and meaningless.

Slowly, the blindfold came off. The faintest light cut through the darkness, harsh against her eyes. She squinted, trying to adjust, fighting panic as she tugged on the restraints.

"Careful now. Wouldn't want you to hurt yourself," he said softly, a cruel calm in his voice.

Her wide eyes tracked his every move as he reached into a bag and pulled out a large pair of scissors. Her breath hitched, terror flooding her mind.

"April, will you be a good girl for me?" His words dripped with sick patience.

She froze. No nod, no answer.

"Listen carefully." He shook her gently, demanding her attention. She nodded, eyes locked on the cold steel.

"I'm going to remove your gag. You can scream all you want. No one will hear you. And if you try to make a sound, I'll make the gag tighter. Understand?"

This time, a hesitant nod.

The tape peeled away, leaving her lips numb and dry as dust.

"Please... let me go. I won't tell anyone. Please." Her voice cracked, fragile and desperate.

"You've just arrived, April," he whispered. "Behave, make me happy, and I might let you go soon. Do you understand?"

Tears traced silent paths down her cheeks. Another nod.

"Now, let's get you ready." The scissors glinted as he carefully cut away her skirt and top, then her red thong and lace bra. She was left exposed, vulnerable beneath the cold light.

He sat back, eyes fixed on her bare skin, then slowly pressed the blades of the scissors against her nipple.

A scream tore from her throat. "Please, no! I'll do anything, just don't hurt me!"

A dark smile crept across his face. "I know you will, April. But don't worry. This is just a tease."

He nodded toward a corner. "There's food and water there. Behave, or you get nothing."

"Please... what have I done to you?"

"Nothing, my dear April. Nothing at all." His voice dropped low. "If you need the toilet, there's a drain over there. Some snacks, water, and even a bit to wash with."

He removed the restraints that held her to the bed, then added a chain to her ankle.

The heavy chain clicked as he locked it around her ankle, the other end secured to the bed. It was just long enough to reach the necessities, but no further.

No more words. The door slammed. The key turned. The bolts slid into place.

Darkness swallowed the room, except for a faint glow near the meagre provisions.

She waited, listening.
No footsteps.
No returning presence.

Summoning every ounce of courage, she swung her legs over the bed's edge.

The chain's weight pulled at her ankle, heavy and unyielding.

She stumbled forward, dizzy, hands searching blindly until she reached the chain's limit.

Cold seeped into her skin, raw and biting. Naked. Exposed. She tried to cover herself, but it was futile.

Her hands found the water bottle, the chocolate bar, the packet of crisps, and a small pack of biscuits.

She slid down the wall, the cold floor biting through her skin. Sobs shook her body.

She screamed. Shouted into the void. But no one came.

Chapter 6

The station felt colder than usual.

David Owen stared blankly at the wall. The images of the burnt-out van burned deeper into his mind than the smoke had scorched the metal. That was it. Nothing else. No leads. No clues. Just ashes and silence.

Brooke Daniels hovered nearby, her fingers drumming restlessly on the desk.

"We've scoured the area. No footprints. No tyre tracks. Like it never happened."

Owen shook his head, voice low and bitter. "He's a ghost. Moves through the city unseen. Untouchable. And every time we get close, it's like he disappears."

The weight of helplessness pressed down on them both. The van, the only tangible piece of the nightmare, was nothing but a burnt-out shell.

Brooke's eyes flickered with frustration. "What if there's no pattern? No logic to follow?"

Owen didn't answer. He lit a cigarette. The smoke curled in the dim light. The growing cold inside him spread.

The killer was still out there. Watching. Waiting.

And they were nowhere near catching him.

"We must have missed something." Brooke flipped open her laptop and began typing.

Owen looked over. "What are you searching for?"

"I don't know. I just have a gut feeling. I'm cross-referencing missing women from the past two years with age, physical description, and location. Something's bothering me."

A few tense moments passed. Then she stopped.

"Bingo. Owen, take a look at this."

She turned the screen toward him.

"Three other disappearances in the last eighteen months. Different boroughs. Different circumstances. But one similarity. Single women. Similar age. Same physical build. Each vanished without a trace. No ransom. And the first body turns up two weeks later. Beaten. Raped. And left with a mark."

"A mark?" Owen asked, leaning closer.

"A tattoo," Brooke said quietly. "A blue tattoo. Same place each time. Just under the right breast."

Owen stared at the screen. "You think it's him?"

"Yes. I think he's been doing this longer than we thought."

The office door opened. Patterson stepped inside, coffee in hand.

"The higher-ups are breathing down my neck. The media's already sniffing around. What have we got?"

Brooke straightened. "Sir, we found the van, but it's been torched. Probably nothing usable. That said, we've pieced together a rough timeline. She left the coffee shop at five ten. A regular habit. Same time every day. We believe he was watching her for a while. He timed it. Ninety seconds. Grab her, drug her, disappear."

She glanced at Owen, then back at Patterson.

"Sir, we'd like access to cold case files. Women matching this profile."

Patterson frowned. "You think this is a serial?"

Brooke nodded. "I think we've only seen the tip of it."

Owen lit another cigarette, ignoring the no-smoking sign. "He's not going to stop. He enjoys the chase."

Patterson paced the room.

"Alright. Put a couple of the others on the van. You two start pulling cold files. If there's a pattern, I want to know about it fast."

He turned and left without another word.

Brooke looked at Owen. "If he's that precise. That organised. What if he's watching us too?"

Owen didn't reply. He stared at the cigarette burning between his fingers, the smoke drifting into the still air.

Chapter 7

The room was a tomb of shadows, broken only by the faint light near the meagre supplies. April's heart hammered like a trapped bird as the door creaked open again. His presence was a cold wave, crushing her hopes.

She flinched instinctively and lowered her eyes. It was now or never. She sprang up, striking him with her fists.

It had no effect. He slapped her hard across the face, sending her crashing back onto the bed.

"Now that was silly, wasn't it? What did you think you could achieve by doing that? Now, you must pay."

He came to her side, rough hands grabbing her arms and dragging her back down. She struggled as he re-tied her to the bed. The ropes bit cruelly into her wrists, silencing her frantic resistance.

Her muffled cries and sobs were swallowed by the thick silence. Every desperate plea went unheard. He didn't speak. He only moved with a chilling calm that made her blood run cold.

When the blows came, they were sudden and sharp. Fists pounded into her body, bruises blooming beneath her skin. She curled inward, trembling, every breath a ragged gasp against the relentless pain.

She wanted to scream, but the gag smothered her voice. The room spun. Darkness pressed in as tears streamed unchecked, mixing with the sting of fresh wounds.

Then came the unbearable weight of violation. The shadow of control seeped into every corner of her being, a desecration that shattered what was left of her will.

There was no consideration for how she felt. He forced her legs apart without care. She held her breath as he entered her.

When it was over, she lay broken and trembling beneath him, the cold sweat of fear and pain coating her skin. She felt his semen run from her.

But he wasn't finished.

The needle gleamed wickedly in the dim light as he reached into his bag once more.

"Your mark," he whispered. His voice was soft but filled with menace. "A reminder."

The tattoo needle bit into her skin. Sharp. Burning. Unforgiving. She bit her lip until it bled, tears blurring her vision as the dark symbol took shape.

Each puncture was a cruel promise. This was not just pain. It was ownership. A brutal brand on a broken soul.

When it ended, he stepped back, cold eyes lingering on the fresh wound. Without a word, he untied her, then turned and locked her away in silence once more.

April lay there, trembling and aching. The mark burned beneath her skin—a cruel reminder that her nightmare was only just beginning.

She lay on the cold, hard mattress, her body a map of pain. Bruises bloomed in dark purples and blues. Fresh cuts stung with every shift. The fiery ache of the tattoo throbbed just below her ribs. Every breath was a jagged shard. Every movement, a fresh reminder of the torment she had endured.

Her mind spiralled in a whirlwind of fear and confusion. How had it come to this? How had her world shattered so completely in just hours?

Tears welled, but she swallowed them down, terrified that any sound might bring him back. The silence was a fragile shield. But it pressed down on her like a weight too heavy to bear.

She traced a trembling finger over the tattoo. A dark, twisted mark etched into her side. The pain of the needle pulsed faintly beneath the surface, and with it came the crushing truth. This was no random act. It was a message. A claim.

Her sobs caught in her throat. She was trapped. Marked. Utterly alone.

But somewhere deep inside, beneath the terror and the agony, a spark flickered. A fragile ember of resistance.

She refused to let him erase who she was. Somehow, she had to hold on.

Chapter 8

Back at the station, Brooke Daniels sat at her desk, fingers dancing across the keyboard. Rain hammered the windows, blurring the city into a dull grey.

Her case board was slowly filling. Photos. Maps. Timelines. Red string stretched like a spiderweb, connecting the abductions.

Owen stepped quietly into the room behind her.

"Anything?"

Brooke didn't look up. "I might have something."

She tapped her screen, enlarging a document.

"Three unsolved missing persons. All young women. Same height range. Similar hair colour. All disappeared late at night, leaving work. No witnesses. No trace."

"Well, tell me something we don't know."

She glanced over her shoulder at him, unimpressed. "What bothers me are the gaps."

"Gaps?"

Owen stepped closer. He caught a faint trace of her perfume. Pleasant. Familiar. Something he hadn't smelled in years.

"There's no pattern to the time between abductions. Which is strange, because everything else lines up. Each victim was roughly the same age. All three were beaten, raped, and left with a tattoo."

"A tattoo?"

She nodded. "The first had one. The second had two. The third, three. Then nothing. For twenty-two months. Until now."

Owen frowned. "So, he went dormant? Or it's not our guy?"

"Or he moved. Or something interrupted him."

She pulled up another screen. Maps of boroughs highlighted in red.

"I checked property records. Two of the earlier disappearances happened within fifteen miles of where our Transit vanished."

"Warehouse districts," Owen said, recognising the areas.

"Old industrial zones. Quiet. Easy motorway access. No cameras."

Owen rubbed his jaw. "It's a hunting ground."

Brooke leaned back, unaware of how close he'd moved. Her shoulder brushed lightly against his arm. She tensed for a second, but didn't pull away.

"It gets worse," she said softly.

She opened another window. A grainy photo from a cold case file.

"One of the earlier missing women. This is the only case where a body might have been found. It was never confirmed. File was closed fast, labelled gang-related. But look."

She zoomed in on an autopsy photo. A crude tattoo. Small. Simple. But unmistakably deliberate.

Owen stared.

"The tattoo is his mark."

Brooke nodded. "His signature."

He stayed quiet for a moment, the photo casting a shadow over both of them.

"If the others followed the same pattern, he's keeping them alive for weeks before killing them."

"Exactly. We need to recheck the cold cases. See what might have been missed."

Owen's eyes darkened. "Then we're already on borrowed time."

Brooke turned to him fully now, voice low but steady. "We don't have long. If she's still alive, we need to find her."

Owen nodded slowly. But his gaze lingered. Not just on the board.

He looked at her like he wanted to say something more, but didn't.

Instead, he said, "I'm with you. All the way."

Their eyes held for just a beat too long before Brooke turned back to the screen.

"All right," she said, quieter now. "Let's get to work."

Chapter 9

Brooke sat in front of her computer, steaming coffee in hand, flipping through page after page of cold case files from the last five years. The words blurred together. At some point, she must have dozed off. Her coffee was cold, and Owen was asleep too, his head tilted sideways on top of his mobile.

Rubbing her eyes, she opened the next file. Her brow furrowed. Unease crawled beneath her skin. Her neck ached from hours at the screen, and her fingers trembled slightly from too much caffeine and too little rest.

"Here," she said suddenly, tapping a grainy photo. "This one was found six months after her disappearance.

Dumped in a canal near an abandoned mill. Cause of death: blunt force trauma. Case closed with no follow-up."

Owen stirred and leaned in, scanning the report.

"No suspects. No witnesses. And no one connected it to the other disappearances?"

"No," Brooke replied, pulling up the crime scene photos. "But look. Just above her right thigh."

She zoomed in. The resolution was low, but clear enough. Two small tattoos. Crude. Symbolic. Not decorative. Intentional.

"She has two," Owen murmured. "The first girl had one."

Brooke nodded. "And the third had three."

They both stared at the screen.

"It's not coincidence," she added. "He's counting them."

They exchanged a glance. The silence between them was heavy. Not just from shock, but from something deeper, unspoken.

"There's something else I want to show you," Brooke said. She turned her monitor toward him, pulling up a timeline. "This is what I've pieced together."

She pointed at the screen.

"First victim—Sandy. Went missing on December 4th, 2023. Found two weeks later on December 19th. Beaten, raped, and marked with a single blue tattoo."

Owen leaned closer, eyes scanning the data.

"Terri," she continued, "disappeared January 10th, 2024. Found in a canal six months later—July 12th. Two tattoos. But here's the strange part. The autopsy showed she'd only been dead for two days."

Owen blinked. "So, she was alive for nearly the whole time."

"Exactly." Brooke's voice tightened. "Then there's Alena. Went missing May 8th, 2024. Found August 8th. Three tattoos. Same thing. She'd only been dead a couple of days."

"They were both held alive for months," Owen muttered, shaking his head. "It's methodical."

Brooke exhaled. "And now, April. Missing since June 11th, 2025. Ten months later. So far, no sign of her."

"I don't get it," she added, more to herself. "He treats the women the same, but the gaps between them keep changing. It's like he's rehearsing. Perfecting it. But then changing things just to throw us off. Do you understand what I mean, Owen?"

He could see how stressed she was. Her hands were clenched. Eyes rimmed red from lack of sleep. He reached out and gently held her by the shoulders.

"Brooke. Breathe. You're doing great. Just slow down."

She looked up at him, startled, but didn't pull away.

"He's counting them," Owen said quietly. "Marking them. One. Two…"

"Three," Brooke finished, her voice flat. "Which means April is number four. And he's not finished."

She stood abruptly, grabbing her coat. "We need to find out who handled Alena's case. If someone saw the tattoos, we can backtrack it. There has to be a mistake in the report. Something they missed. Why hasn't anyone looked further into these cases?"

Owen rose beside her. "And we're already running out of time."

The car ride was mostly silent. The engine hummed softly, the rain a steady rhythm against the windscreen. Grey skies stretched overhead as they crossed into the borough where Alena's body had been found.

Owen glanced over at Brooke. She looked focused, eyes fixed on the road, but he noticed the tension in her jaw. The way she flexed her fingers on the wheel.

"You alright?" he asked.

She didn't look at him. "Yeah. Just thinking about the third case. It's bothering me that no one put this together before."

"Or didn't want to," Owen said.

They turned off the main road onto a narrow road flanked by derelict warehouses and rusting fences. An overgrown park bordered the canal nearby. Brooke checked the address again, then parked.

"This is it. They found her just under that bridge."

They stepped out into the drizzle, breath fogging in the cold air. The area was silent, thick with rot and neglect.

Brooke led the way down the gravel path along the canal. Owen stayed close behind.

"You think he brought them here after?" he asked.

"I think it was convenient," Brooke said. "Quiet. Forgotten. And I think we're dealing with someone who plans everything, but changes things just enough to stay unpredictable."

Owen knelt by the water's edge, staring at the bridge. "Still doesn't explain the tattoos. What do they mean?"

Brooke hesitated. "That's what's gnawing at me. They're not for the victims. They're for him."

She trailed off, lost in thought.

Owen looked at her. Really looked. The fire in her. The discipline. But also something raw. A heaviness in her eyes she kept hidden well.

"You know," he said gently, "you don't have to carry this alone."

She turned to him, surprised. Their eyes met. For a moment, the silence between them deepened. No longer just professional. Charged, but quiet.

"I know," she said, her voice low. "But it's easier that way."

Owen gave her a small smile. "Yeah. I used to think that too."

They stood there a moment longer, rain soft on their coats.

Then Brooke turned away and motioned toward the path. "Let's find the scene report. I want to speak to the original detective. Someone must have seen the tattoos."

Owen followed her, still watching as she moved ahead.

He'd seen many partners come and go. But this—this was different.

The case was heating up.

But so was something else.

Not ready to surface.

Not yet.

But definitely there.

Chapter 10

The room stank of sweat, blood, and fear.

April no longer knew how many days had passed. Time didn't move in here. It pressed down. Smothering. Eternal.

Her wrists burned from rope abrasions. Her throat was raw from screaming into nothing. She no longer begged. No longer cried. But deep within, something still flickered. Weak, but alive.

She heard him before she saw him. The routine never changed. Heavy boots on concrete. The rattle of keys. A creak of hinges. Then the light died behind him.

He stood in the doorway, watching her like a collector inspecting his prize.

She didn't bother to cover herself anymore. Resistance only made it worse.

"You're quieter now," he said. His voice was even. Almost pleased. "I like that."

She said nothing. Couldn't. Her lips were cracked. Mouth dry as sand. Her eyes stayed down. Her face expressionless.

He moved to the bed, unbuckling his belt. His breath came thick and slow.

"You know how this goes."

April lay still. Like a corpse.

The belt came first. Three lashes, maybe four. She barely reacted. He lifted her legs and entered her, hard and without pause. Still, she didn't respond.

He slapped her. Once. Twice. Then again and again. A final grunt. It was done.

But something shifted inside April.

Perhaps it was the exhaustion. Perhaps the rage.

Or maybe it was a quiet certainty. She wasn't leaving this place alive.

As he leaned over her, satisfied, her hand, loosened just enough after nights of careful wriggling, shot upward. Fingernails raked across his cheek, carving deep.

He gasped and stumbled back. Blood welled on his face.

She kicked, catching him in the ribs.

"You little bitch," he hissed, clutching his cheek as blood dripped through his fingers.

April screamed. Not in pain, but fury. She reached for the lamp. Her fingertips brushed it and knocked it over.

It was enough.

He snapped.

With a roar, he lunged. The first punch shattered her nose. The second drove the air from her lungs. Then came the storm. Fists. Elbows. Kicks. Like he was trying to erase her from existence.

She stopped moving long before he stopped hitting.

But somewhere inside, she swore that if she lived, if she ever got out, he wouldn't win.

When it ended, he stood over her, panting. His knuckles were split and raw. Blood smeared across his hands. Some hers. Some his.

April's body lay still. One eye open. Glassy. A hand twisted beneath her. Her lips moved once. Barely.

Then nothing.

"Damn you, April," he muttered. "I hadn't planned for this yet."

He wiped blood from his cheek. The sting was sharp.

Time to work.

He fetched the tattoo gun. Three small symbols. Each blue. The final one, a blue rose. Her mark.

A final insult carved into her body. Not for her, but for him. To remember what he had done.

When he finished, he stepped back, admiring his work. Then cursed under his breath.

She had ruined his timing. The next one wasn't meant for two more weeks.

He paced, grumbling, jaw tight. Then he turned back to the tools.

"Four for you, April," he said coldly. "Including the rose."

He had fallen asleep in his office, but the job wasn't done.

Time to say goodbye.

From the back of his van, now reeking of bleach and old blood, he retrieved a roll of black sheeting. He spread it on the floor beside her. Then, without ceremony, dumped her body onto it and wrapped her like waste.

He checked the surroundings. Quiet. No one around.

He hauled her into the back.

He knew the police were closing in. This one had to go far.

He had a plan. M25. M3. M27. Then the A31. The New Forest. So many lay-bys. So many people stopping for nothing.

He pulled into one. Engine idling. Watching. Waiting.

Then, calmly, he opened the side door and rolled her out. She hit the gravel beside a bin. Wrapped in black. Silent. Discarded.

It was just after seven a.m. when Brian pulled into the lay-by off the A31. The one he always used on early courier runs between Southampton and Bournemouth.

Mid-forties. Hardened to road life. He had seen his share of mess. But nothing like this.

He parked up, lit a cigarette, stretched his legs. The birds were chirping. The summer sun rose gently through the trees.

He wandered toward the bins, empty coffee cup in hand. That was when he saw it.

A shape. Wrapped in black. Too big. Too still.

He frowned, slowing his steps. The air smelled wrong. Metallic. Thick with something he couldn't name but his gut recognised instantly.

He moved closer, cautiously. A pale foot protruded from the torn sheeting.

His hand went slack. The coffee cup hit the ground.

"Shit."

He stumbled back, heart pounding, and fumbled for his phone.

"Yeah. I think I've found a body. A woman. Just off the A31. Lay-by near the forest. Please. Send someone."

He didn't go near it again. Just stood there. Pale and shaking. Eyes fixed on the plastic that fluttered slightly in the breeze.

Chapter 11

Detective David Owen stepped out of the unmarked car, the soft crunch of gravel beneath his boots the only sound in the early morning hush. The lay-by had been sealed off with police tape, a crime scene unit working quietly under a washed-out sky. The sun cast long shadows through the trees, making everything feel colder than it should.

Brooke Daniels followed close behind, notepad in hand, eyes scanning the perimeter.

"Male driver. Name's Brian Travers," she said, low. "Courier. Found the body just after seven. Called it in right away. Still shaken, but cooperative."

Owen gave a small nod and moved toward the white tent where the body had been moved.

A tech peeled back the sheet. April's body lay curled, the black plastic she'd been wrapped in folded nearby like discarded skin. Her face was a ruin of bruises, and her limbs were twisted in unnatural directions.

Brooke crouched, one hand covering her mouth. "Bastard did a real number on her."

Owen's eyes were already scanning. "There. Right thigh."

Brooke leaned in. "The blue rose."

"It's different," Owen said. "Sharper. Cleaner. That's not like the others."

She nodded slowly. "And it's the only tattoo he's repeated."

He stood silent; brows furrowed. "She's also the first with four marks."

"He lost control," Brooke said, flipping through her notes. "The others, he kept them longer. This one, he dumped fast."

"But he still made time for the tattoos," Owen muttered. "That rose wasn't rushed. That was deliberate."

They stared at the ink. It was delicate, carefully done. A soft blue bloom above a brutalised body.

Owen stared for a long moment.

"It's beautiful," he muttered. "And that makes it worse."

Brooke looked up. "It's a message."

"Or a mistake," Owen said grimly. "Let's talk to the witness."

Brian Travers stood near the cordon, arms folded across his chest. A paramedic had given him a blanket and a bottle of water. He hadn't touched either.

"I didn't go near her," he said as Owen approached. "I just saw something. A black bag, way too close to the bin. Thought it was a dead dog or something."

Owen gave a small nod. "Start from the top. What time did you get here?"

"Just after seven. Same run I do every morning. Pulled in for a quick smoke. Walked toward the bins. Saw the shape. It looked wrong. Plastic, but part of a foot was sticking out. Pale. Still."

"Any other vehicles around?" Brooke asked.

Brian shook his head. "No. Quiet. But I wasn't really watching the road, just trying to beat the traffic."

"Did you move anything?" Owen asked.

"No. Swear to God. As soon as I realised it was her, I backed off and called 999."

Owen studied him for a moment. "Do you have dashcam footage?"

Brian nodded quickly. "Yeah. Front and rear. You can have the footage."

"Good," Owen said. "Might catch someone leaving the scene."

Brian looked away, face pale. "It's not something you forget. Her face... Jesus."

"Thank you, Brian. We'll need a full statement with the officer over there," Owen said, turning.

Brooke hesitated; her brow furrowed. Something wasn't sitting right.

"Brian, just a minute. You've been asked twice if you touched anything. You said no. Right?"

"Yes. I said no. Didn't go near her."

Brooke folded her arms. "Funny. You said the bag was wrapped up, foot sticking out. So how'd you know it was a woman?"

Brian froze.

"And how'd you see her face?" she added, voice sharp.

Brian's eyes darted.

"Your phone. Now," Brooke snapped.

"This is bullshit."

"Shut your mouth and give me the phone."

Brian, grumbling, handed it over. It wasn't locked. Brooke opened the gallery. Her face changed instantly.

She grabbed him and slammed him against the car.

"Owen."

He stepped over. Brooke handed him the phone. The screen showed a photo of April's face, bloodied and bruised. Another shot of her body, zoomed in.

Another officer moved in. "Got him."

Owen didn't hesitate. "Get this piece of shit out of my sight. Tampering with a crime scene. And being a fucking pervert."

The officer cuffed Brian and led him away, still protesting. Brooke stared after him in disgust.

Owen and Brooke walked back toward the tent in silence.

Brooke opened her notebook. "What are you thinking?"

Owen's jaw tightened. "This tattoo. He's done it before, but never like this."

"Same image. Different execution," Brooke said.

"He's escalating," Owen muttered. "Or slipping."

She glanced at him. "Or both."

He didn't answer. His eyes were fixed on the blue rose.

South Central CID was quiet. The kind of quiet that came with dread. Evidence boards lined the walls. Photos. Maps. Timelines. All of it pointed to the same shadow.

David Owen rubbed his temple, watching the dashcam footage load. Brooke sat beside him, arms crossed.

The technician brought up the rear camera feed. The timestamp read 06:45.

"There," Brooke said, pointing. "Lay-by entrance."

Brian's van pulled in. The footage showed the shape by the bins, just barely visible. No other vehicles parked.

"Roll it back," Owen said. "Ten minutes earlier."

The tech rewound to 06:35. A quiet road. One car sped past, useless. Then another vehicle. Slower. A red van. No visible rear plates. The driver, a male silhouette, was just out of clear view.

"Pause it," Brooke leaned in. "That's him."

"Can't see his face," Owen muttered.

The van disappeared offscreen.

"Enhance the frame," Owen said. "I want everything. Paint job. Markings. Shape. Anything that gives us a lead."

"I'll flag it with ANPR," Brooke added. "Red panel van, early hours. Might be custom. Might already be repainted."

The tech nodded and got to work.

Brooke turned to Owen. "Did you see how he drove? No panic. No speed."

"He's done this before," Owen said. "He has a routine. But April changed something. He killed too early. Dumped her too soon. And that rose... he wanted it found."

Brooke's voice softened. "You think she fought back?"

"I hope so," Owen said quietly. "I hope she made him bleed."

He stepped to the board and pinned a new photo of April's body. Beneath it, a print of the blue rose tattoo.

"Same design," he said, tapping the image. "But this one was different. Clean. Intentional. We need to find out where it came from."

Brooke already had her phone out. "I'll get prints out to every tattoo parlour within fifty miles."

"Not enough," Owen said. "Make it a hundred."

"Now we've got another job," Brooke said quietly. "Patterson wants us to speak to the family."

Owen rubbed his face with both hands, weariness sinking into every line. "God, I hate this job sometimes."

They drove in silence. The kind that fills a car like fog. Thick. Heavy. Impossible to ignore.

The only sound was the hum of the engine as they approached April's family home.

Brooke parked outside a modest three-bedroom semi on a quiet residential street. A couple of kids' bikes rested against a low wall. Curtains twitched. Life continued here. Curtains fluttering. Bikes abandoned on lawns. All except for the house where grief waited behind the door.

She glanced at Owen. "You ready?"

"Are we ever really ready for this?" he murmured. "What's the surname again?"

"Thomas. April Weaver. Mother's Susan. Father's Joe. Little brother's Tommy. He's only eleven."

They stepped out. As they walked up the short path, Owen's hand brushed Brooke's. Instinct. Comfort. Then he pulled away, unsure why he'd reached for her at all.

Maybe he just didn't want to face what was coming alone.

The door opened almost instantly, as if Susan Thomas had been waiting, sensing what was coming.

Her eyes widened. "Oh my God. No. Please, no. Not April. Not our baby girl."

Joe appeared behind her just in time to catch her as she staggered. He held her tightly.

"Come in," he said, his voice raw. "Please. Just come in."

Inside, the home was warm. Lived-in. A family home. Photos lined the hallway. April in a school play. April grinning in a party hat.

Brooke took the lead, with Owen stepping in when her voice faltered. They explained gently, carefully, choosing their words like surgeons.

"Susan. Joe. We wanted you to hear it from us first. Before it ends up in the news."

Susan clutched a tissue in her hand, shredded from tears. "Thank you. Thank you for that, Brooke. But please, please catch him. Don't let him get away with what he did to her. She was kind. She was funny. She was so brave."

Joe's face twisted in rage. "Whoever did this, he didn't just kill her. He tortured her. I want him dead. I swear to God, if I ever find him before you do, I'll kill the bastard myself."

"We understand," Owen said gently. "And we promise, we will catch him. He will pay for what he's done."

He handed Joe his card. "The family liaison officers are just arriving. They'll stay with you. Help you through all this. And keep the press away as best they can. If you do speak to them, be honest. But be careful. They'll twist anything to sell a headline."

They shook hands, though it felt like a cruel formality after what had just been shared.

As they stepped outside, the buzz of voices rose like wasps. Cameras snapped in rapid bursts. Reporters jostled for position behind the tape.

"Shit," Owen muttered. "Press. Just what we need."

Brooke nodded grimly. "Stick to the script. No comment."

A man in a rumpled jacket stepped forward. "Detectives. Micky from The Sun. Can you confirm, was April Weaver murdered by the same man as the other women? Are we looking at a serial killer?"

Both detectives answered, firmly and together.

"No comment. A statement will be released in due course."

They walked away without another word, the camera flashes lighting up Owen's face. Tired, hollow eyes that had seen too much death and not enough justice.

Chapter 12

South Central HQ – Incident Room – 11:30 a.m.

The air hummed with quiet focus. Coffee steamed in paper cups. Crime-scene photos blanketed the evidence board. A muted TV in the corner looped the headline:

Sky News: Fourth Woman Confirmed in Suspected Serial Case – "Blue Rose Killer" Claims Another Victim.

April Weaver's Facebook profile picture flashed across the screen, followed by a close-up of the Blue Rose tattoo. Clean. Razor-sharp. Sinister.

Detective David Owen stood with arms folded, eyes fixed on the image.

Brooke Daniels entered with a manila folder. "Lab results just came through."

"Tell me."

"She was raped. Multiple times. No surprise there, but the trauma was extensive. Broken nose. Fractured ribs. Internal bleeding."

Owen scanned the pages, his face tightening with each line.

"There's more," Brooke added, her voice gentler now. "Skin under her fingernails. Male DNA. Clean sample. No hit yet."

Owen exhaled slowly. "Good girl. She fought him."

Brooke stepped closer, her shoulder brushing his. "You think he's watching all this? The news, the reports?"

Owen was quiet for a moment. Then: "I'd bet my life on it."

Unknown Location

In a dark, cluttered garage, the man stared at an old tablet propped against a rusted toolbox. He rewound the news clip, pausing it on April's face.

"She's beautiful like this," he whispered.

He turned the screen toward a glass jar on the bench. Inside, a copper lock of hair floated in cloudy liquid.

"They're calling me the Blue Rose Killer," he said, amused. "You should be proud."

The tattoo image flashed again.

"She made me bleed," he murmured. "That wasn't supposed to happen. She ruined things. But that's okay. It gave them hope... and now I get to take it away again."

He smiled. Small. Restrained. Satisfied.

Back at South Central CID, Owen and Brooke stood side by side in silence. A flicker passed between them. Acknowledgement. Connection. Something not yet spoken aloud.

Brooke broke the moment. "Do you remember a case in Kent, 2017? Sharon Elliot?"

Owen frowned. "The name's familiar."

"She was attacked walking home from work. Gloves. Tape. No sexual assault. She scratched him. Left DNA, but no match back then. I pulled the file this morning."

Owen's eyes sharpened. "Could be his first strike."

Brooke nodded. "Exactly. She got under his skin."

She glanced back at the board where photos were pinned in chronological order. Her fingers traced the image of April's tattoo.

"What's this?" she muttered. "I'd forgotten. Look at this shape."

Owen followed her gaze. A triangle-shaped smudge, once dismissed, stood out on an older photo in Sharon's file.

His brow furrowed. "Didn't stand out back then."

"Maybe it should've."

Broadstairs – 11:55 a.m.

Sharon Elliot stood outside her narrow-terraced house; a chipped mug clutched in both hands.

The news had been relentless. April's name. That tattoo. Now dubbed a calling card.

Her phone buzzed again. More alerts. More images.

April's tattoo looked painfully familiar.

Her breath caught. A memory surfaced. Cold air. Panic. Silence.

A hand clamped over her mouth.
The sharp chemical reek of alcohol wipes.
The burn of a needle digging beneath her skin.

That triangle.

Her chest tightened. The man who'd taken her night wasn't finished.

He was just getting started.

Her phone rang, making her jump. CID flashed on the screen.

She answered with a shaky, "Hello?"

"DI David Owen. Am I speaking to Sharon Elliot?"

"Yes?"

"I was wondering if we could visit today?"

"Is this about that poor girl... April?" Her voice cracked.

"Yes. April was the fourth. We're trying to make sure there's not a fifth."

There was silence on the line. He could hear her breathing. Trembling.

"Okay. But I don't know how much help I can be."

"Thank you, Sharon. DC Brooke Daniels and I will be there around 2:30 p.m."

Broadstairs – 2:40 p.m.

They arrived at a modest terraced house. Sharon was pacing the front path, hands wringing together.

"Good afternoon. Sharon? Is it all right if we call you that?" Brooke asked.

"Yes, that's fine. Are you the two police officers?"

Owen introduced them formally. "May we come in?"

"Of course. Please, take a seat. Can I get you a drink? Tea? Coffee?"

They both politely declined.

"Sharon," Brooke said gently, "thank you for seeing us. I know this must be incredibly difficult after all this time. Can you tell us, in your own words, what happened?"

"Well... I was walking home from work. Around five-thirty. Same route I always take."

"Anything different that day? Did you take a new way, or notice anything unusual?"

"There was a man on the corner, fumbling in his pocket. Then he bumped me. Next thing I knew, I felt something jab into my arm. I just collapsed."

"Do you remember anything after that?"

"I think... I heard a sliding door slam. I found out later it was a van. I woke up in the back."

She stood, arms folded, pacing toward the fireplace.

"I'm sorry. I still get nightmares."

"That's okay," Owen said softly. "Take your time."

"He'd taped my hands together. Covered my mouth. Told me to stay quiet or else. I screamed. He punched me hard in the face. Everything went dark. When I came round again, he was tattooing me. Under my right breast."

"Do you remember the pain?" Brooke asked quietly.

Sharon nodded; eyes distant. "It was the burning that woke me."

"You're doing really well, Sharon. Go on if you can."

"I waited for him to turn away. Then I kicked him. I just kept kicking. He looked stunned. Then... he opened the door and threw me out. Just like that."

"You were incredibly brave," Owen said. "Did you get a look at him?"

"He wore a clown mask. I managed to grab it. Scratch him. But not enough. I could tell he was white. Strong. Taller than average. He lifted me like I weighed nothing."

"Do you still have the tattoo?" Owen asked gently.

"Yes. I... I never had it removed. I don't know why. Maybe part of me needed to remember."

"Would you mind showing us?"

She hesitated, then nodded. "If it helps."

She lifted her top slightly on the right. Just below her ribs sat a small gold triangle.

Owen knelt. "Do I have your permission to take a photo?"

"You do."

He raised his phone and took a clear close-up. Flash.

"Thank you, Sharon," he said, standing. "Please call us if you remember anything else. No matter how small."

She nodded and followed them to the door. As they got into the car, she stood watching, lifting a tentative hand in farewell.

Brooke glanced at Owen. "You didn't say much in there."

He nodded. "I was listening. I think Sharon was the first. He wasn't prepared. She wasn't tied up. He was sloppy. And that triangle... what's that about?"

"He was experimenting," Brooke replied. "Testing how to brand them. That triangle—it's like a test run for the rose."

Owen sat in the passenger seat, pulled up the photo of the tattoo, and zoomed in.

"Here," he said, handing the phone to Brooke.

She leaned in, squinting. Inside the triangle, almost hidden, was a faint outline. An intricate gold rose.

"Is that what I think it is?" she asked.

Owen nodded. "His first signature. Version one point oh."

5:31 p.m. – Winchester

She stepped off the train, brushing long auburn hair over her shoulder as she adjusted the strap on her bag. Tall. Slender. Early thirties. Her stride was confident, heels clicking softly against the pavement.

Her name was Rosie Osbourne. She lived just under a mile away. This was her routine. Train home. Quick walk through the quieter side streets. Keys in hand. She liked the calm. It made her feel safe.

Until tonight.

Behind her, a figure stepped out from the far end of the platform. Dark hoodie. Backpack. Distance carefully measured. Pace deliberate.

Rosie didn't notice.

The sun was still high—a warm summer evening. Traffic buzzed along the main road, but the path she chose—a shortcut through a wooded footpath—was quieter.

She paused to reply to a message, to her friend.

Wine or Thai tonight?

She smiled, typing back.

Behind her, the figure moved again. Close enough to see the glint of copper in her hair.

Close enough to know she was alone.

5:52 p.m. – Edge of the Woods

Rosie glanced over her shoulder. Empty. Just trees and birdsong. But her steps quickened.

She thought she heard something. A crack of a branch. Soft breathing behind her.

She stopped. Nothing.

She laughed to herself, shaking her head. "Get a grip, Rosie."

But she didn't see the figure slip behind the tree line. Watching her. Waiting.

7:00 p.m. – CID Lab

Owen watched as the technician zoomed in on the flakes of skin from beneath April's nails.

"We'll get a profile soon," the tech said. "Still nothing in the major databases. We're going wider."

Brooke handed Owen a coffee without a word. He took it gratefully.

"You sleep at all during the drive?" she asked.

He shook his head. "Not really."

"You don't have to carry it all yourself."

He looked at her. Not distant. Just tired. "I know."

They stood close. Quiet. The hum of equipment the only sound.

"You said April made him bleed," she said. "That means there's a piece of him out there now. That's hope."

He nodded. "Yeah."

Their fingers brushed. Neither said anything.

Brooke glanced down, then back up. Just for a second, her eyes lingered on his. Then she looked away.

7:35 p.m. – CID Incident Room

They arrived back looking shattered to find Patterson waiting.

"Bloody hell, you two look like shit. When was the last time you had a proper night's sleep? A decent meal?"

They glanced at each other and shrugged.

"Right," Patterson said firmly. "Both of you—go home. Eat. Sleep. And for God's sake, take a shower. That's an order."

"Yes, boss."

Later That Night – Brooke's Flat

It was close to 10 p.m. They managed to grab Chinese on the way. Owen hauled a holdall of clean clothes through the door—kept at the office for emergencies.

Brooke flicked on the light. "Come in. Make yourself at home."

He paused, taking in the warm, book-lined space. "Nice place. I figured you'd be all filing cabinets and cold pizza boxes."

"You're thinking of your own flat," she smirked.

He raised both hands. "Fair."

They ate quietly until Brooke set down her chopsticks.

"So... who was she?" she asked gently.

Owen looked up, surprised. "Who?"

"The woman. You wear it like armour."

He exhaled. "Emma. My wife. Died three years ago. Cancer."

She reached across and touched his arm. "I'm sorry."

He nodded, eyes down. "We fought it hard. Thought we were winning. But it came back angry."

"She made me promise I wouldn't stop living. But I've not exactly nailed that one."

"You're still here," Brooke replied. "Still fighting. That counts."

Next Morning – Early

A phone rang.

Owen stirred as Brooke entered. "You awake? We've got to go. Looks like he may have struck again."

"Bloody hell. Okay—I'm up. Give me ten minutes."

Ten minutes later, he was ready.

"Who called?"

"Patterson."

"What did you tell him?"

"I said he had just woken us up and you were getting dressed."

"You what?"

Brooke burst out laughing, nearly spilling her tea.

"You should've seen your face," she grinned.

Owen paused, then smiled. "You all, right?"

"Yeah. Much better after that rest."

7:05 a.m. – CID Incident Room

The place was chaos.

"Right—everybody stop what you're doing!" Owen's voice cut through. "Rushing won't help. Mistakes happen when you panic. Stop for five minutes, then start from the top."

Brooke grinned. "Nice speech. Officer White's compiled everything from last night. Ready to look, unless you need five minutes?"

Owen gave a faint smile.

Rosie Osbourne was now officially a missing person.

7:30 p.m. – Remote Location

The van stopped.

Rosie whimpered as the back doors opened. Cold twilight air seeped in. Birds faded into silence.

A shadow climbed in and pulled the doors closed behind him.

"Shhh," he whispered, brushing damp hair from her face. "No noise, Rosie. I've waited too long to ruin this now."

His breath was warm. Calm. Practised.

She trembled as he tightened the restraints.

Everything was clean. Gloves. Tape.

No blood.

Not yet.

This time, he wasn't rushing.

This time, he was back in control.

Chapter 13

The air was cold. Damp. Still.

Rosie stirred; her cheek pressed against the concrete floor. Her wrists throbbed, tied tightly behind her back, the rope biting into her skin. For a moment, she didn't know where she was.

Then it came flooding back. The van. The man. The needle.

"Hello?" she called weakly. Her voice echoed.

No answer.

She lifted her head and tried to sit, but her ankles were bound too. She winced as the coarse rope scraped against her skin. Somewhere behind her, a drip of water hit metal with the slow rhythm of a leaking pipe.

The room smelled of dust, engine oil, and something burnt. Not fresh. Industrial.

"I'm Rosie," she called again, trying to steady her breathing. "Please… I'm not going to scream or fight you. Just talk to me."

Still nothing.

But she could sense someone. Watching. Listening. Breathing.

She shifted, pressing her back against the wall. Her throat was dry, heart hammering, but she kept her voice steady.

"I won't try anything. I just want to understand why you picked me. If we talk, maybe it doesn't have to be so bad."

From the shadows, something stirred. A shuffling step. Then silence again.

Back at South Central CID, it was only 8:15 a.m., but for Brooke and Owen it felt like they had been there all night.

Brooke stood over a desk cluttered with reports. Owen was beside her, arms folded, brow furrowed. The CCTV footage from Rosie's last known movements looped on the screen. Still nothing new.

"She's been missing twenty hours now," Owen muttered. "Too long."

Brooke glanced over. "I know. There's not much to go on. The only CCTV caught her at the railway station. Then she vanished. Her friend, the one she was supposed to meet for that takeaway, said Rosie always cuts through the edge of the woods. Bit of a shortcut."

"Any word from the dogs?"

"Nothing yet, but they're still searching."

Owen stepped away and returned a moment later with two coffees.

"You all right, Owen? You seem pissed off about something else."

"No, I'm good. I guess... Brooke, let it lie. For now."

"Okay. Well, I'm here if you need anything." She glanced down at a notepad. "There was a report. Her sister called in. Said she missed several calls, didn't show up to work. But no sign of struggle. No evidence of foul play yet."

Brooke softened her tone. "You've been here all night."

"I couldn't sleep," he said. "Every time I close my eyes, I see that tattoo."

She reached toward him, hesitated, then lightly touched his wrist.

"We'll find him."

Their eyes met. A pause. Just a second too long.

Owen pulled back. Not cold, just cautious.

"Let's follow up on that van paint tip. Maybe it connects back to April's Street."

Back in the shadows

He watched her from behind the partition. Silent. Still.

Rosie had been clever. Friendly. Not hysterical. It intrigued him.

She reminded him of someone. Not April. Someone else.

He turned away and picked up the spray cans. The van had to change. No more red.

He worked quickly. Grey primer first, then a dusty navy. He swapped the plates too.

By the time he was done, it looked like something entirely different.

It was time to move. Take Rosie. Get to the backup location.

She heard him before she saw him.

"Please, just talk to me," she said. "I won't scream. I promise."

He stood there for a moment, just looking at her.

"Come on, Rosie. Time to move."

His voice was low. Calm. Not unkind.

He didn't drag her. He was gentle. Almost careful.

"Where are we going?"

"Somewhere different." He paused. "Now get in the back of the van. I'm going to gag you and tie you down."

Rosie didn't argue. She did as she was told.

Inside, she stayed quiet.

He lit the fire with precision. Drenched the rags. Trailed them through the corners of the abandoned garage.

The flames caught fast, spreading with a dry whoosh.

He didn't look back as he drove away.

Chapter 14

They arrived at the new location, a good ninety minutes from London. A rental property with a large garage, deep in the countryside. No neighbours. No light.

He unlocked the chains with gloved hands, carried Rosie inside, and left her on the floor.

It was an old mansion. He had checked in advance. It was a six-month lease. The owners were abroad. A quick look around confirmed two floors, four bedrooms, all fully furnished, with a kitchen and a very large lounge.

He picked her up and dragged her upstairs to one of the bedrooms. She stirred again as he laid her on the mattress, tying her to the bed. Her hands and feet were still bound.

"Where are we now?" she asked quietly. "Is this... it?"

He looked at her, really looked. Calm eyes. No screaming. Just watching him.

"You'll stay here for a while," he said. His voice was soft, almost kind. "Be good and it'll be easier."

She swallowed hard. "Are you going to hurt me?"

His fingers brushed her face, then her neck, as if checking for a pulse. His touch lingered.

"No," he said. "Not yet."

He stood, moving slowly around her. She trembled but didn't cry.

"I'll be back in a moment with some food and drink for you."

Keeping his word, he returned with a pack of water, sandwiches, biscuits, and a couple of pies.

Taking a long chain, he clipped it around her ankle and fastened it to the heavy bed frame.

"Now, Rosie, you be good. This chain will let you use the bathroom and eat your food. That's all. There are cameras in here, so I'll see what you're up to."

Her voice was shaky. "Thank you... do you have a name?"

There was no answer. He turned and shut the bedroom door behind him.

She lay there in the quiet, as darkness fell. Wondering what he was going to do. She didn't have to wait long.

He came to her after nightfall.

There was no rage. No shouting. He was clean, controlled. Cold in a way that felt worse than violence.

Rosie flinched when his gloved fingers brushed her arm but didn't scream.

Stay calm. Breathe.

She tried not to look at him, focused instead on the wallpaper behind his head. The design repeated, like a maze with no exit.

He whispered things she couldn't understand. Called her beautiful. Said she was special.

He undressed her as if it were a procedure. Precise. Silent.

Her firm, round breasts rose. Her nipples hardened at his touch, which seemed to amuse him. A pulse of shame fluttered in her throat. She hated that she could feel anything.

He ran his fingers up her legs, pausing over the recently shaved skin. She jerked away and the chain rattled.

"Please be gentle," she pleaded.

"How do you like your new home, Rosie? Nice soft bed?"

"It's... nice. Not what I expected."

"Oh? And what did you expect?"

"I... I don't know."

"Then just lie still."

It happened quietly, almost tenderly. He caressed her breasts.

My body is betraying me.

Then his mouth was on hers. She froze, torn between revulsion and some reflexive urge to respond.

Don't move. Don't give him anything.

His hand slid lower. She wanted to scream but pictured the cattle prod in his bag and bit her lip instead.

Somewhere safe. Think of somewhere safe.

A childhood beach. Sunlight. Salt air. The sound of gulls. Her dad laughing. Gone in a heartbeat.

First his fingers, coaxing a sound from her throat she hated. Then he entered her and began to thrust. Methodical. Silent.

Her muscles clenched. Sensation surged despite her horror. An unwelcome climax rippled through her. She gritted her teeth and squeezed her eyes shut.

I hate this. I hate that my body feels anything at all.

He said nothing. Rode it out. Finished.

Warm fluid seeped from her.

It was over, she thought.

He shifted. Pinched her nose. Forced himself into her mouth. Held there until she gagged. Then it was truly done.

He wiped a thumb over her cheek and kissed her forehead.

"Sleep now," he murmured. "You'll need your strength."

The door clicked shut. Darkness swelled. Thick as tar.

Rosie stared at the ceiling, counting the red dots of the cameras. One. Two. Three.

Stay alive, she told herself. Over and over. She mouthed the words until the counting dulled her heartbeat and the room slid into hush.

He looked back at her, almost relaxed.

This feels right. I'm back in control.

Somewhere near Oxford, the sun was rising.

Rosie Osbourne stirred. Bright sunlight shone through the windows. She could just manage to get close enough, with the chain still tightly locked to her ankle, to see the countryside.

Birdsong drifted through the walls. It felt unreal.

She sat on the edge of the bed.

Did it really happen?

He raped me.

Yet it wasn't what I expected, she thought. But I've never been raped before.

She looked down. Her thighs were sore. Her stomach hollow. She still hadn't cried.

Rosie looked around the room. He had been back. There was more food. Something to drink.

A bottle of water stood neatly beside a clean plate. A folded napkin.

Realising her nakedness, she looked for her clothes, but they were nowhere to be seen.

She pulled the blanket over her chest and sat in silence.

In the background, she could hear low classical music. The notes were soft and eerie, like the soundtrack to something she didn't want to remember.

Chapter 15

It was nearly 9:30 a.m. when Brooke and Owen arrived at the station.

They had barely stepped through the door when Patterson approached, holding a stack of fresh printouts.

"New tip just came in," he said. "Anonymous call. Woman said she saw a van parked near the woodland path Rosie used. Red, possibly maroon, but spray-painted badly. The caller said the paint was still wet. Plate was obscured."

"Did she leave a number?" Owen asked.

"No. Line went dead after she gave the street name."

Brooke frowned. "Why report it anonymously?"

Patterson shrugged. "Scared, maybe. We get plenty of that when these cases get media heat."

Owen scanned the report. "Cedar Lane. That's close to where her phone last pinged."

"I've already sent a team to canvass the area," Patterson said. "You two might want to visit the caller's location. She didn't leave a house number, but said she was near the corner shop. CCTV might have caught her calling."

Brooke nodded. "We'll head there now."

The morning air was warm. Summer was turning. That strange point in the season where the sun still shone, but the shadows started to stretch longer. They parked near the shop and approached on foot.

"Think it's legit?" Owen asked.

"Not sure," Brooke replied. "But why make a call like that if you're lying? She sounded scared."

The shop owner, a woman in her sixties with sharp eyes and a cleaner's apron, had already been spoken to by uniformed officers.

Brooke flashed her badge. "DC Daniels. This is DI Owen. Mind if we ask a few questions about the call that came in?"

The woman nodded. "She stood over there, near the noticeboard. Used the pay-as-you-go phone, then hurried off. Didn't buy anything."

"Did she look upset?" Owen asked.

The woman hesitated. "She looked... nervous. Like she wasn't sure she should be here."

"Do you remember what she was wearing?" Brooke asked.

"Dark jeans. Grey jacket. No bag. Hair was tied up, I think."

"Did she speak to anyone else?" Owen said.

"No. Came and went."

"Do you have CCTV?"

"I do. The council made us put it in a couple years ago."

Brooke smiled. "Good. Can we see it?"

An hour later, back at the incident room, they reviewed the footage.

The woman had her back to the camera, but it was clear enough to show her using the payphone, glancing around, then walking off toward a bus stop. She didn't wait for a bus.

"Something about her looks off," Owen said, narrowing his eyes. "She doesn't want to be seen. See that? She ducks her head every time someone walks by."

Brooke slowed the footage. "She came here for one reason. To report that van. Why not stay longer or leave a name?"

"Maybe she's connected to him," Owen said. "Or afraid of him."

Brooke looked uneasy. "You think she knows who he is?"

"It's a possibility," Owen replied. "Maybe even someone who got away once. Or someone he let go."

Brooke didn't respond, just stared at the screen.

Rosie sat huddled on the floor, wrapped in the sheet she had pulled from the bed.

The food was untouched.

She couldn't bring herself to eat. Every time she tried; her throat closed up.

The room smelled of soap, damp wood, and her own fear. The music played constantly. Strings and piano. Slow and haunting.

She rocked gently, arms around her knees. Trying not to think. Trying not to feel.

A camera blinked at her from the far corner. She could see the red light. Watching.

Every movement. Every breath. Recorded.

At some point, he entered again. Quiet as ever. She didn't hear him until he was standing over her.

Rosie flinched but didn't scream.

"Not eating?" he asked.

She shook her head.

"You'll get weak."

She said nothing.

He crouched beside her, resting his gloved hand on the bedpost.

"I brought you something else." He held up a dress. Pale blue. Clean. New. Her size.

Rosie stared at it. Her voice cracked. "Why are you doing this?"

He didn't answer. Just laid the dress on the edge of the bed and stood.

"You'll wear it later."

She lowered her eyes. "Am I the only one?"

There was a pause.

"No," he said simply.

He walked out without another word, and the lock clicked behind him.

Back at the station, Brooke leaned over the case board, eyes scanning each photo and document.

Owen sat across the room, jotting notes, but watching her.

"She's still alive," Brooke said quietly.

Owen looked up. "You sure?"

"She didn't fight back," Brooke replied. "That's what he wants. Someone who gives in. He's not done with her."

Owen didn't argue.

"She's buying time," Brooke added. "Trying to survive."

"We need something to work with. Anything," he said. "He's getting smarter. That van's gone now. Painted. Plates changed."

Brooke looked down at her notes. "But he kept Rosie. He didn't dump her like April."

Owen stood. "Then let's figure out why."

Chapter 16

Just after 7:50 p.m., the team pulled up together. Owen and Brooke were told to hold position as the armed response unit moved in. It only took minutes before the call came through.

"All clear," the radio crackled.

Owen stepped forward immediately. "Anything, lads?" he called to the team as they emerged.

"Not a thing, sir. Clean as a whistle."

Owen swore under his breath. "Thanks."

He turned to Brooke. "Come on. There must be something. Anything."

"Owen, wait. Just wait a minute. What's the matter with you? Keep it together… or go home."

He froze. The words hit harder than they should have, but she was right.

"Sorry, Brooke. This is just getting to me. We get a lead, and it's always nothing."

They stepped into the property. A small industrial unit, the windows painted black. Empty. Silent. It smelled faintly of bleach and something metallic. Too clean. There were no personal items, no dust, no fingerprints. Even the walls looked recently wiped down.

"Jesus," Brooke murmured. "This place has been scrubbed top to bottom."

Owen crouched beside a metal drain in the corner, peering down. "He's not just gone. He's erased himself."

One of the ARV lads poked his head back in. "You alright, sir? You shouted earlier…"

Owen didn't respond. He stood up slowly, tension behind his eyes.

They spent the next two hours combing through every room. Twice. Even three times. But it was sterile. No fibres, no hairs, no receipts, no DNA.

"Fuck," Owen muttered, slamming a locker door shut.

"Come on," Brooke said, rubbing her temples. "We're wasting our time. Let's get back."

Owen didn't answer. He just walked to the car and slid into the passenger seat.

"I guess I'm driving, then," Brooke muttered, slamming her door.

She paused, glanced at him, then snapped, "You're coming to mine tonight. I don't care if you sleep or pace the floor—you're not doing it alone."

He opened his mouth to argue, but the look on her face shut him down. She was properly pissed off with him.

Back at Brooke's flat just before midnight.

"Well, at least you got a little sleep," she said sarcastically as they sat in the parked car. "You coming?"

Owen got out slowly, feeling like a schoolboy being told off.

Inside, the flat was warm, lived-in, softly lit. She kicked off her boots and dropped her keys in the bowl by the door.

"I hope you like pizza," she added, flicking the oven on.

"Brooke… wait. Just… wait."

He rubbed the back of his neck. "I'm sorry for being an ass. I don't know what got into me. And yes, I love pizza."

She looked at him for a long moment, then gave a faint smile. "Come on, you. What am I going to do with you?"

He followed her into the kitchen.

As she handed him a slice, he held her gaze a moment too long.

Owen looked at her hand resting on his arm, then back into her eyes. Something shifted.
"If we don't catch him soon…" he began, his voice quieter now, "I don't know what I'll do."
She didn't reply straight away. Her fingers pressed just a little more firmly. "You're not on your own, Owen. Not anymore."

Owen looked at her hand again, then leaned forward and kissed her on the lips.

For a moment, she kissed him back.

Then she pulled away slightly, a small smile on her lips.

"I think we should eat, don't you?"

Chapter 17

Rosie woke to a knock at the door.

Strange, she thought, blinking into the half-light.

"Yes?"

"Good morning, Rosie. Did you sleep well?"

"I guess so, thanks."

She was confused. What is going on? But deep down, she knew she had to stay with it—play along. For now.

"I was wondering if you'd like a shower?"

She hesitated, taken aback.

"Ah… yes, please. Excuse me for asking, but what should I call you?"

Call me, he thought. Interesting. Then an idea came to him. They called him the Blue Rose Killer.

"You can call me Blue."

"Blue. Okay. Thank you, Blue."

He knelt in front of her, eyes never leaving hers, and unlocked the chain securing her ankle to the bed.

"Come, Rosie. This way."

She followed him, her bare feet padding across the cold floor, knowing full well she had no choice.

"Here we are then. There's shampoo and shower gel. If you need anything else, just let me know."

Rosie stood still, expecting him to leave. But instead, she saw a chair in the corner that hadn't been there before. He must have placed it earlier.

She thought better than to question him and stepped into the shower.

The hot water poured over her like a blessing. For a moment, it felt like she could wash everything away.

Please, she thought. Wash it all off. Wash me clean.

When she was done, she reached for a towel, but he stepped forward and held out his arm, helping her out.

"Thank you, Blue. That was… nice. Can I have the towel, please? And maybe some clothes?"

"Allow me, Rosie."

He began drying her, rubbing the towel over her face, arms, and chest. She tensed as his hands passed over her breasts, but forced herself to show nothing.

He knelt and began drying her legs, starting with her feet and moving slowly upward. He paused between her thighs. Her jaw tightened.

"Turn around, Rosie."

She obeyed, her heart pounding.

He placed her hands on the washbasin against the wall, then roughly spread her legs. His hand thrust up between them.

At first, he touched her with his fingers. Then, without warning, he entered her fully. His thrusts were harsh, almost lifting her off the ground. One hand reached around to grab her breast, squeezing hard.

Deep down, she hated him. Hated this. Hated herself for not fighting.

But if pretending meant staying alive, she would pretend.

She locked her mind onto the ring of keys clipped to his belt. One had a strip of red tape wrapped around it. Small, meaningless maybe—but different. She would remember it.

He grunted and stepped back. She could feel him finish inside her, warmth trailing down her legs.

He calmly adjusted himself, breathing quietly. As he turned to leave, she kept her eyes on the key ring.

"When you're ready, Rosie, we can have breakfast together."

"Okay, Blue. Thank you. I won't be a minute. I did ask if I could have some clothes?"

He turned back, his face calm.

"No, Rosie. I like seeing you naked. Always ready. Always mine."

Chapter 18

Rosie opened the bathroom door. He was standing there, just looking out of the window.

"Are you ready? Good. Let me get that chain."

His voice was calm, almost polite. That somehow made it worse.

Rosie watched as he unlocked it from the radiator and carefully carried it for her, instead of making her drag it.

"Well, Rosie, feel any better after that shower?"

"Yes, thank you, Blue."

He sat down and spread his legs.

"So, Rosie... how can you show how grateful you are?"

Rosie knew exactly what he wanted, and what might happen if she didn't comply.

"Well, Blue, I think this might show how grateful I am."

He smiled as she knelt in front of him and unzipped his trousers. She carefully removed his erect penis and began performing oral sex.

Her stomach churned. Don't gag. Don't flinch. Just get through it.

"There's a good girl. You know what old Blue likes."

After a short while, he pulled her closer. She gagged as he finished, forcing her to swallow. She felt sick, but wiped her lips with the back of her hand and stood.

"Was that alright, Blue? Is there anything else?"

"Not now, Rosie. Let's eat."

Rosie moved to the window and looked out. A breeze stirred the trees, and sunlight danced on the long grass.

Are people looking for me? she wondered. Are they worried? Searching?

What were her family and friends doing? She thought of an unfinished project at work—her laptop still open on her desk, coffee ring staining the paper beside it.

"Beautiful, isn't it, Rosie?"

"Yes, Blue. I've never seen so much green grass in my life. Is this your house?"

"No, Rosie. Just somewhere to stay for a while. Come eat. Egg and bacon, hot coffee, and a slice of bread."

"Thank you, Blue. I'm really hungry."

She glanced at him, searching his face for any sign of warmth. Nothing. Just a blankness she couldn't read.

She wondered what his next move would be. Would this be her last night, like the others?

She felt his eyes on her as she lifted the hot coffee to her lips.

"Blue, that's a great cup of coffee."

She smiled back. Not because she meant it, but because it gave her a second to breathe.

He said nothing, just gave a sly smile.

"Now, Rosie, I'm popping out for a couple of hours. Is there anything you need, not want—need?"

"I'm good, thanks, Blue. You seem to have thought of everything."

"One more thing, Rosie. Here. Make sure you take these."

He tossed her a packet of birth control pills.

She caught them, her hand trembling. "Yes, of course. Thank you."

As she looked down at the blister pack, her stomach twisted. The pink tablet reminded her of being fifteen, laughing with her best friend the first time she took one. Now it had become something else entirely. Something foul. Something forced.

"Okay, come on, Rosie. Back to your room. I'm sorry, but I have to restrain you."

"I understand, Blue."

She lay back on the bed, the chain clinking against the frame. He tied both arms and legs to each corner, then gagged her.

"I won't be too long, Rosie."

He bent down and placed a kiss on her forehead.

Moments later, she heard the door slam and the sound of an engine fading into the distance.

Rosie lay there, trying to make sense of it all.

Giving him what he wanted seemed to be working. But was it? Was it just another part of his twisted game before he killed her?

Two nights so far. How many more?

The taste of him still clung to her mouth, bitter and vile.

The smell of his skin still clung to her fingers.

She clenched her fists against the mattress, helpless.

No, she tried to scream, but the gag swallowed her voice.

She would do whatever he wanted.

She would smile.

She would survive.

I'll give him what he wants. I'll smile.
I'll win his trust.
And when the time comes, I'll be ready.

Chapter 19

He read the paper while sipping lukewarm coffee in the café's corner booth.

He was making headlines again. A grainy photo of a male suspect stared back at him from the front page.

He laughed softly to himself.

They fell for it.

He paid for the paper and the shopping. He was surprisingly good at hunting for bargains. He knew which stores had markdowns and what time they hit the shelves. He made a mental note to grab more bottled water next time.

Pulling out his notebook, he turned to a marked page.

Sarah. Long black hair. Good body. Works in estate agents.

He wrote the time beneath her name.

12:35 p.m. Lunch break.

He sat opposite the bus stop and waited. It wasn't long before he saw her, just as expected. Stepping out for lunch, brown paper bag in hand, her phone pressed to her ear.

Not today, Sarah.

He smiled.

But we'll play soon. You're going to be my reward. My little celebration. A proper treat after all this running around.

He drove into a multistorey car park and circled slowly until he found just what he needed. A black van. Almost identical to the one he had torched. He parked nearby, checked his surroundings, and quickly swapped the plates with a set he had brought in a Tesco carrier bag.

He stood back and admired his work.

Then, managing to open one of the doors, he placed a few key items inside. April's boots. A reel of duct tape. Some rope smeared with her blood.

A cruel little smile played on his lips.

"Perfect," he muttered. "Let Brooke sort that one out. Let's see how clever they really are."

The open-plan room at the CID buzzed with quiet intensity. Phones ringing. Keyboards tapping. Evidence photos pinned across whiteboards. A muted television in the corner showed a local news update, its captions crawling silently across the screen.

"Owen, Brooke. My office. Now."

Paterson's voice cut through the noise like a whipcrack.

They exchanged a look. That tone meant business.

They followed him in. He was already seated at his desk, sleeves rolled up, eyes tired but sharp.

"Close the door. Sit. Now tell me you've got something worth my time."

Owen pulled out his notebook and sighed.

"Well, sir… not much, if I'm honest. The raid was a bust. If he was ever there, he was long gone. We've got a rough description of the suspect, and there's a strong

DNA match, but no sign of Rosie Osbourne. This'll be her third night missing."

Paterson tapped a pen against his pad, frowning.

"Damn it. Brooke?"

She sat forward.

"We think we've traced his first victim. As you know, sir, he tattoos them. April was the fourth and had four tattoos. But the last one stood out."

"Different how?"

"Well… aside from the first woman, they all had multiple tattoos. The first had a single blue rose. The second had two, one of them another blue rose. But April's fourth tattoo was different."

"How?"

"It was bigger. More intricate. The work was better quality. More like a signature piece. It felt deliberate. Almost proud."

Paterson narrowed his eyes.

"You think he's evolving?"

"Maybe," Brooke said. "Or getting bolder. Either way, it's a lead. We're also working on tracing his previous cases in more detail."

"Well, work harder," Paterson snapped. "Because if you two don't bring me something real, and soon, I'll have you both back directing traffic in Croydon. Clear?"

Before they could respond, a constable knocked and stepped inside.

"Sir, Detective Owen. This just came in."

Brooke scanned the report. Her eyebrows shot up.

"Bloody hell. Owen... they've found a black van. The plates match the partial registration from the CCTV."

"You're kidding. What else?"

"They've recovered April's boots, rope with her blood on it, and an old reel of duct tape. The forensics team is all over it."

"They're bringing the van in?"

"Yes. But there's more. They arrested a man who approached the van just before it was secured."

Owen straightened.

"Does he match the suspect?"

"Not even close. White male. At least fifty. Overweight. Balding. Doesn't fit any profile we've got."

She tossed the report onto Paterson's desk with a shake of her head.

"He's screwing with us," she muttered.

"Or," Owen added grimly, "we've completely misjudged him."

Paterson stood, rubbing his temples.

"Recheck everything. Start again if you have to."

Owen nodded.

"We also need to canvas every tattoo parlour in the region."

Brooke groaned.

"That could be thousands. He's going all over the South."

"We don't need thousands," Owen replied. "We need one."

Rosie had drifted off again. The air was cold, stale, but her body welcomed the silence. She knew he wasn't there. That was the only time she could sleep without fear pressing on her chest.

Then… the door slammed.

Her eyes snapped open.

Should I scream? What if someone found me? But what if it's him?

She held her breath and stayed still.

Footsteps.

The door creaked open.

"Hello Rosie," he said cheerfully. "Sorry, that took a bit longer than planned. Let me take that gag off. Did you miss me?"

She blinked, then nodded slowly.

"Of course, Blue. Did you get done whatever it was you were going to do?"

"Yes, I did. Thanks for asking."

She forced herself to sound calm. Light. Even curious. He was watching her too closely for her liking.

Don't overdo it. Be sweet. Be curious. Not scared. That's what he wants. That's what keeps you alive.

"I might have a surprise for you soon," he said, sitting beside her. "I think you might like her."

Her heart skipped.

"Thank you for the magazines… and the newspaper," she said gently, accepting them. "That's really thoughtful."

He smiled.

"You can ask a question if you like."

She hesitated, then said, "Who might I like?"

He gave a sly grin.

"Now, Rosie, it wouldn't be much of a surprise if I told you, would it?"

She offered a small laugh.

"No, I suppose not."

He reached down to untie her wrists.

"There we go. Now relax."

"Thank you."

He looked her in the eyes.

"Now Rosie... you know what I like."

He sat beside her, watching. Always watching.

And Rosie smiled.

A little lie.

A little longer.

She would wait.

Because waiting was surviving.

Chapter 20

The office felt heavier than usual. Files stacked like monuments to unfinished business. The board was still cluttered with photos, maps, and red string. Rosie's face stared back at them, beneath April's, beneath Sharon's.

Owen leaned over his desk, rubbing his eyes with the heel of his hand.

"Tell me we're not just chasing our tails again," he muttered.

Brooke didn't answer immediately. She was knee-deep in the cold cases, files stretching back nearly a decade. Victims mislabelled as suicides, junkies, or simply gone missing. The forgotten ones.

"There's something here," she said at last, flipping a page.

He looked up. "Something, or you're desperate?"

Brooke didn't smile. "Both."

She slid the file across the desk. "Lucy Baines. Reported missing in 2017. Found two weeks later. Disoriented, malnourished, claimed she'd been taken. Said she escaped. Nobody believed her."

Owen frowned. "Why not?"

"Her story didn't add up. No visible injuries except rope burns. Her ex had a history. They charged him. She retracted. Case fell apart."

"Tattoo?"

"No mention. But get this…" Brooke tapped the page. "She refused to be examined. Said, and I quote, 'I don't want anyone else touching me again'."

Owen exhaled slowly. "Christ."

"Southampton."

"That's not far from the others."

Brooke nodded. "Pattern fits. Short-term abduction. Release or escape. And ignored because she didn't play the victim the way they expected."

Owen pushed back in his chair. "We missed her."

Brooke looked at him. "So did everyone else."

They sat in silence for a moment, the kind that hums with frustration.

The board was covered in women's faces. Young, smiling, alive. Before.

Owen stood and paced. "What if she was the first? Or one of the first? Maybe he didn't kill back then. Maybe he was just... testing the water."

"Then Lucy could be the key," Brooke said. "If she'll talk to us."

The door opened. Paterson stepped in, holding a mug and a mood.

"Tell me you've got something, or I swear I'll start flipping desks."

Brooke held up the file. "Cold case. 2017. Lucy Baines. Sounds like she was taken but slipped through the cracks. Lines up with the timeline and location."

Paterson sipped his coffee. "And?"

"She might've escaped the guy. If we can get to her, we might get a face, a name, something."

Paterson considered it. "And?"

Brooke raised an eyebrow. "That's not enough?"

"It's a start," he said finally. "But if the press doesn't get something soon, they'll eat us alive. You want me to keep the higher-ups off your backs, then find something concrete. Fast."

He left without another word.

Owen turned back to Brooke. "I'll try Lucy. You keep digging."

Brooke was already opening another file. "What are we even looking for?"

"I don't know. A pattern. A mistake. Anything."

Two hours later

The desk was littered with takeaway coffee cups and half-finished notes. Brooke stared at a name that had popped up twice in different cases. "Bluebird Ink", a tattoo parlour just off the coast in Brighton. She circled it. A coincidence, maybe. But nothing about this case felt random.

Owen returned, dropping into his chair.

"She moved to Leeds. Took some convincing, but she said she might be willing to talk—by phone. Doesn't want to meet in person."

"Good," Brooke said. "Because I might have something too."

Owen slid his phone across the desk. "Here. Give it a shot now, if you think it's worth it."

Brooke didn't hesitate. She dialled.

After a few rings, a cautious voice answered. "Hello?"

"Hi, Lucy? This is Detective Constable Brooke Daniels, Surrey Police. You spoke earlier with my colleague, DI Owen."

A pause. Then, "Yeah. I remember."

"I was hoping you'd be willing to speak now. It won't take long. I just want to ask a few questions about what happened to you back in 2017."

Another pause, longer this time. "That was a long time ago."

"I understand. But we're working on a case that might be linked. Anything you can tell us could be important."

Brooke kept her tone soft, reassuring.

Lucy sighed. "Look, I already told people what happened. Nobody believed me. They thought I was crazy. Or trying to frame my ex. He wasn't perfect, but he didn't… he didn't do what I said he did. Not really."

"Do you still believe someone else took you?"

"I don't know what I believe. I was confused. Out of it. Maybe I just wanted attention. Maybe I made more of it than it was."

Brooke frowned. "But you said you escaped. You had rope burns. You refused an exam."

Lucy's voice dropped. "Because I was ashamed. Embarrassed. I didn't want people touching me. But it doesn't mean I was abducted by some serial guy, okay? I've moved on. Please don't bring it all back."

Brooke was quiet for a moment. Then she said gently, "Thank you for your time, Lucy. That's all I needed."

She ended the call and stared at the phone.

"Well?" Owen asked.

Brooke shook her head. "She's either covering, or it really was nothing. Either way, she's not going to help."

Owen nodded slowly. "One less name on the board."

Before Brooke could say more, Owen's mobile buzzed. Unknown number. Local area code.

He answered. "Detective Owen."

A young female voice spoke on the line. "This the guy dealing with the blue rose stuff?"

Owen's brow furrowed. "Yes. Who's this?"

"Tattoo artist. Been in the game a few years. Someone came in about eight weeks ago, asked me to design a blue rose."

Owen sat up straighter. "Go on."

"Said he wanted it done a certain way. Real specific. Almost obsessive. But he never booked the appointment. Then two nights ago, he walked past the shop again. Didn't come in—just looked through the window. Like he was checking I was still here."

Owen already had a pen in hand. "What's your name, and where's your shop?"

Brooke looked up as Owen hung up.

"Well?"

He grabbed his coat.

"We're going to Brighton."

Chapter 21

It took a couple of hours to reach Brighton, and they had to rely on the GPS to find the tattoo shop.

"Brighton. Blimey, not been here in years. Not since…"

"Not since what, Owen?"

"Nothing. Forget it."

Brooke glanced over. There was something in his eyes—a flicker of memory, maybe sadness. She couldn't tell which, but she made a mental note.

One day, I'll find out what that was.

She turned her attention back to the row of shops ahead. "Well, would you look at that. I didn't realise it was the same place I'd looked up earlier. Bluebird Ink."

"Sorry, Brooke. I should've said something."

She shot him a look that could kill.

They parked nearby and took a short walk to the shop. Its windows were crammed with tattoo designs—arms, legs, backs, even faces. Every body part had its place in the display.

"So," Owen said casually, "do you have any ink?"

"Ink?"

"You know—tattoos."

"I might have," she replied, letting the corner of her mouth curve into a mischievous smile.

Owen hesitated. That look she gave him—it always threw him off, like she was hiding more than she let on. And maybe she was.

They stepped inside. A heavily tattooed man was working on a customer's arm, focused and silent. The buzz of the tattoo machine hummed through the space.

"Good afternoon," Owen said, flashing his ID. "I'm DI Owen, and this is DC Daniels. We believe you may have some information related to the Blue Rose Killer."

"No, mate," the man replied bluntly, without looking up.

Just then, a young woman stepped out from the back office. Slim, with tattoos on her arms—stylish, not overdone.

"Ah, you're the Old Bill I spoke to earlier. I'm Zoe. I own this joint. I'm the one who called you."

"Yes, I'm—" Owen began, but she waved him off.

"Yeah, love, I heard you the first time. You're here about the guy asking for the blue rose tattoo, right?"

Brooke took out her phone and showed her a photo of the latest blue rose design found on the victim.

"Have you seen anything like this? Or did he show you any examples?"

Zoe raised a brow and grinned. "You want a quick tattoo while you're here, love?"

"No, I'm good, thanks," Brooke said with a polite smile. "So why did you call us?"

"He was weird," Zoe said. "Kept banging on about how he wanted a blue rose tattoo. Said it had to be perfect. Ten petals. He was really specific. Wanted it deep blue on the edges, fading into a lighter blue."

"Thank you, Zoe," Owen said, notebook already in hand. "What else can you tell us about him?"

"Well, here's the strange bit. Look at my arms, then look at Bert's—my partner over there. You see what they are, yeah?"

Brooke and Owen exchanged a quick glance.

"Sorry, Zoe," Brooke said. "That's not quite making sense."

"No idea," Owen added. "Can you explain?"

"Sure. I'm getting ahead of myself. Here—take a look at these two photos." She handed them two laminated sheets. "Spot the difference."

They leaned in, studying the sheets. Owen was the first to spot it.

"Okay, this one… something about the ink. It doesn't look quite right. Cheap, maybe?"

"Exactly," Zoe said. "That sheet you're holding? Those are temporary tattoos. Some come off in days, others last a few weeks—but they all wash off eventually."

"Right," Brooke said slowly. "And you're saying the man who came in… was wearing temporary ones?"

"Yeah. Had a few on his arms and neck. But here's the thing—anyone seriously into ink wouldn't be caught dead with fake ones. They're a joke to real artists."

"That is strange," Owen said. "Trying to pass as someone he's not."

"Exactly. And he spoke like he knew everything—what he wanted, how it had to be done. Like he was obsessed with the design. But those tats were all fake."

"Can you describe him?" Brooke asked.

"Not in detail, love. Muscular—looks like he works out. Maybe six foot, white, clean-shaven. But he had one of those COVID masks on, so the bottom half of his face was covered."

Owen handed her two cards. "Thanks, Zoe. Please call us if he comes back or you remember anything else."

"Sure thing."

They were halfway out the door when Zoe called after them.

"Wait—almost forgot something. I think he was trying to cover a real tattoo on his neck. Something just didn't look right. We get cover-up jobs all the time—old names, mistakes people regret. This looked like one of those."

"Could you see what it was?" Brooke asked.

"No, not really. It was blue. Maybe a name. But it looked like he was trying to hide it under a temporary design."

Brooke's pulse quickened. A name. Blue. Maybe that's the thread we need to pull.

"Thanks again, Zoe. We'll be in touch."

Chapter 22

The sea glinted silver beneath a low Brighton sky as Owen and Brooke walked back to the car.

"That was something," Owen said, flipping through his notes. "A blue tattoo. Maybe a name."

"She said it didn't look right," Brooke added. "Temporary ink over something permanent. That's not random. He's hiding something."

They got in the car, and Brooke pulled out her tablet as Owen started the engine.

"We might be able to trace it," she said, already typing. "Tattoo artists don't always keep official records, but they post photos. Cover-up jobs, fresh ink, customer tags. We search for blue neck tattoos, names, anything similar."

Owen glanced at her. "You think he's been walking around with this thing for years?"

"Maybe. Or maybe it's recent. Something he regrets. Either way, it mattered enough to hide."

They drove in silence for a few moments, both deep in thought.

"You know," Brooke said eventually, "the ten petals. It keeps coming back. Every victim's tattoo is the same. It's not just a signature. It's a statement."

Owen nodded. "A ritual."

"Or a memorial."

"Yes, but hang on. Are they all exactly the same?"

"What are you on about, Owen? You've looked at them as much as I have. Of course they are. We've said that from the start."

"You're missing the point. We've been calling it the same Blue Rose tattoo without ever actually checking. We took it for granted."

"Owen, get to the point."

"She said he wanted ten petals. Have you counted how many are on each tattoo?"

Brooke froze, a look of shock crossing her face.

"Bloody hell. You're right. I haven't. Never even thought to check."

"Remember. Ritual, or memorial."

Those words hung between them.

Later they made their way to Brighton Police Station.

They were given a desk to work from. Brooke settled in, tapping into databases and public image repositories, while Owen stood at a whiteboard, pinning up copies of the tattoo images, including Zoe's sheet of temporary designs.

"Okay, let's go through every Blue Rose we've got," Brooke said, loading the images onto a large monitor.

She magnified the first one. "Here. We thought this was a stylised rosebud. But it's just one petal, curled in."

Owen leaned forward. "Second one has two. Christ, how did we miss that?"

Brooke clicked through. "April has four."

Owen exhaled. "That means he's building to ten. That's six more victims if we don't stop him."

Brooke swallowed. "He's counting down. Or up."

"Marking them," Owen said. "Piece by piece."

"Wait. Look closer." Brooke highlighted an image. "There's a mark on this petal. Is that a squiggle or…?"

Owen squinted. "Could be an S. Childlike. Or rushed."

She moved to the next image. "Here. What about this one?"

Owen tilted his head. "Looks like an H."

Brooke's fingers paused over the keys. "What if they're not just marks?"

"What are you thinking?"

She looked up slowly. "What if they're letters?"

He stared at her. "Each petal. Each new victim. A new letter."

"Oh God," she whispered. "He's spelling something."

"Not something," Owen said grimly. "Someone."

Ping.

A notification flashed on Brooke's laptop.

"Found something. Tattoo posted two years ago by a shop in Crawley. Blue rose on the neck, same fade pattern. Ten petals. It's tagged to a guy named Ryan K. Melanie commented on it."

Owen moved in quickly. "Crawley's what, forty minutes?"

"Thirty-five if you drive like you usually do," Brooke muttered, smirking.

He grinned. "Show me."

She opened the profile. "Ryan Kingsley. Mostly private, but the image is still public. That's Melanie Granger next to him. Same age. Probably a couple back then. Her account's been inactive since March 2015."

"Inactive?

"Dead, in social terms. But here's the kicker. Melanie Granger was reported missing. March twelfth, 2015."

Owen's face tightened. "Who reported it?"

"Not Ryan. A co-worker. Said she stopped showing up. No calls. No messages. No signs of travel. Filed as a missing adult. Cold case status."

"No statement from Kingsley?"

Brooke shook her head. "Not a word."

Owen grabbed his coat. "Let's pay him a visit."

Later that day, they arrived in Crawley.

The flat block was unremarkable. Three floors of beige brick, a cracked intercom box by the main door. Flat 2B.

Owen rang the buzzer. No answer.

He rang again. Still nothing.

Brooke glanced up at the windows. "No movement."

"Let's try the neighbour."

The woman in 2A answered in slippers and a dressing gown. Her eyes squinted behind thick glasses.

"Sorry to bother you, ma'am," Brooke said. "DC Daniels. This is DI Owen. We're looking for a Ryan Kingsley. Did he live next door?"

"Oh yes, dear. He did. Moved out over a year ago. Didn't say goodbye. Just up and left. Quiet lad. Strange though."

"How so?" Owen asked.

"Odd hours. Heard him talking to himself sometimes. But never saw a woman come or go. Not once."

"Did the police ever come round?" Brooke asked. "About a missing person?"

"No. I'd remember that."

Back at the car, Brooke sighed. "Dead end."

"No," Owen said. "It's a lead. A man with a rose tattoo matching the others. A girlfriend who disappeared. He covered up the tattoo. Never reported her missing. He's hiding something."

Brooke stared out the window. "You think Melanie could've been the first?"

"Maybe. Before the pattern started. A prototype."

They sat in silence.

"I'm pulling his financials," Brooke said, already back on her tablet. "Let's see where he last showed up."

Two hours later and several cups of coffee.

"Got him," Brooke said. "Used a gym membership card in Redhill three weeks ago. Paid in cash but swiped his keycard. That's the only recent trace."

Owen stood. "Get CCTV. Reopen Melanie's case officially. I want her DNA compared to the partial sample under April's fingernails."

"She wouldn't match."

"Not if she's the victim. But if he killed her and later touched April, we might find transfer."

"We'll need permission from Melanie's family for a full reference sample."

"Find them," Owen said. "We dig until there's nothing left."

Brooke nodded. "There's one more thing."

"What?"

"The profiler's next door. She's got something for us."

"About time, Brooke." Owen stood and followed her.

Brooke led the way into a side office. A woman in her late thirties stood by a whiteboard, a thick file in her hands.

"Nicola, this is DI Owen," Brooke said. "Nicola's a criminal psychological profiler. She's been working on the background for us."

"Hello. Nice to meet you." Nicola offered a firm handshake. "I take it you two have worked together before?"

Brooke nodded. "Yeah. A couple of years back."

Nicola smiled knowingly. "Ah. I see."

Owen frowned. "You see what?"

"You two are a thing," she said, matter-of-fact. "Relax. Your secret's safe with me."

Brooke looked away quickly. Owen gave a tight smile.

Nicola opened the file. "Let's get to it. This killer of yours. He's one sick bastard. But you already know that."

"We're looking for what we don't know," Owen said. "Something useful."

"Understood. Some of this may repeat what you've already guessed, but let me walk you through it. This is the short version. I'll leave the full profile for you."

She clicked a remote and brought up a slide on the monitor.

"Victim selection appears deliberate. He's choosing based on a specific type. Age range, physical appearance, behavioural traits. Possibly vulnerability or perceived purity. His signature—the blue rose tattoos and increasing petal count—is not necessary to the crime. It's a psychological compulsion. The escalation in petals suggests either a countdown or a build-up to a final victim."

Owen nodded. "We thought the same."

Nicola paused, eyes on him. "Let me finish."

He held up a hand in apology.

She continued, flipping the page. "Offender profile. Likely male, aged twenty-five to forty-five. Exhibits obsessive-compulsive traits. Possibly a perfectionist. Could be delusional. Very likely experienced early trauma. Specifically involving a maternal figure or a romantic relationship that ended badly. This kind of pathology points to someone who wants control, obedience, and emotional ownership."

Brooke glanced at Owen. "Fits."

They spent another hour working through the rest of the profile. Patterns, possible triggers, behavioural predictions. Until Nicola stood to leave.

"I'll leave the full report," she said. "It's not pleasant reading."

Once she was gone, Owen leaned back. "Well. That was revealing. Confirmed a lot of our theories."

"Yeah," Brooke agreed. "One seriously twisted bastard."

She turned her laptop toward him. "I've got something else. Cold case from Kent. Twenty twenty-three. Woman found in woodland. No ID. No confirmed sexual assault. But look here."

She zoomed in on the photo.

A faint tattoo. Blue ink on the neck. Faded. Smudged. But visible.

Ten petals.

"Shit," Owen muttered. "We missed her."

"Maybe," Brooke said. "Or maybe she was the first. And after her, he got smarter."

They looked at each other.

The game had changed.

Chapter 23

He had left Rosie back at the house. She knew the drill. It didn't matter anyway—she couldn't go anywhere, still chained to the bed, which in turn was bolted to the floor. He was sure Rosie would enjoy the surprise.

He fumbled for his phone and dialled the number.

"Good morning, Town Estate Agents. How can I help you today?"

"Good morning, it's Mr. Taylor. I called yesterday regarding a property viewing."

"Oh yes, Mr. Taylor. It's Sarah. I spoke to you yesterday. How are you?"

"I'm well. You said you could meet me today at 23 Duncan?"

"Yes, Mr. Taylor. I can be there in thirty minutes. Would that be okay?"

"Perfect. I look forward to meeting you."

He was already waiting, his van parked a few miles away in a quiet car park near the river. There were several other vehicles, so it didn't stand out. Neither did the blue Ford Fiesta with false plates.

He was dressed smartly. Collar and tie. Suited and booted, as they used to say. A false beard, long black wig, and dark glasses completed the disguise.

It started to pour with rain. He sat in the Fiesta until he saw a black BMW pull into the driveway. He watched Sarah get out and run to the door, unlocking it and going inside.

Perfect, he thought.

He pulled the Fiesta onto the driveway and parked beside her car. His hands were shaking. Doing things differently made him tense. This was a risk, but a risk worth taking.

He rang the bell. The door opened.

"Good morning. Mr. Taylor, I presume?"

"Yes, good morning, Sarah. I've been looking forward to viewing the property."

"Well, let me show you around, Mr. Taylor."

He followed her inside, noting the way her fitted clothes hugged her frame. She moved with easy confidence, unaware of the danger standing behind her.

"This way, Mr. Taylor. I want to show you the beautiful garden."

She stepped to one side and gestured outward.

"Yes, very beautiful," he said, smiling. "Just like you."

She turned, startled.

She never saw the needle.

Her body went limp and collapsed into his arms. He held her there for a moment, breathing in the scent of her perfume.

"Oh, Sarah," he whispered. "We're going to have so much fun."

He made sure the coast was clear. Inside the Fiesta, he had already prepared restraints. He gagged her, tied her hands behind her back and ankles together, and slipped a cloth bag over her head. Then he secured her to the seat so she couldn't move.

Twelve and a half minutes later, he pulled into the car park where the van waited. The rain had driven everyone away.

After a final check, he transferred her to the van, tying her to the steel support post in the back.

The drive to the house took ninety minutes. By the time they arrived, Sarah was awake and kicking at the floor of the van.

He opened the side door. She fell still.

"Now, Sarah. You must listen to me. Nod if you understand."

She nodded slowly.

He removed the bag from her head.

"There you are. Oh, you've been crying. Don't worry, you may like it here. I have someone I want you to meet."

He dragged her upstairs to the room next to Rosie's and tied her to the bed. Then he left her there and crossed the landing.

"Hello Rosie, are you okay?"

"Yes, thank you, Blue. May I ask… who was that?"

"That? That's your surprise. Her name is Sarah. Come and meet her."

He unfastened the chain from Rosie's bed and held it tightly, leading her next door.

"Rosie, meet Sarah. Sarah, meet Rosie."

Sarah, gagged and tied, lifted her head just enough to see Rosie standing in the doorway. Her eyes widened in confusion and fear.

"Now Rosie, sit down and watch."

Rosie obeyed. Inside, she felt sick. She didn't know what he had planned, but she had learned long ago not to resist. Every inch of her wanted to run. But she sat and waited.

He stood beside Sarah, running his hand slowly over her shoulder, down her arm, along her side. She flinched beneath his touch.

Then he picked up a pair of scissors and began cutting away her clothes. Rosie turned her face away.

"No," he said firmly. "You need to see this."

She forced her eyes back open, locking her stare onto Sarah's face instead of what he was doing. The tears on Sarah's cheeks mirrored her own.

Once Sarah was fully undressed, he crouched beside her, speaking softly.

"I'm going to remove your gag now. But if you scream, it won't end well. No one will hear you. Understand?"

Sarah nodded, lips trembling.

He removed the gag.

"Say hello to Rosie."

A whisper escaped her. "Hi."

"Rosie," he said, without looking at her, "say hello back. Nicely."

Rosie stepped forward, the cold floor biting at her bare feet. She forced a smile.

"Hello, Sarah. I'm Rosie."

"Now show her how you say hello to me."

Rosie froze. Her heart thudded against her ribs.

"Blue… please…"

His voice hardened.

"Now."

Rosie moved to Sarah's side and reached out. Her touch was light, her hand brushing over Sarah's body. That was all. A gesture. A lie they both had to tell.

He watched, satisfied. For now.

Then he turned his full attention to Sarah.

Rosie turned her head away instinctively.

"Don't," he said. "You watch."

She obeyed, numb. Detached. She had to be.

The minutes crawled by like hours. She didn't cry. Didn't scream. Just sat, eyes open, heart breaking for the girl on the bed, and for herself.

When he was done, he threw her a towel.

"Clean us up."

Rosie took the towel silently. She wiped his skin, then Sarah's, her hands trembling. Sarah stared blankly at the ceiling, motionless, barely breathing.

Blue stood watching them both, his arms folded, his breathing steady now.

"Good girl," he said softly.

Rosie froze. It wasn't praise. It was possession.

He stepped closer, placing a hand gently on her head.

"See, Rosie? I knew you could be trusted."

She didn't respond.

"You and Sarah are going to get along well," he added. "But remember, you were here first. That means something."

Rosie nodded, but her stomach twisted. He wasn't angry. That scared her more.

Because it meant he had plans.

Not just for Sarah.

But for both of them.

Chapter 24

The room was dark except for the faint glow from the hallway light seeping under the door. Rosie sat on the floor, her back against the cold wall. She heard the faint rustling of movement in the room next door—Sarah, likely trying to adjust her restraints or just breathe quietly through the fear.

A soft knock came. Not on the door. On the wall.

Three gentle taps.

Rosie hesitated.

Then answered back—three taps.

A few moments later, the door creaked open.

Blue stood there with his arms crossed, his eyes calm but cold. "No talking," he said. "But since you're both being good girls, you can be in the same room. For a little while."

He unfastened the chain from Rosie's ankle and led her down the hall, then into the next room where Sarah was still tied and naked on the bed.

"Be polite," he said, and then shut the door behind them.

Rosie looked around the room. He hadn't chained her up as usual. Then she noticed the bars on all the windows.

Just like a prison, she thought. But it was.

Rosie stood still for a second. Sarah's eyes followed her every move.

"Are you okay?" Rosie whispered.

Sarah looked away. "No."

Rosie lowered herself beside the bed. "I know what he's like."

"No, you don't," Sarah snapped. "You're still alive. You play along."

Rosie's lips parted, but no words came.

Sarah continued, her voice sharp with trembling fury. "You touched me. You helped him."

"I didn't want to," Rosie said quickly. "He makes you choose between that and pain. I've seen what happens when you don't listen."

"Why has he put you in here with me? Why are you not tied up like me?"

"First, because I do as I'm told. He has a little trust in me. But not enough to be let out. The room is locked, and the windows are barred."

"And what's the other reason he put you in here?"

"Because…"

"Because what, Rosie?"

"He wants me to make love to you."

"What? No. No fucking way. Don't you lay a finger on me, bitch."

"I won't. But it means he'll be back sooner, and much more forceful. In the end, Sarah, you do what you're told. Without question."

Sarah didn't respond. Her eyes brimmed with tears, but they didn't fall.

They sat in silence for a while. The quiet was heavy, like the air before a storm.

Then Sarah leaned slightly closer. "Does he sleep?"

Rosie blinked. "What?"

"You heard me. Does he sleep?"

Rosie swallowed. "Sometimes. On the sofa downstairs. He locks everything at night."

Sarah's voice lowered. "He has blind spots. Everyone does."

Rosie looked at her carefully. "You're planning something."

"Of course I am," Sarah hissed. "A man like that doesn't keep us alive forever. I'm not waiting around for him to decide I'm used up."

Rosie felt her heart thud. "If you try something and it fails, he'll kill us both."

"I'd rather die on my feet than wait in a cage."

Silence.

Then Rosie asked, "What if we both don't make it?"

Sarah looked her dead in the eyes. "Then you better decide now—are you going to survive, or are you going to watch me bleed?"

Rosie couldn't answer.

Not yet.

Chapter 25

"Good morning, ladies. How are you both?" Blue said cheerfully. "Now, Rosie, come here."

Sarah watched as he sat down, trousers already around his ankles.

"Rosie, show Sarah what I like in the morning."

"Yes, Blue."

Rosie dropped to her knees without hesitation and began to perform oral sex on him until he finished. She didn't leave a drop.

Blue exhaled with satisfaction. "So, Sarah… let's get you untied. But first, this ankle chain's going on the end of the bed, so don't get any silly ideas."

Sarah looked at Rosie—she wasn't chained at all.

As soon as Blue released her, Sarah yelled, "Now, Rosie!" and leapt at him. She threw punches and tried to kick, wild with adrenaline.

"Rosie, do something! This is our chance!"

But Rosie didn't move.

"I'm sorry, Sarah. I have to do what I'm told."

Sarah's struggle didn't last long. Overpowered and alone, she gave up, breathing hard, fury in her eyes.

"So," Blue hissed. "You little bitch. You thought you could escape? That deserves a punishment."

He pulled off his belt and started whipping her hard. She screamed, covering her face, but her thighs, buttocks, and chest bore the brunt, bleeding from the lashes.

"Blue, please stop!" Rosie begged. "You're killing her. Please. I'll do anything for you."

He paused, staring down at Sarah, then at Rosie.

"For you?" he said thoughtfully. "Alright, Rosie. I'll let her live. But she needs to learn what I like—and when I want it."

"Yes, Blue. I'll do my best," Rosie said softly.

He stepped up to her and kissed her on the lips. Rosie didn't mean to respond—but she did. They kissed like lovers.

"I know you will, Rosie. But if all else fails, there are plenty more to choose from."

When he left, Rosie went to the bathroom and returned with a wet cloth and towel.

She knelt beside Sarah, who lay curled up, bruised and bleeding.

"Sarah, I'm sorry. I just couldn't—"

"Get the fuck away from me, bitch."

Rosie didn't flinch. "No, Sarah. You listen to me. Because if you don't, you'll end up tattooed and dumped in a ditch somewhere. Do you hear me?"

Sarah rolled onto her back. She didn't speak as Rosie gently wiped the blood away.

"Do you mean that?" she finally asked. "He'd really kill me, just like that?"

"Oh, come on, Sarah. Don't be stupid. You talk a good fight, but you've got no idea what this is. Why do you think I'm still alive? Because I do what he asks. And honestly... I'm starting to like it."

"You what? Are you serious?"

"I've been here nearly a week now, I think. He took me, like he took you. But now I give myself to him."

"This is mad. You're mad."

Rosie ran the towel over Sarah's chest.

"What are you doing, Rosie? Stop. Stop now."

"You're beautiful," Rosie murmured. "Firm breasts. He'll like you."

Rosie let the towel fall and ran her hands over Sarah's chest. Sarah's nipples hardened in response.

"See? It's nice, isn't it?"

Sarah's breath caught. She didn't want to respond, but her body did.

Neither of them knew Blue was watching through the CCTV. He smiled.

"Good girl, Rosie," he whispered to himself. "Just as I wanted."

The next morning, Blue unlocked the bedroom door and stepped inside.

"Well, well, well. Just look at you two," he said.

Rosie and Sarah were curled up together, asleep in each other's arms.

"Did you have fun last night?"

"Yes, Blue," Rosie replied. "Thank you."

"And you, Sarah?"

Sarah hesitated, then nodded. "Yes, sir. I did."

"You can call me Blue now."

He dropped his trousers and sat down again.

"Remember what Rosie did for me yesterday?"

Sarah looked to Rosie, who gave a subtle nod.

"Yes, Blue," Sarah said quietly.

She moved in front of him, took a deep breath, and knelt. She did what was expected—and finished cleanly.

Blue sighed with satisfaction. "Very nice. You're learning fast."

He stood and reached for the ankle chain.

"Time for breakfast. Let's get your chain, Sarah. And no funny business this time."

"No, Blue," Sarah said quietly.

He walked behind them both as they left the room. He still didn't trust either of them completely, not yet.

But Rosie...

Rosie was turning out to be something special.

Chapter 26

Both Owen and Brooke stood looking at the timeline.

"Owen, I want to clear the board and go over everything again. There are still things we haven't heard back on yet."

"OK, Brooke. I guess it's going to be another late night. Let's make a start."

"No, Owen. It's nearly 11 p.m. We're both tired, and that's when mistakes happen. We want this bastard. Let's get some sleep and start fresh tomorrow."

Owen let out a deep sigh. "Yeah, OK. You're right. Your place or mine?"

"You really want me to answer that, Owen?"

There was little talk on the short drive. They picked up some sandwiches and coffee from a petrol station.

"Brooke, are you sure you don't mind me staying over again?"

"Of course I don't mind. I've also noticed you haven't been smoking."

"Yeah… I gave it up."

He thought about it. He hadn't even realised he'd stopped smoking since the day he met Brooke.

They looked at each other, both waiting for the other to make a move.

"Good night, Brooke. Sleep well."

"And you, Owen."

Brooke felt a little disappointed. Maybe the timing wasn't right.

The next morning, Brooke was about to knock on his door with a coffee when she heard him. It had been six days since Rosie Osbourne disappeared. They were running out of time, and the weight of it pressed on both of them. She wasn't sure if he was talking to someone or dreaming. But the sound of him sobbing like a child made her heart twist.

"Owen, are you OK?"

She didn't wait for an answer. She opened the door.

He sat up in bed, startled. "Good God, Brooke, what's wrong?"

"You. Were you having a nightmare?"

"I don't know what you're talking about."

"Bullshit, Owen. Remember who you're talking to. If you don't want to talk about it, fine. But I'm here when you're ready."

She left the coffee on the side and walked out, leaving him to think.

Brooke sat drinking her coffee with her back to the door when Owen walked into the kitchen. He put his cup down, then walked up behind her, wrapping his arms around her and pulling her back toward him. She didn't pull away.

"I'm sorry, Brooke. I just don't know where to start."

She gently removed his arms. For a moment, he thought he'd gone too far. But she turned to face him, stood up, and ran a hand over his sad, tired face.

"What am I going to do with you?"

She pulled him close and kissed him on the lips.

For a moment, he froze. Then responded. Their tongues met. He kissed her again, and then her neck. She let out a soft moan.

"Oh, Owen… we shouldn't, but… oh God."

He slipped her robe off her shoulders, revealing just her underwear and a beautiful, toned body.

He caressed her breast. Her head fell back, pushing her chest toward him. Slowly, he eased her down onto the sofa. They lay in each other's arms as he ran his hands over her body, feeling the strength beneath her skin.

"Owen… I need you. I need you now."

Afterwards, they sat side by side.

He reached for her hand. She looked at him and kissed him again.

"Owen… I don't know what to say. But that was… really wonderful."

"It was, wasn't it? You're so, so beautiful. But where do we go from here?"

"Owen, don't worry about that. We enjoyed each other — and to be honest, I hope we'll continue."

She watched him carefully.

He turned to face her. "The day I first saw you, I felt something. And I liked it. Brooke, I'm not going anywhere. And neither are you. But I guess we need to get to work."

"I think we should keep this between us for now. Especially while we're working this case."

Owen looked at her, then kissed her one more time. "I agree. But we'd better get going — otherwise people might start talking."

Chapter 27

The station was already alive with phones ringing, keyboards clacking, and voices overlapping as Owen and Brooke walked in. They were nearly an hour late, but no one raised an eyebrow.

Owen slid into his chair, taking a sip of lukewarm coffee. "Told you no one would notice."
Brooke smirked behind her cup. "Let's not get cocky."

They exchanged a quick look. It wasn't awkward. Not yet. But it carried weight. What they'd shared that morning felt real, but fragile.

Before either of them could settle, Owen's mobile buzzed. Unknown number. He answered.
"Owen."
"DI Owen? Sergeant Fields here from Surrey. We've got a missing person's report. Woman named Sarah Whitmore, twenty-eight, estate agent. Reported missing late last night by her flatmate. She didn't come home after work."
Brooke glanced over, instantly alert.
"Last seen where?" Owen asked.

"She had a viewing at a house on Duncan Street. Number 23. According to her agency, she showed up for the appointment but never checked in afterward. No CCTV nearby, and no neighbours recall anything suspicious. We assumed it was just a routine report until this morning."
Owen's fingers tensed around the phone. "Go on."
"One of our officers returned to the property. Garden gate was unlocked. Her car's still in the driveway. And inside, painted on the rear wall of the lounge, is a blue rose. Same style you've flagged in your bulletins."
Owen stood. "No victim?"
"No, sir. No sign of a struggle or a body. Nothing. It's like she vanished. There was one thing I thought was odd. Especially for an estate agent. Her phone, iPad, and bag were locked in her car. Her car keys were left under the painted rose."
"Text me the address. We're on our way."

He ended the call and looked at Brooke.
"He's got another one."
"Sarah Whitmore," she said, grabbing her jacket. "How the hell was this missed? It happened yesterday, and we don't get told until nearly lunchtime?"
"He changed his method. Took her from a house viewing. Not on the way home. This was well planned. I didn't expect a body, but just a painted rose? That's new."
Brooke's voice lowered. "He's evolving."
Owen nodded grimly. "And we're behind him."

Duncan Street – 11:40 a.m.

The house at number 23 was a red-bricked semi, empty and echoing with years of neglect. The front door was locked, but the estate agent's key box hung loosely from the handle, cracked open. They circled around the back, where a narrow garden path led to an overgrown lawn.

There, on the faded brick wall, was the rose. Blue, ten-petaled, glistening slightly. Still drying.
He hadn't rushed it.

Brooke crouched beside the wall, her eyes scanning the base.
"He painted it here after taking her. He wanted it seen."
"No struggle. No blood," Owen muttered, glancing at the window. "This place is quiet. She probably let him in thinking he was a buyer."

Inside, dust clung to the air. The living room was bare except for two folding chairs and a brochure left on the windowsill. Sarah's name badge from the agency lay nearby.

Owen picked it up, frowning. "She never left this behind. It's like it's been left for us."
Brooke looked around the room, uneasy. "He didn't just take her. He watched. He made arrangements getting her to come so she was alone."

They were quiet for a moment. Then Brooke turned to him.
"We slept together this morning, and now we're standing in the middle of a crime scene, knowing another woman is probably chained somewhere, praying someone notices she's gone."
Owen met her eyes and, for once, had no answer.

They continued moving slowly through the house.
"Owen, come here a second. What's that up there?" Brooke pointed to something on the ceiling.
Owen looked up but couldn't reach it. "Hang on. Forensics are here now."

He called across the room. "Sergeant Miller, can you check that out?"
"Hey Owen," Miller replied, walking over. "Let's take a look. Oh, hi Brooke. Didn't see you there."

He returned a moment later with a small set of steps, just enough to reach the ceiling.
"Well, I'll need to get this back to the lab, but it looks like something's been stuck up here. Also, look how dusty it is in here. Check out that plug socket over there. Don't touch it yet. Could be evidence."

Owen and Brooke knelt down. The socket looked clean. Unnaturally so. As if something had been plugged in recently.
"Any ideas, Sergeant?" Owen asked.
"Well, you two are the detectives, last time I checked," Miller said. "But if I had to guess, someone used this for a camera. Probably a small CCTV feed."

Owen and Brooke locked eyes.
"He recorded it," Brooke whispered. "He recorded the whole thing."
Owen straightened. "Right. Everyone, look for something very small. Hidden camera, bug, whatever. And I mean small."

Everyone was already in gloves and shoe coverings, combing carefully, not touching anything they didn't have to.

Then,
"Sir, I think I've found something," one of the forensic techs called, pointing to a small hole in the ceiling. He carefully removed a tiny black square, less than an inch across, with a small battery unit attached.
"Sir, I think it's still recording."
"What?" Owen barked, snatching it from him. He yanked the battery off.
"I don't want that bastard knowing more than he already does. Get this checked immediately. Pull every frame of footage from it."

From his private room in the new house, he watched the footage again.
Sarah, unlocking the door. Smiling. Saying something about the downstairs needing work. So trusting.

She didn't scream when he stepped in behind her. That part always fascinated him. How shock stole their breath before fear could even begin.

She was in the new place now. Still adjusting. Not quite obedient like Rosie. But she would learn.

He glanced at the blue paint still on his fingers and smiled.
"They're going to find that rose, and they'll realise how much closer I am than they think."

He sat watching the footage like it was a trophy. Then, the other laptop beeped.
There you are, Brooke.
And of course, Owen.
Nice to see you finally turn up.

He watched them from the feed. The live one.
From another hidden camera.
"I could do with some popcorn," he muttered, laughing.

Chapter 28

Brooke led the way into the estate agency. It was nothing special — just the kind of place you'd find on any high street. Glossy window displays of houses for sale, slightly faded, sat behind the glass. Inside, the atmosphere was quieter than expected.

"Good morning. DC Daniels, and my colleague DI Owen," she said, showing her badge. "May we start by seeing the manager, please?"

The young woman at the desk looked up. Her eyes were red and puffy from crying.

"Is this about Sarah?"

"Is your manager available?" Brooke asked gently.

Just then, a tall Asian man appeared from an adjoining office.

"Good morning, officers. Please, come in. Can I get you anything? Tea, coffee, bottled water?"

"Water would be great, thank you," Brooke replied.

He returned moments later with two chilled bottles.

"Please, take a seat. My name is Rohan Vyas. Please tell me you have good news about our Sarah?"

"I'm sorry," Brooke said softly. "We're still following leads. We were hoping you could tell us more about who she was meeting at 23 Duncan Street yesterday."

"Of course. Let me pull up her schedule."

As Rohan turned to the computer, Owen quietly stepped out of the office and approached the receptionist.

"Hi. How are you coping?"

"I'm not," she whispered, her voice trembling. "She's my friend and..." Her breath caught, and she broke into tears.

From across the room, Brooke watched Owen pause, grab a box of tissues, and hand them over with a quiet word. She noticed the way he softened his tone — calm, grounded. The side of him that rarely came out.

He really cared.

Brooke looked away.

"Thank you," Mel sniffed, taking the tissues. "Please… is she — is she dead?"

"We don't know yet, Mel. I'm sorry — I didn't catch your name?"

"Mel Smith. Just call me Mel."

"Alright, Mel. Can you tell me a bit about Sarah?"

"She's kind. Would do anything for anyone. I don't think she feared anyone or anything."

"What makes you say that?"

"I've seen her stand up to people. We've gone out for drinks, and if anyone tried anything dodgy… well, not with Sarah. She never took shit from anyone."

"Is that her desk there?" Owen asked, nodding toward a corner workstation. "Mind if I take a look?"

Mel hesitated, then shook her head. "No, it's fine. I don't think she ever locked it."

"Thank you."

He moved to the desk. She was right — the drawers opened easily. Just stationery, loose pens, gum, a compact mirror. Then, tucked near the back of the middle drawer, he spotted a sticky note.
Mr Taylor – 23 Duncan – 11:30

He glanced back toward Mel, but she was dabbing her eyes with a tissue.

"Mel, this Mr Taylor — have you ever spoken to him yourself?"

She wiped her nose and nodded slowly. "He called once or twice. Always asked for Sarah by name. Said he'd only deal with her."

Brooke re-entered the reception area, catching that last part.

"He insisted on Sarah?" she asked, eyes narrowing.

"Yeah. Said she'd helped him before and he trusted her. But she didn't mention anything about that to me."

There was a flicker of something cold in Owen's eyes. "Thank you, Mel. That helps more than you know."

Back in the office, Rohan called out, "Here we are. Yesterday, 11:30 a.m., a viewing booked at 23 Duncan Street. Client listed as 'Mr Taylor.' We've been trying to shift that place for over a year, needs a ton of work."

"Do you remember meeting this Mr Taylor yourself?" Brooke asked.

"No," he admitted. "Sarah handled the appointment directly. We don't always meet the clients unless there's a follow-up."

"Do your staff usually show houses alone?"

"Well… yes. We've never had any reason not to. It's common practice."

Owen returned and joined Brooke. "Maybe that's something to think about," he said flatly.

Rohan looked uneasy. "Yes… yes, of course. I'll review our procedures."

Brooke pulled a card from her wallet and handed it over. "If you remember anything else, anything strange at all about this 'Mr Taylor' or the call that booked the appointment, give us a ring."

Rohan nodded slowly. "Of course. I will."

As they walked out, Owen muttered under his breath, "You think that's even his real name?"

Brooke didn't answer.

She didn't have to.

Chapter 29

The evidence room was dim, lit only by the glow of the screen.

Owen leaned forward as the footage rolled, his face tight with tension. The angle was fixed, slightly elevated, giving a perfect view of the lounge inside 23 Duncan Street. Sarah walked in smiling; unaware she was being recorded. She set her bag down, checked her clipboard, and moved toward the window to open it.

Then, she turned toward the front door as it opened.

"Hi, you must be Mr Taylor. Come in," she said, stepping aside with a polite smile.

Owen's stomach flipped. His right fist closed against his thigh, knuckles whitening.

There he was. Not his face, that stayed hidden, but his presence: calm, silent, gloved. No hesitation. He closed the door behind him.

"Pause it," Owen said.

Brooke tapped the keyboard. The screen froze on Sarah's face, still mid sentence, caught in a half smile before any fear had time to register.

"She had no idea," Brooke whispered.

They had seen victims before. They had seen bodies. But this was different. This was intimate. Real. A moment of trust captured and violated.

"Anything else on the device?" Owen asked.

The tech, hunched nearby with headphones, looked up. "No audio on the clip. What we recovered was stored to internal memory, about thirty minutes' worth. Standard buffer for this model."

"That's all?"

He shook his head. "Not quite. This unit's WiFi enabled. It can livestream with remote access. The camera is sensor operated. As soon as someone entered, it started recording and streaming. He could have been watching in real time, or pulling the footage remotely afterward."

The tech angled the device so they could see the casing. "Also, it's been modified. Overclocked memory, custom firmware. Whoever set this up knew exactly what they were doing."

Brooke swallowed, blinking hard. "He was watching her," she said quietly, "and probably watching us too."

Owen rubbed the back of his neck. "What about the Waltham house? The car park near April's flat?"

"We'll check them all," the tech said. "If he planted cameras there, we'll find the traces."

Owen exhaled sharply and turned to Brooke. "We sweep every recent scene. Not just for what he left behind, but for what he might have seen."

Brooke nodded, eyes still on the frozen image of Sarah's trusting smile.

Owen stared at the screen a moment longer, feeling the killer's gaze like static in the room.

"Feels like he's always a step ahead," he muttered. "Because he's been in the room the whole time."

Later that night at Owen's flat, the mood was quieter. He didn't pour a drink. He didn't put the telly on. Brooke sat at the table staring into her tea. Neither of them spoke at first.

"You alright?" he asked gently.

She nodded. "Yeah. Just..." She looked at him. "It's like he's taunting us. Not just by taking them, but by watching us. Knowing our moves. Playing a step ahead."

"I hate that he sees us," Owen said. "I hate that we don't see him."

Brooke stood up. "We will. We just have to hold our nerve."

She walked to the window and pulled the curtain slightly aside.

Just in case.

"Owen, are we jumping the gun?"

"What do you mean?"

"Well, this is the first time, and we are letting him get to us. Just what he wants. Look at us, Owen. We're here in your horrible flat. Sorry, but it is. We can't do this. This is stupid. We must carry on as normal."

"Yes, you're right. I feel bloody stupid now."

"Look, we know April was taken in the street. So was Sharon. And so was Rosie. No camera set, nothing."

"Well Brooke, I'm going home. I can't stay here. Are you coming or what?"

"OK, Owen. But is my flat really that horrible?" She turned to face him.

"Yes. Yes, it is."

Back in his private room, with Rosie and Sarah locked away, he sat there replaying the CCTV feed. One feed played Sarah. He loved seeing the look on her face when he put the needle in, how she collapsed into his arms. He played it over and over. It made him feel good. He was disappointed they had found the second feed at 23. He had left it running, but that was expected. Still, it was great to watch.

One last look, he thought. The feed blinked into view. His smile widened.

One day, Brooke. You never know what is around the corner.

"You're catching up," he muttered, sipping his drink. "But not fast enough."

He saved both clips. The second he marked: Owen and Brooke Live.

It was getting late, but he wanted to see what Rosie and Sarah were up to. It was Sarah's second night, and Rosie was standing in front of her. It looked like she was having a go at Sarah. He wasn't sure if his original plan of keeping both of these two...

He leaned back, satisfied.

Rosie and Sarah.

"Sarah, look, if you want to survive then you must do as he says. You now know what happens if you don't."

"Yes, Rosie. I know. I can't depend on you. You're his little favourite. Just a little whore. The master calls and you run."

"Sarah, that's not nice. We need to get along. He won't trust you unless you do."

"Oh, I see. He trusts you, does he?"

"No. But he treats me better. And it's been over a week. I'm still alive. How long will you survive?"

"So, what you're saying is that I must be like you. Fuck, suck, whenever he says without question? You are sick. You even said you enjoyed his kiss."

Rosie went quiet for a moment, thinking about that kiss. She had plans of her own to get away from him, and as much as she wanted to, she couldn't trust Sarah.

"Sarah, I don't know what to say. When he kissed me... it felt, I don't know, natural. Yes, I did enjoy it. And I guess you won't understand this, but I hope he kisses me again that way."

Rosie asked, "Why do you care?"

Sarah replied, "Because if you crack... I'm alone."

Chapter 30

The door opened with a slow metallic creak.

Blue stepped inside, dressed in dark clothes, sleeves rolled, hands gloved. Rosie stood immediately, head down. Sarah remained seated, her glare steady from across the room.

"Good evening, girls," he said smoothly, locking the door behind him. "Isn't it nice to see everyone behaving?"

Rosie nodded.

Sarah didn't move.

Blue walked between them, letting the tension stretch like wire. He stopped beside Rosie, resting a gloved hand gently on her shoulder. She flinched but stayed still.

"You've been good," he said softly.

Sarah scoffed. "Of course she has."

Blue turned his head slowly.

Sarah stood, eyes defiant. "She does everything you say. Fetches, bends, smiles. Is that what you like? Little trained pets?"

"Sarah…" Rosie whispered.

"No. Let her speak," Blue said, his voice low and dangerously calm. "Tell me what you really think."

Sarah's expression tightened. "I think she's a coward. She thinks if she plays along, you'll spare her. She even enjoys it. Don't you, Rosie?"

"Stop," Rosie said, voice trembling.

"I saw you last night," Sarah snapped. "That look on your face when he kissed you. You liked it."

Rosie's breath caught.

Blue smiled faintly. "And did she?"

"She melted," Sarah said through clenched teeth. "Like a child playing at love. Pathetic."

Blue stepped closer to Sarah. His tone chilled. "And what does that make you?"

"I'm not pretending," she shot back. "Whatever you do to me, I'll never be that."

Without warning, he struck her hard across the face. She stumbled into the wall, blood at her lip, her cheek flushing red.

Rosie flinched.

Sarah steadied herself and stared him down. "Go ahead. Prove me right."

He seized her by the hair and threw her onto the mattress.

"Watch," he said to Rosie, not turning. "Learn what happens when you forget your place."

Rosie stood frozen, body tense. He didn't ask again.

The room filled with quiet rustling and sharp breathing. Blue moved deliberately; each action cruelly measured. Rosie turned her face to the wall, trying to block it out. But the sounds found her anyway. The grunt of force. The gasp of pain. Then silence.

When it ended, Sarah curled into herself, trembling, her back to the room.

Blue stood and turned to Rosie.

"Lie down."

Her legs shook as she stepped forward. He guided her to the same mattress, beside Sarah's crumpled form. He was slower this time. Whispering. Stroking her hair. Kissing her like she belonged to him. Like she had chosen this.

Rosie didn't fight. She lay still and endured it, letting it pass over her like water over stone.

Because survival meant silence.

Sarah didn't move.

When it was over, Blue pulled on his clothes.

"You see the difference?" he said, voice smooth and quiet. "Obedience is rewarded. Defiance is not."

He walked to the door.

"Rest well, girls. Tomorrow, we try again."

The door clicked shut behind him.

Silence lingered in the room like smoke.

Rosie lay on her side, eyes wide, her heart hammering in her chest. But she had made it through another night.

Behind her, Sarah's voice came in a hoarse whisper.

"You let him."

Rosie didn't answer.

Because maybe, for a moment, she had.

Chapter 31

Brooke's flat was small but warm, soft yellow lamplight casting long shadows against the walls. Rain ticked against the windowpane, steady and calm, a rare, welcome peace.

Owen sat on the edge of her sofa, nursing a mug of tea. Brooke moved around the small kitchen, barefoot, hair tied up, more relaxed than he was used to seeing her.

"You sure you don't want anything stronger?" she asked, glancing over her shoulder.

"I think I've had enough strong things for one day," he said with a faint smile.

She came over and sat beside him. Their knees touched. Neither moved.

"You've been quiet," she said.

"Just thinking," he replied. "The house in Duncan Street. The camera setup… it wasn't random. Someone knew how to place that tech without being seen and how to pull the footage."

"I've started a list," Brooke said, reaching for her notepad on the coffee table. "Anyone who had access to the property, landlords, previous tenants, neighbours. Also, people with IT or surveillance backgrounds."

"Someone ghosted that place," Owen said. "They went in, prepped it, waited. That's not impulse. That's a plan."

Brooke nodded. "And it's not the first time he's planned."

They sat in silence for a moment.

Then Brooke said, "Melanie Chambers. I went back through the files from her case."

"From 2015?"

She nodded. "There were inconsistencies. The crime scene photos, the layout of the room, the bindings, the sedation, they all match recent victims. But the Blue Rose wasn't there."

"No tattoo?"

"Not at the time. But I found a note in her old therapy records from before she vanished. She mentioned waking up once with a sharp pain in her back. Said she thought it was from a fall, but her counsellor noted what looked like a half-finished scar. No follow-up. No explanation."

Owen frowned. "So, she was marked, but not in the usual way?"

"Maybe. Or he was experimenting. Still refining his method. And get this, she registered under at least three different names while moving through the system. Melanie was just one of them."

They exchanged a look.

"He's been doing this longer than we thought."

Brooke nodded slowly. "And if Melanie was a trial run, then someone slipped her through the cracks."

Owen leaned back, rubbing his jaw. "We need to find everyone she spoke to. Her counsellor. Anyone she confided in."

"I've already sent a request," Brooke said. "Waiting to hear back."

He glanced around her flat, the warmth, the lived-in feel, the quiet tension between them. For once, the case didn't fill every corner of the room.

"You know," Owen said, "we don't always have to talk about work."

Brooke raised an eyebrow. "Are you saying that… here… in my flat?"

He smiled.

She smirked, then leaned her head gently on his shoulder. "Just for tonight," she whispered.

They sat like that for a while. Not lovers. Not detectives. Just two people in a moment of peace, before it all started again.

It was well past midnight when Brooke looked at the clock.

"Well, I've had enough, Owen. I'm going to bed. You coming?"

"How could I possibly refuse?"

Brooke turned and gently slapped his hand. "Naughty." She laughed as she led the way.

They didn't speak much as they moved through the flat, brushing teeth side by side, peeling off layers of the day's clothes like armour. By the time they slipped under the covers, the tension had changed shape. Not gone, but gentler. The kind that lingers between people who already know what the other feels like in the dark.

Her hand found his beneath the sheets.

"I missed this," she whispered.

"Me too."

He leaned in and kissed her, slow, unrushed, no urgency. Just contact. Connection.

They made love again. Quiet. Steady. No noise but the rain outside and the occasional breath shared between them. It wasn't escape. It wasn't distraction. It was comfort. Survival.

And when it was over, they lay tangled in each other, the case still out there, but for once, not in the room.

It was still early when Owen's phone buzzed.

He stirred, blinking in the half-light of dawn. Brooke shifted beside him, one arm across his chest.

"Sorry," he muttered, reaching for the phone on the nightstand.

A message from the tech team:
MATCH FOUND – DUNCAN ST. CAMERA HARDWARE ID LINKED TO REPAIR JOB. NAME FLAGGED: B. KINGSLEY.

Owen sat up straighter.

Brooke rubbed her eyes. "What is it?"

He showed her the screen.

"Kingsley," she said, heart sinking. "I thought he was a dead end."

"Apparently not."

She pulled herself upright beside him, suddenly wide awake.

"Right," she said, already moving for her clothes. "Let's find out what else he's hiding."

"No, Brooke, wait."

"What is it, Owen?"

"Just a few minutes more." He gently pulled her back into bed. No talk. Just a quiet cuddle.

For a moment, it felt like the night before hadn't entirely slipped away.

Then Brooke's phone went off.

"DC Daniels."

"Yes, sir. I'm on my way to pick him up, then we're going to see Kingsley again. Yes, sir."

"I take it that was Patterson?"

"Yeah. He's not happy. Says we're moving too slow. Come on, hurry up, or we'll both be pounding the beat."

They had Kingsley's details from the first visit. Less than forty minutes later, they were outside his garage again.

Chapter 32

Kingsley's garage sat at the edge of town, tucked between a boarded-up butcher's shop and a tyre depot. It looked even more tired in daylight. A rusting sign hung crooked over the shuttered front: Kingsley Electrics and Repair.

As they waited outside, the cold morning felt a million miles from the warmth of Brooke's flat. Last night had already faded into memory, like all their stolen moments did.

Owen stepped out of the car first. Brooke followed, scanning the front windows.

"No CCTV," she said.

"Bit ironic for someone who worked on surveillance gear," Owen muttered.

They knocked twice. Nothing. Owen rapped harder, then tried the handle. It opened with a reluctant squeal.

The interior smelled of metal and stale coffee. A cluttered workbench stood against the far wall, scattered with disassembled hard drives, motherboards, and two half-gutted Wi-Fi routers. A small monitor blinked softly in sleep mode. The stillness inside felt too still.

"Police," Brooke called out. "Mr Kingsley?"

A figure emerged from the back, Barry Kingsley, late fifties, pale, scratching his temple, sweat beading on his forehead.

"I thought you lot were done with me," he said, voice tight.

"Funny," Owen said, stepping forward. "So did we."

Brooke held up her phone. "The camera used at 23 Duncan Street? The serial number matches a unit you logged for repair six months ago. Ring any bells?"

"How do you know that?"

"Come on, Barry. You work in electronics. That should be the least surprising part of this conversation."

Kingsley hesitated. His eyes darted to the desk.

"I get loads of jobs."

"Not like this one," Owen cut in. "The unit was modified. Custom firmware. Overclocked memory. That's high-end work. Yours?"

Kingsley shook his head. "I just fixed the power supply. That's all I did."

"Who brought it in?" Brooke asked.

He licked his lips. "Didn't give a name. Paid cash. Looked normal. Bit quiet. Didn't say much."

"Did you log the device anywhere?"

Kingsley nodded. "Yeah… hold on."

He moved to a rusted filing cabinet, flipped through a stack of faded receipts, and pulled one out.

"Here. Wi-Fi HD Cam, Model 2X. Drop-off ID: 119-KT. Initials T — that's all I had."

"T?" Brooke repeated.

"I assumed it was for pickup. That's what they gave me."

Owen looked over at her. "Taylor?"

She nodded. "Mr Taylor."

"Did he come back?" Owen asked. "To collect it?"

Kingsley nodded slowly. "Yeah. Picked it up just before closing. Quiet guy. Wore gloves. Thanked me and left."

"Can you describe him?" Brooke asked.

"Hood up. Cap low. Soft voice. Kept his head down the whole time."

"But you saw part of his face?" Owen asked.

Kingsley didn't answer.

Owen stepped in. "Barry, if you're lying and this man kills again…"

"I saw something, alright?" Kingsley snapped. "A scar. Pale. Ran down the right side of his neck, just under his jaw. Looked old."

Brooke made a note.

"Do you have any family? Kids?" she asked.

Kingsley paused, then gave a short laugh. "A daughter I haven't seen in years. No idea where she is now."

"Thanks, Barry. If anything, else comes to mind, you know how to reach us."

"Sure," Kingsley muttered. "And don't let the door hit you on the way out."

"That's something," Owen said as they stepped outside.

"Is it enough?" Brooke asked quietly.

"No," Owen replied. "But it's a start."

They walked back to the car in silence.

Then Brooke said, "So… the family questions. Barry's Barry — but who the hell is Ryan Kingsley?"

"Good point," Owen said. "Last I heard, it was a dead end. The system came back with nothing. No trace of him since 2015."

Chapter 33

The file on Melanie Chambers was thinner than it should have been. Sparse notes, mismatched dates, an incident report marked as "unresolved." No family contacts. No permanent address. Just a vague trail leading nowhere.

Brooke sat in front of her desk, frowning at the computer.

"None of this makes sense," she said.

Owen leaned over her shoulder. "Still think it's a copycat?"

"No. The sedation method, the bindings, the silence, it's too specific. He was still learning back then, but it was him."

"Then why the fake name?"

Brooke clicked into a redacted section of the therapy notes. It had just come through from Melanie's former clinic. Most of it was generic, but one line stood out.

Client referred to herself as 'Melanie' – no ID ever confirmed. Possible alias due to trauma response.

"She gave a fake name," Brooke said.

"Deliberately?"

"Looks that way. She never used NHS services under that name. Never filed official paperwork. There's no record of her before or after that brief window."

Owen leaned back. "So, who is she really?"

"That's what I'm going to find out. And she didn't just give one false name. The notes suggest she may have used more than two or three. Melanie might have been just the one she gave the therapist."

A knock at the door pulled them both from the screen. A young officer stepped inside, a slim file in hand.

"Got something from the original 2015 missing persons batch," he said. "There's a girl who vanished four weeks before the 'Melanie' report came in. Her name was Lesley Cordery. Nineteen. Dropped out of college, no permanent address, no bank records or NHS contact after she disappeared, but the physical description is close."

Brooke took the file and stared down at the black-and-white photo clipped to the front. Pale eyes. Messy dark hair. A small scar under the chin.

"Could be her," Owen said.

"She didn't use the name Lesley with the therapist. Or with the hostel where she stayed for a while. But the description lines up." Brooke frowned. "If she changed her name more than once, maybe she wasn't just hiding from him."

"Someone else?"

"Or maybe she had her own secrets," Brooke said.

Owen crossed his arms. "If she was his first, maybe he let her go."

"Or maybe she got away," Brooke said quietly. "And if she did, we need to find out who helped her… and why she never came forward."

Chapter 34

The private counselling centre was tucked between a dental practice and a nursery, the kind of anonymous space that blended in easily. Inside, it smelled of lavender and old books.

Dr Miriam Caldwell welcomed them with a polite smile, her hands clasped neatly in front of her. Late forties, tidy, sharp-eyed.

"I remember her clearly," she said, leading Owen and Brooke into her office. "She called herself Melanie. But I suspected from the start that it wasn't her real name."

They sat opposite her, the sound of a distant ticking clock marking time between questions.

"She came here in early 2015. Traumatised. Disassociated. She refused to go to police, insisted she wasn't ready to face anything. But she did talk. Slowly."

Brooke leaned forward. "Did she ever describe her attacker?"

"Not in detail," Caldwell said. "She described the room, the darkness, the cold. She said she remembered a van. Said he sedated her more than once. She would wake up confused. Moved. Always chained."

Owen scribbled notes. "Did she say how she escaped?"

Dr Caldwell shook her head. "She didn't remember. Or maybe she didn't want to. She only said, 'He let me go. I think he wanted me to talk about it.'"

Brooke's eyes narrowed. "He released her to spread the fear?"

"Possibly. Or he was testing her. Seeing if she would go to the police. When she didn't, maybe it reinforced his control."

Owen nodded. "We believe her real name is Lesley Cordery. Can you confirm?"

Caldwell blinked. "Lesley. Yes. That sounds right. I remember she slipped once, signed her name on a form. She quickly scribbled over it, but I saw the 'L'. She said she didn't trust the system. She was hiding from someone. Possibly him."

"Do you know where she went after she stopped therapy?" Brooke asked.

Caldwell shook her head. "She disappeared. Missed two sessions, then nothing. Her phone number went dead. I assumed she had either left the city or something worse."

Brooke's voice softened. "If she's alive, she may be the key to everything."

Dr Caldwell nodded slowly. "Then you'd better find her."

Chapter 35

The chain around Sarah's ankle was lighter now.
Not removed, just looser. A sign.
Blue had noticed her shift.
She smiled more. Didn't argue. Let him speak without flinching. Played the game.
Rosie had noticed too, but she wasn't sure whether to believe it. Or trust it.

Sarah sat on the mattress, folding the thin blanket with care. Her voice was quiet, almost soft.
"I think he likes me now. Maybe I misjudged him."
Rosie looked up sharply. "You don't believe that."
Sarah shrugged. "I don't know. Maybe if I keep my head down, I'll get through this."

The door opened without warning. Blue stepped inside. Both women stood immediately, naked as always, their arms at their sides.
"Good girls," he said, voice smooth and deliberate. His eyes lingered on Sarah. "You're learning."
Sarah smiled faintly. "You were right. Resistance just hurts."

He walked to her slowly, gaze scanning her face like he was looking for cracks.
"No more clever talk? No insults today?"
She shook her head once.
He tilted her chin up with his fingers. His touch made Rosie tense.
"Tell me you're mine," he said.
Sarah paused for a breath, then met his eyes. "I'm yours."

His smile widened.
That twisted, satisfied grin that made Rosie's stomach turn.

Blue pulled up a chair in front of her and sat down, watching her with quiet expectation. Rosie's eyes darted to the glint of metal in his hand.
A knife.
Small. Hidden. But definitely a blade.

Is he going to kill her?

Sarah knelt in front of him without hesitation and took him in her mouth.
His morning ritual.

Rosie turned away, the bile rising in her throat.
She wanted to scream, to look away completely, but something made her keep listening.
Survival, maybe.

When it was over, Sarah sat back on her heels, opened her mouth to show it was empty. Just like he liked.

He left without a word.
The door clicked shut behind him.

Sarah exhaled and dropped back onto the mattress. Her hands trembled as she tucked them under her thighs.
Rosie sat beside her. "Was that real?"
Sarah looked up, her eyes cold and sharp again.
"No. You fucking stupid?"
Rosie let out a shaky breath, part relief, part regret.
Sarah leaned in slightly. "But he has to believe it is. If we're going to survive, I need him to trust me."
"You're playing him?"
"I'm trying."
Rosie nodded slowly. "Then I'll back you. Just… don't get too good at pretending. I won't risk myself."
Sarah didn't smile.
"That's what scares me."

The door creaked open again.
He was standing there. Watching. Listening?
Rosie's blood ran cold.

"Rosie. Come with me, please."
She swallowed. "Yes, Blue."
She glanced back at Sarah, who stayed frozen in place.
As they walked out, Sarah's chest tightened with panic.
Had he heard them? Had Rosie said too much?
Was she about to lose everything she'd built?

Down the hallway, Rosie forced calm into her voice.
"Is everything alright, Blue?"
"Yes, Rosie. I want you to spend the night with me. You're different from Sarah. There's something about her

I don't like."
She didn't respond. Not yet.

They entered the other bedroom.
He stood by the bed, watching her, then silently unfastened his belt and let his trousers fall to the floor. He removed his shirt slowly, never taking his eyes off her.
"Join me, Rosie."
It wasn't a command. Not quite. But the implication hung in the air like smoke.

She didn't want to think about what would happen if she said no.
Rosie stepped forward, already naked.
Then she lay on top of him, skin to skin.
She kissed him.
It wasn't forced.
She made herself mean it.
And maybe, for just a second, she did.

She needed him to believe it.
To stay safe.

For the next hour, she gave herself to him in every way.
When she climaxed, it was real. And she hated herself for it.
When it was over, she rested her head on his chest and listened to his heartbeat.

And in the steady rhythm of that monstrous pulse, she drifted into sleep.

Chapter 36

A young constable rushed into the CID office, looking slightly lost but determined.

"Good morning. I'm looking for DC Daniels and DI Owen," he said, holding a manila file.

Someone pointed him in the right direction, and he made his way over quickly.

"Good morning," he continued, slightly out of breath. "You must be Daniels and Owen. I've got some information on the leads we've been working on for you."

"OK, thank you... uh?" Owen asked, giving the young man a once-over.

"Oh. Constable Jones. Just transferred in from the Met." He straightened up. "So, how's it going?"

"Thank you, Constable. We'll take it from here," Owen said, taking the file from his hands. Jones gave a quick nod and retreated without another word.

Owen turned to Brooke. "So, Brooke, what have we got? Please tell me there's something."

Brooke opened the folder and tapped the top sheet. "The body found in Kent? Turns out it was a domestic. Her ex did it. He's already confessed."

Owen let out a frustrated sigh. "Great. Another dead end."

"Wait," Brooke said, flipping the page. "But look at this. There's something else—possibly a breakthrough. A connection to that photo of Melanie Chambers. Or Lesley Cordery. You remember the image Kingsley had, the one with the two teenagers?"

"Yeah," Owen said, frowning. "What about it?"

"We double-checked the school records from the area and matched them with a partial name found in Kingsley's archived files. It looks like the girl in that photo is his daughter."

Owen blinked. "His daughter. The one he claimed he hadn't seen in years?"

Brooke nodded. "Yes. If we're right, then Melanie—or Lesley, whatever name she was using—wasn't just a housemate or runaway. She might've been his kid."

A heavy silence fell.

"That lying bastard," Owen muttered. "He's been holding back since day one."

Brooke closed the file. "We need to bring him in. Properly. No more doorstep chats."

Owen nodded. "Agreed. I'll get the paperwork started. He's coming in, today."

Brooke stood. "This time, he answers everything."

Chapter 37

Rosie woke up beside Blue. He was still asleep, or at least pretending to be. She sat up slowly, eyes fixed on him, her thoughts spinning.

Was this it?

Was this her chance?

Or was this just another trap?

She hated him. Despised everything he was. But she had survived this long for a reason. She knew what he wanted, what he needed to believe.

Swallowing the bile rising in her throat, she leaned over him and ran her hand across his chest, then down between his legs. She kissed his cheek, then his chest. Her eyes flicked down. Still soft.

She took him in her hand, gently stroking, then lowered her mouth onto him, covering everything. Slowly, he began to respond. She glanced up. Still no movement. His eyes remained closed.

Is he asleep? Or just seeing what I'll do?

She moved across his body, straddling him, and lowered herself onto his now firm erection. A small gasp escaped him. His eyes fluttered open.

Good morning, Rosie, he murmured. This is a nice surprise. That's it, Rosie. Yes, just like that.

She leaned forward and kissed him deeply, pouring everything into it. The only way to make it look real was to make it real.

Let him believe it. Make him feel safe.

He rolled her onto her back and took over. She moaned, half acting, half reacting. Her body betrayed her. Her climax hit faster than she expected, and that terrified her even more.

When it was over, she lay there panting, shaken by how real it had felt.

Thank you, Rosie, Blue said warmly. That was truly wonderful. But now… now we have to find out the truth.

The truth? she whispered. Blue, I don't understand.

Oh, you will, he said. Come on. Let's see what Sarah's up to.

They walked the short distance to the other bedroom. Rosie's gut twisted. Dread curled in her belly. Was this a trap? Had she just failed another test?

Blue unlocked the door with a faint smile.

Good morning, Sarah. Hope you weren't too lonely on your own. We had a great time, didn't we, Rosie?

Ah… yes, Blue. It was really great, Rosie replied, her voice flat.

She stood back as Blue walked into the room, calm and controlled.

So, Sarah, he said, dragging out a chair and sitting down, I've been thinking. Rosie's been very loyal to me. Or… she wants me to believe that. And you… well, you've been rather eager to escape.

He folded his arms.

So, here's my problem. I don't know who to trust. Is Rosie for real? Or are you both playing me?

He turned to Sarah. So, I'm going to test your loyalty. Tell me. Is Rosie planning to escape?

Sarah looked at Rosie, just for a second, and then said, yes. She told me to pretend, just like she's doing. She's planning to escape as soon as she gets a chance.

Rosie's stomach dropped. Her heart hammered in her chest.

He turned to her. So, Rosie. Is that true?

Rosie didn't blink. Not anymore, Blue. When you first brought me here, yes, I planned to escape. But not now. I've seen a different side of you. You're not just a monster. You've shown me care. Protection. That night when you held me after the storm…

She paused, then went on. It's Sarah who's been plotting. She stole a screw from the wall. She's been trying to pick the lock.

Blue smiled. Yes, Rosie. I know.

Both women stared at him in silence, stunned.

Now, Sarah, he said, rising to his feet, to prove your loyalty, I'm giving you a choice.

He walked slowly toward her.

Either hurt Rosie… or I'll kill you both.

No, Blue. Please, Rosie started, stepping forward.

Silence, Rosie.

Sarah looked at Blue, then at Rosie. Her eyes had changed. There was fear, yes, but something else now. Hatred.

You fucking whore, she spat. Trying to grass me up? Fine. Take this, bitch.

She slapped Rosie hard across the face, knocking her sideways.

Come on, Rosie. I'll fucking hurt you, I swear.

Another slap.

Rosie reeled, the taste of blood in her mouth. Her instincts screamed move, but she held her ground.

Sarah lunged again. Rosie struck first, hitting her in the chest and winding her slightly.

Sarah laughed, breathless. Is that the best you've got? He won't have to kill you. I will.

She launched into a fury of punches. Rosie blocked, retaliated, driving her back. She landed two clean hits, one to the chest, another to the jaw, sending Sarah stumbling.

Get up, Rosie yelled. You don't scare me.

Sarah saw an opening, charged, tackled her to the floor. They wrestled, grunting, biting, clawing. Rosie used her elbow, driving it hard into Sarah's back. Sarah rolled away and scrambled toward the bed, reaching underneath.

From the shadows, she pulled a rusted metal bar, broken from the bed frame.

She turned and ran at Rosie, swinging it overhead.

Before the blow landed, Blue was there. His hand snapped around Sarah's throat, lifting her like she weighed nothing, and he hurled her across the room.

Are you okay, Rosie? he asked, helping her up.

Yes, Blue, she gasped. Thanks to you…

Blue stepped over Sarah's crumpled body and picked up the metal bar. He turned it slowly in his hand, almost admiring its weight.

So, this was meant for me, was it? You get the screw in the lock, wait till I come in, then strike?

No. I wasn't. Blue, I swear. I would never, Sarah gasped. She was on her knees now, hands outstretched in desperate surrender. It was Rosie. She wanted to escape. I was just protecting myself.

Shut up, Sarah.

Please, Blue, don't…

He didn't answer. He hurled the bar with a sudden, fluid motion. It slammed into her chest with a dull thud, the force driving her backward.

Sarah gasped; eyes wide in shock. She looked down at the jagged metal protruding from her, her mouth opening in a silent cry. Blood welled up instantly, dark and thick.

She looked to Rosie, her eyes pleading, confused.

Then her body swayed, and she toppled sideways, hitting the ground hard, eyes still fixed on Rosie as the last breath left her body.

Rosie didn't move. Couldn't.

She had imagined escape a hundred times. Fighting, running, tricking him.

But not this.

Not standing by while someone died.

Come on, Rosie, Blue said calmly. You've proven yourself to me.

He took her by the arm, dragged her into the other room, and chained her back to the bed. He leaned down and kissed her softly on the forehead.

I'll be a little while, Rosie. Try to rest.

He left the room, locking it behind him.

Rosie sat in the dark, her body trembling. What could she have done differently? Could she have saved Sarah? Or had she already picked her side?

The silence was broken by a soft, steady buzzing.

She blinked, confused.

A fly.

Then another.

The sound grew louder, from the room next door.

Her eyes filled with tears, and this time they didn't stop.

Goodbye, Sarah, she whispered. I'm sorry.

She couldn't hold back the tears, part of her wondering what she had become.

Chapter 38

The camera's red light blinked steadily from the ceiling corner. Cold, quiet, clinical.

Kingsley sat in the middle of the room, back straight, hands folded tightly in front of him on the metal table.

His expression was unreadable. Defensive. Like a man who had already rehearsed his story too many times.

Owen leaned against the wall while Brooke paced slowly behind Kingsley, setting the rhythm without saying a word. They let the silence stretch. Let him feel the weight of it.

Kingsley finally broke. "I've told you everything I know."

Owen stepped forward. "You've told us something. But the more we dig, the more it stinks of something else entirely."

Brooke dropped a photo onto the table. It slid to a stop in front of Kingsley.

It showed two teenagers in a school courtyard. A girl with long brown hair and guarded eyes. And a boy, maybe a year older, with a lean frame and the same sharp jawline as Kingsley.

Kingsley glanced at the photo, then looked away.

"Recognise them?" Brooke asked.

"No."

Owen stepped in. "Really? That's odd. Because the girl—Melanie Chambers, or Lesley Cordery, depending on the year—was listed as living at your address. And the boy—records suggest he might be related to your family."

"I never had a son."

"DNA will clear that up," Owen said calmly. "We've already applied for a match."

Kingsley's face tightened.

Brooke spoke more softly now, circling behind him again. "You said Melanie was a lodger. That she moved out. That she wasn't your daughter. But we have school records under your name. Guardianship forms. Old social worker notes. Did you forget about those?"

"I didn't forget," he said, voice tightening. "I tried to forget."

Owen folded his arms. "What happened to her, Kingsley?"

Kingsley was silent. Then: "She ran away. At fifteen. Left in the middle of the night. Never came back."

Brooke didn't blink. "But we know she didn't run away. You're hiding something."

He sighed. "Fine. She didn't run. She was taken into care. I didn't want that coming out—not after everything else."

"That's convenient," Brooke said. "Because around that same time, a child sex abuse inquiry involving your family quietly disappeared."

He looked up sharply. "That case was dropped. There was no evidence."

"There was a girl who wouldn't talk," Owen said. "And a man with enough pull to keep it quiet."

Kingsley's face twisted—not with rage, but shame. His throat worked to swallow words that didn't come.

"I didn't touch her," he said hoarsely. "But I wasn't a good father. I was angry. She reminded me of her mother. Of everything that went wrong. I was hard on her. Too hard, maybe. But I didn't…"

He stopped.

"Then who did?" Brooke asked.

Kingsley hesitated.

"There was someone else," he said slowly. "Not what I would call close family. My older brother. He used to visit. He drank. Wasn't right in the head. Always said things to her that made me uncomfortable. I told him to stop coming round. After she went away into the home, where he worked. He fell—or some say he was pushed—down the stairs. Died at the bottom. Broken neck. And I wasn't sorry that he did."

Owen narrowed his eyes. "Name?"

"David Taylor."

Brooke and Owen locked eyes. That name again. Mr Taylor.

"How come he has a different name to you, Barry, if he is your older brother?"

"He got into all sorts of shit when he was younger. No one would give him a job, so he changed his name and forged other things. Driving licence, bank account. Lived a secret life."

"Did she ever mention him again?" Brooke asked.

Kingsley nodded. "Once. A letter came maybe a few months later. No return address. Just a few lines. No signature. But she wrote: 'He found me again. I thought I was safe.'"

The room fell silent. The only sound was the faint whirr of the camera in the ceiling.

Owen leaned in. "That girl—your daughter—she's at the heart of all this. The victims. The pattern. The lies. She might have changed her name again. She might even be dead."

Kingsley's mouth twitched. "No. She's not dead."

"How do you know?"

He hesitated. "Because I still dream about her. Every night. And she's always running."

Brooke tapped the table gently. "Did she ever draw? Keep journals?"

"She used to write stories," he said quietly. "Dark stuff. Girls locked in basements. Monsters wearing friendly faces. I thought she was just imaginative."

"Did she ever draw anything like this?" Brooke asked, sliding another photo across the table.

It was a close-up of a tattoo, the Blue Rose.

Kingsley's reaction was instant. A sharp inhale, then complete stillness.

"I've seen that before," he whispered.

"Where?"

"She sketched it once," he said, almost to himself. "A rose with ten petals. She said it meant... ten pieces of herself. Ten lies, maybe. Or ten men. I didn't understand it then."

Brooke froze. "Ten petals?"

Kingsley nodded. "She coloured one petal black. Told me each one would turn dark eventually. One for every time someone betrayed her."

Owen spoke gently now. "Do you think she's still alive, Kingsley?"

He looked up at them, eyes rimmed red, voice thick. "I think she became someone else. Someone colder. Someone dangerous. And if she's still out there... then someone's going to pay."

He hesitated, then added, "By the way... her name—her real name, a name never used—was Shawnnessy. An old Irish name."

Brooke frowned. "Why was it never used?"

"She didn't like it," Kingsley said. "Because he used to call her Shawny."

"He being David?" Owen clarified.

Kingsley gave a slow nod.

Brooke leaned in a little. "One last question. You say the boy in the photo wasn't your son. Then who was he? He had to be someone you knew."

She reached out, gently touching his arm. A small gesture of compassion.

"His name is, or was, Ryan Kingsley. David's son."

Owen's brows rose. "Your brother's son? And he kept the Kingsley name?"

Kingsley nodded slowly. "David wanted people to think I was the father. That was his way of punishing me for trying to shut him out."

Brooke lowered her voice. "When was the last time you saw him?"

Kingsley looked between them, then dropped his gaze, shaking his head slowly, mumbling to himself.

"2015. The last time I saw my daughter."

Brooke's voice softened. "Do you think they ran off together?"

Kingsley exhaled. His voice cracked. "Look… I've told you everything this time. This is all stuff I wanted to forget. Did they run off together? I don't know. I really wish I did."

He slumped back in the chair, eyes on the cold steel of the table.

Owen stood. His tone was calm but firm. "We're holding you as a person of interest."

Chapter 39

The buzzing was gone.
So was the body.

Rosie sat in silence, still chained to the bed, staring at the shadows cast by the bars on the window. Her cheeks were stiff with dried tears. Her body ached, her face, her arms, her soul.

Sarah was dead.

And Blue had kissed her on the head like she was a good girl.

The weight of it all pressed down on Rosie's chest. She hadn't just witnessed a murder, she had become part of it. She had stood there. Done nothing. Said nothing.

And a part of her still felt grateful it hadn't been her. A part she hated.

The door unlocked. She flinched.

Blue stepped in, a towel over one shoulder. His hair was damp from a shower, his face clean-shaven. He looked… ordinary. That somehow made it worse.

"You doing okay, sweetheart?" he asked gently, walking over.

She nodded, robotic. "Yes, Blue. Did you… um… move Sarah?"

"Yes, Rosie. I have. I need to pop out for a few hours, but I'll bring you back something nice."

He sat beside her on the bed and reached for her wrist, checking the chain. His fingers lingered.

"I'm sorry you had to see that," he said. "But I had to be sure. About you. About her."

Rosie said nothing.

"She failed. You passed."

He leaned in and kissed her cheek. She forced herself not to recoil.

"You're not just another girl now, Rosie. You're… more."

She looked at him then. "What am I?"

He smiled. "You're mine."

She lowered her gaze. "I want to be."

He beamed, pleased by the answer. "Good girl."

He stood and walked to the dresser. Rosie noticed something, a book tucked into the corner, its spine cracked and worn. Something he'd been reading. She couldn't see the title, but made a mental note of where he kept it.

"Are you hungry?" he asked.

"Yes."

He turned, visibly pleased by her obedience. "I'll bring you something warm before I go out."

He smiled again. "Now that Sarah's gone, we need to find someone new to play with."

She blinked. "We…? You mean you want my help?"

Blue paused at the door. His head tilted slightly. "Is that going to be a problem, Rosie?"

She shook her head quickly. "No, Blue. Not at all. I was just surprised, that's all. But thank you."

He walked back and kissed her on the forehead.

As he left, Rosie finally let out the breath she'd been holding.

This was her new game.
Not resistance. Not escape.
Not yet.

She had to become what he needed. Let him believe she was his. Let him trust her.

But could she really do it?
Could she sit beside him, smile at him, laugh at his jokes
And help him pick a victim?

She hadn't even let herself think about that.

How could she help him choose someone, knowing what he'd do to them?
What he'd already done to her. To Sarah.

Her stomach turned. But if she didn't play the part, she was next.
And if she was next, there'd be no one left to stop him.

So she would play it.
Perfectly.
She would become whatever he needed her to be.
And maybe, just maybe, she could take it all from him.

He returned twenty minutes later with two plates of food, spaghetti Bolognese.

He sat beside her again on the bed and handed her one plate, with a proper knife and fork. Not plastic. Not disposable. It felt almost… civilised.

"I hope you enjoy this," he said. "It's something I haven't had in a while."

"Thank you, Blue. It looks and smells great. I didn't realise you could cook."

Inside, she felt sick.
With every mouthful, she wanted to gag.
But she smiled. She chewed. She swallowed.

For a brief second, as the flavours hit her tongue… she almost wanted more.

They talked, books, movies. He asked if she could draw. What she used to do. Where she worked.

He said something he thought was funny. She giggled, just enough to please him.
Not too much. Never too much.

When they'd finished, he stood and gathered the plates, walking toward the door.

"Blue, wait, you forgot the knives and forks."

He turned and smiled. Took them silently.

Another test, she thought.

And she'd passed again.

Chapter 40

The car was quiet as they drove away from the station.

Brooke was still holding the sketch of the blue rose between her fingers. The photocopy had started to curl at the edges. She couldn't stop staring at it.

"Ten petals," she said aloud. "Each one for someone who betrayed her."

Owen nodded slowly; his eyes fixed on the road. "And Kingsley said she coloured them in as they turned dark. If that's true, she's not the killer."

"She's the reason for him."

They were both thinking it but didn't say it.

Brooke leaned forward. "You realise what this means, right? Melanie, or Lesley, was Shawnnessy. She might have been the first victim. Emotionally, if not physically. He's not just killing random women. He's killing symbols of her. Pieces of her life."

Owen glanced at her. "A trail of revenge."

"Or obsession. But, wait, I just thought of something. Everything revolves around the number ten. Ten petals. Ten people who betrayed her… but there's one more. Shawnnessy. That's ten letters."

"You're right," Owen said, frowning. "But we're still missing something. We've got all the pieces of the puzzle, but not the one thing that connects them."

He pulled into the car park outside the station and cut the engine.

"We need to dig into Kingsley's brother. David Taylor. The name's too much of a coincidence."

"Owen, I don't want to jump the gun here, but the killer used the name Mr Taylor. David Taylor's son was Ryan Kingsley. So, what if Ryan isn't dead? What if he murdered Shawnnessy? Or... what if he's the one still doing this?"

"I like your thinking, Brooke," Owen said. "But there's no evidence. Not yet. Everything we've got is circumstantial. It lines up, sure, but it wouldn't hold in court. And it's thin. Very thin. We need to connect the dots."

Brooke opened the file on her lap. "Already started. I ran a basic background on him. Died in 2016, officially from a fall. But here's where it gets strange. He was suspected in the disappearance of a young woman that same year. Case was dropped. No charges."

Owen frowned. "Do we know her name?"

Brooke flipped a page. "Maggie Smith. Seventeen. Went missing after reporting harassment at her job. When the local station investigated, they found there was no way to identify the body. Some say it was Maggie Smith, but she was recorded as a Jane Doe. The paperwork for her employment was all forged."

She looked up. "Guess who her employer was?"

Owen sighed. "Taylor."

"Exactly. Says here she had a bust-up with a Mr David Taylor, who fired her. A week later, she was found dead."

"Okay, but was there any tattoo? Anything to connect her to these murders?"

"No," Brooke said. "But get this, about the fall Taylor had. The witness listed at the time was Eddie Brooke."

Owen raised his eyebrows.

"He said he saw someone push Taylor, but there was no evidence to back it up."

Owen sat forward. "I'm starting to think that maybe Maggie Smith, Melanie Granger, Lesley Cordery, and Shawnnessy might all be the same person."

Brooke blinked. "If that's true, Owen, how many names did she have?"

"Jesus," he muttered. "It's a web. This isn't just about kidnapping and killing. This is legacy."

Brooke leaned back, tired but wired. "Generational damage. Kingsley's abuse. Taylor's perversion. Melanie caught in the middle, and then someone comes along. Someone broken. Someone who sees her pain as gospel."

Owen looked at her. "You think the killer knew Melanie?"

"I think he worshipped her. Or what she became. She survived everything. He didn't."

They sat in silence a moment.

Then Owen said, "So what now?"

"We need to speak to the people who were there when Maggie got sacked, anyone who worked with her or saw what happened that day."

"And the witness," Owen added. "Eddie Brooke. If he saw Taylor pushed, maybe he didn't tell us everything. Or maybe someone made sure he didn't."

Brooke nodded. "We track him down. See what else he knows."

Owen reached for the ignition again. "Alright. Let's dig up the dead. If we're lucky, someone still breathing will tell us the truth."

Brooke glanced down at the blue rose sketch in her lap. "The petals aren't random. I think he leaves one on each victim. Just like she did, on paper."

"A death for each petal," Owen murmured.

Brooke closed the file and looked at him. "How many petals have we found so far?"

"Four," he replied. "But if there are ten…"

They didn't finish the thought.

Brooke stared out the window. "Six more women might be out there. Still alive. Or not yet taken. Let's not forget Rosie and Sarah. If they turn up dead, that would leave four."

Owen looked away. "We're running out of time."

Chapter 41

Rosie found it strange to be free to walk around the large bedroom.
No chains to hold her back.
He had taken away all the clothes he had given her, leaving her naked again, a deliberate reminder that freedom was only ever partial.
She knew the door was locked securely from the outside, the windows bolted shut. Thick metal bars made escape unthinkable.
Blue had been gone for at least a couple of hours, she thought. Without a clock, it was hard to keep track. Time had become slippery here.

Now, where is that book?
Ah, yes. I remember.

She muttered quietly to herself, stealing a glance out the window. Then she pressed her ear to the door. Nothing. Silence.
Carefully, she pulled the book from its hiding place. It was old, the cover frayed, the spine cracked. She opened it to the first page, expecting blank pages or gibberish.

Instead, she read:

My love, my first and only, Shawnnessy. Then you hurt me… and became the first to die.

Her stomach turned. She placed the book back gently, making sure it looked undisturbed.

What the hell does that mean? Who was she to him? And the first to die?

Her skin crawled.

Sometime later, the hum of an engine grew louder outside.

He's back. Now what?

She straightened up just as the door unlocked. Blue walked in like a man returning home to his lover, casual and expectant.

"Hello, darling. Did you miss old Blue?"

"To be honest… yes, I did. You were gone a long time."

"Well, I brought you some chocolate. And a puzzle book. I even trust you with a pen."

Rosie took them without hesitation, her movements smooth and rehearsed.

"Wow, thanks, Blue. Just what I needed."

She placed the items on a nearby chair, then walked up to him slowly. Her fingers slid through his hair, and she kissed him gently on the lips.

"Blue… I want you. I want you now."

He didn't hesitate. He stripped off without a word. Rosie took his hand and led him to the bed.

Do it. It's for your freedom.
Don't flinch. Don't resist. Just pretend.
Another voice inside her added, What choice do you have? Just get through it. Maybe even fake your way to the end.

She pushed him onto the bed. Took him in her hand, then her mouth. Then she climbed on top of him and let him inside her. She moved with rhythm, fluid and slow, forcing herself to believe this was right. When he lifted his hips, she let herself climax.

Then he turned her over and continued until he finished. Nothing was rushed. It was almost romantic, like two lovers savouring each other.

Afterwards, she cleaned him. Then herself. Just like she had been taught.

He told her to sit beside him. He pulled a small pad from the bag with the sweets and set it between them.

"So, Rosie," he said, "we need to pick a new playmate."

"Blue… are you sure you want my help?"

"Yes, of course. Just like the old days."

Rosie froze for a second.

The old days? How many others played this same part before me? How many are dead because they didn't play it well enough?

"OK, Blue," she said carefully. "Can I ask you something first?"

"You're full of questions today. Go on then."

"If I'm going to help you pick the next one… why did you choose me?"

He smiled, a little crooked.

"When I'm out looking, I look for beauty. The way a woman dresses, the way she moves. I watched you a few times before I brought you here."

"You think I'm beautiful?"

She leaned forward and kissed him gently on the cheek. A small gesture, loaded with manipulation.

"OK, Blue. Where do we start?"

He laid the pad on the bed and spread out six printed profiles.

"Here are the details of six young women who fit the bill."

Rosie scanned the sheets. All looked like they were in their twenties. All had dark hair. From the notes alone, they seemed nearly identical. He had all their names listed, and where they worked.

Then her eyes stopped.

One name stood out, written in blue ink.

Brooke Daniels.

Her stomach twisted. Why was this written in blue? Who was she? Someone special?

"Blue, why is this one marked in blue?"

"Oh, don't worry about that one. She'll be my last."

Your last...

Rosie felt the panic swell but forced it down. She shrugged.

"Do you have anything else, Blue?"

He opened the gallery on his mobile.

"Here, take a look at these."

Six photos. Three white women. One Asian. One Black. All of them pretty, well-dressed, polished. The kind of women who got second glances in bars.

Their smiles were frozen. Their futures already bleeding away.

But one photo was missing. Rosie kept quiet.

Blue watched her as she scrolled.

"So, Rosie, do you have a favourite?"

Her heart thudded. Don't stall. Don't hesitate. He'll know.
Which one suffers less? Which one fights? Which one breaks fast?

She hesitated. Then pointed.

"Yes, Blue. I like this one, Linda."

"Why Linda?"

"They all look good. But Linda reminds me a little of myself. She's twenty-two, fit, and from your notes, not close to anyone."

"Good girl, Rosie," he said, pleased. "Yes, she fits the bill. If all goes well, you'll have a new playmate tomorrow."

She forced a smile.

"I look forward to meeting her, Blue. Will you want me to teach her too?"

"Yes. When I bring her in, I want you to teach her what I like, and when I like it. Make her ready or she ends up another Sarah."

He paused.

"Rosie, as much as I'd like you to come with me, you can't. Not this time."

"That's OK. I understand. Really, I do. It's not about me running… but someone might recognise me."

"I'm glad you understand."

He leaned in and brushed her hair back.

"Now come on, Rosie. Let's go to bed. I want you again."

She stood. Smiled.

Play the part. Say the words. Stay alive.

She climbed into bed beside the monster and braced herself for another night of pretending.

Tomorrow, Linda would arrive.
And the nightmare would begin again.

Chapter 42

The morning light was cold, barely touching the edges of the room through the barred window. Rosie lay still, listening.

She could hear him moving. Calm. Methodical. Packing something into a bag. Whistling.

It was happening.

Linda was about to lose everything.

"Now, Rosie, I'll be gone most of the day. You've got enough food and drink, and you know the routine."

"No problem, Blue. Have a safe trip."

She didn't need an explanation. The routine was always the same. Locked in. No clothes.

"Wish me luck," Blue said casually, as if heading out to buy milk.

"Good luck," Rosie replied softly, giving him a smile she didn't feel. "Be careful."

He smiled at her like a proud husband.

Then he was gone.

The lock turned. The sound of his footsteps faded down the corridor. A door opened at the far end. Then it shut.

Silence.

Rosie sat up in bed, staring at the door. Her gut twisted. She pictured the girl, Linda, somewhere out there now. At a bus stop. Leaving a gym. Checking her phone. Just doing the everyday things, like Rosie had been, when he grabbed her.

Not knowing how her life was about to change.

The guilt bloomed in her chest.

I chose her. I sent him to her. God, what have I done?

She didn't cry. She couldn't. Not here. But her fingers dug into the bedsheets, her breath shaky, her thoughts racing.

South London, 5:48 p.m.

Linda Aniston was out for her usual evening jog before getting ready for work. Right turn through the outskirts of town, along the river, then down the alley toward her flat.

She wore navy gym leggings, a hoodie tied around her waist, and her hair was pulled into a messy bun. Earbuds in. Music up loud. In a world of her own.

She nodded to the rhythm in her ears, the bass thudding in her chest. The scent of the river drifted across, grimy and familiar.

She never noticed the white van creep past and stop.

She never saw him get out.

Never saw the door slide open.

Just a hand. Sudden and strong. Then a sting in her neck.

A needle.

Then nothing but blur and terror.

There was no struggle. It only lasted seconds.

The van door slammed shut, swallowing her scream.

The street fell silent.

He drove away slowly, keeping to side roads until he found a quiet spot to park. Near Tesco's. Big car park, not too busy. No one would notice.

He climbed into the back. She was unconscious but breathing. Her headphones were missing, must have fallen. Too late now. He couldn't go back.

He hogtied her with duct tape, securing her to the van floor. Then the gag. Tight.

One last look.

Then he climbed back into the driver's seat.

Back at the house

The door slammed.

Rosie had been doing the puzzle book he had given her. The sudden bang made her jump. She moved to the window, trying to catch a glimpse of what was happening outside. Her pulse raced. Her stomach lurched.

She heard the front door open, then footsteps. He was dragging something.

Her heart missed a beat.

It was too late now. No turning back.

Then, muffled cries. A thud. Another cry, high-pitched. Female. Real.

He had done it.

Blue had brought her.

Rosie backed away from the window and sat down on the bed, folding her hands in her lap. She forced herself to breathe evenly.

The cries came again, louder now. A scuffle of feet. More dragging. A door closing.

Then silence.

A few minutes passed.

Then he came in.

He looked flushed. Smiling. Triumphant.

"It went smoothly," he said. "You chose well."

Rosie nodded, keeping her voice light. "She sounds strong."

"She kicked like a mule," he laughed. "Almost bit me."

"I'm sure she'll learn."

"She will. And you're going to help me teach her."

He sat beside her, wiping something from his arm. Blood or dirt, she couldn't tell.

"Do you want to meet her tonight, or wait until morning?"

Rosie hesitated. Her stomach turned.

"Maybe wait," she said gently. "She'll be frightened. Let her settle. I'll be more help in the morning. I'll show her what you like then."

He tilted his head, studying her face.

Then he nodded. "Good thinking."

He stood and stretched.

"I'm going to shower. Then I want you again."

He kissed her forehead and left.

Rosie sat still, every muscle taut.

In the next room, Linda was crying softly. A sound like glass cracking in the dark.

You're not alone, Rosie thought. I'm here. Just stay strong. Don't fight too fast. There might still be a way out.

She closed her eyes.

One of us has to get out of this.

The next morning

It came too quickly.

Blue got up without saying a word.

Was something wrong?

"Morning, Blue. You okay? You seem deep in thought."

"Yes. Thank you, sweetheart, for being so caring. You always looked after old Blue."

She caught the shift in his words. The past tense. As if he were talking to someone else. Someone he had lost.

Who was he remembering? A victim? A ghost?

"Come on, Rosie. Ready to meet your new friend?"

"Yes, Blue."

It's now or never, she thought, as she watched him unlock the door. She followed him to the next room, still naked, still feeling sick, still plotting.

Blue unlocked the door, and they stepped inside.

Linda was still clothed and tied to the bed. Her eyes were wide with fear as she watched Blue approach and remove her gag.

"Now, Linda, no screaming. No one can hear you. And Rosie here will tell you what happens if you misbehave. Now, say hello to Rosie."

Linda didn't speak at first. Her eyes flicked between them, wild and furious.

"Let me go, you fucking bastard. Get away from me. What is this? Some kind of twisted game? You freaks doing this together?"

Blue stepped in and slapped her hard across the face.

She lifted her head, seething, and he slapped her again.

"Now, Linda, we're a happy little family here. So watch and learn. Rosie's going to show you what I like."

"Just kill me, you freak."

Rosie stepped forward.

"Linda, don't talk to Blue like that, or you'll piss me off too. You'll learn to do as you're fucking told."

Blue blinked, surprised. He hadn't expected that from her.

Neither had she.

But it worked. He liked it.

"Now this is how Blue likes to start his day."

She knelt beside the bed and did what he wanted. She didn't flinch. Didn't choke. Didn't let it show when she tasted him.

When it was over, she wiped her mouth and looked at nothing. She hated every word that had come out of her mouth, but if it kept them both alive, it was worth it.

"You think I'm going to do that? You can fucking kill me now."

Blue stepped forward, but Rosie raised a hand.

"Blue, please. Let me handle it. Let me do what you asked of me."

He paused. Then nodded.

"Okay, Rosie. But when I come back, you know what I want."

He turned and left, locking the door behind him.

The silence between them was immediate and sharp.

Linda glared at her. "So… Rosie, right? You're the one who's been all over the news. That cop, DI Owen, he's looking for you, right?"

She laughed bitterly. "And now what, you and this freak working together? You his little apprentice or something? Helping him find the next girl?"

Rosie flinched. "No. It's not like that."

"Really?" Linda snapped. "Because it sure as hell looks like it from where I'm sitting."

"Linda, listen to me. You won't like it. You'll hate it. But if you don't let me do what I have to do, if you don't give Blue what he wants, he'll beat you to death."

"Yeah? Maybe that's better than becoming his pet."

Rosie moved toward her and began removing Linda's clothes.

"What the fuck are you doing? Get off me."

Rosie slapped her. Harder than she meant to. But she had to sell it.

"Shut up. And you might just get through this."

She undressed what she could and sat her up.

"Look, Linda. You can act brave. Resist. He'll beat you. And then he'll beat me for not getting you ready."

Linda went quiet. Her mind spinning. A storm of thoughts behind her eyes.

"So… if I give him oral, he won't beat me?"

"Not if you do it right. And clean up everything when he finishes."

She hesitated.

"But Linda, this won't stop with just your mouth. He'll take every part of you."

Rosie swallowed hard.

And when he's done, he'll still want more.

That was what scared her most.

There was no end to it.

Chapter 43

The rain had started again, thin and whispering against the windscreen as Owen pulled the car to a stop outside a squat brick house on the edge of Mitcham.

"This is it," Brooke said, checking her notebook. "Eddy Brooke. Old friend of Kingsley, according to the care home files. Worked with Taylor too, for a few years."

Owen nodded, the engine ticking. "Let's see if he remembers anything worth knowing."

The house looked tired. Net curtains hung limp in the windows. The paint was faded. A rusty satellite dish clung to the roof like it had given up.

Owen rang the bell.

Nothing.

He knocked again, louder this time.

Eventually, a voice from inside shouted, "Alright, alright."

The door creaked open slowly.

Eddy Brooke looked older than sixty. A lean man in a stained vest, white hair slicked back with something that smelled like petrol and cigarettes.

"You, coppers?"

Owen showed his badge. "DI Owen. This is DC Daniels. Mind if we have a word?"

Eddy eyed them both, cautious but curious. "Depends what about."

"We're looking into some old cases," Brooke said smoothly. "You worked with a man named Taylor. Some years back."

Eddy scratched his jaw. "Yeah. Long time ago. He was a weird one."

"We've had conflicting statements," Owen said. "Some say he got sacked. Others say he was pushed. Literally."

Eddy let out a rough laugh. "Yeah, he got shoved alright. Bloke was creeping on one of the girls in the kitchen. One of the lads saw it, lost it, gave him a shove down the stairs. Two flights. Snapped his neck. Dead on the spot."

Owen raised an eyebrow. "And the guy who pushed him?"

"Ryan Thomas," Eddy said, tapping the side of his head. "Quiet lad. But he saw red that day. I think he had a thing for her. They arrested him, but no one came forward to back it up. No witnesses. No statements. So they let him go."

"You say he had a thing for the girl. Who was she?" Brooke asked, watching him carefully.

"Yeah, well, Ryan was a young lad. Good-looking, I guess. But there was another problem."

"What was that?" Brooke asked.

"Well, look. I don't know if this is true, but that girl was said to be his first cousin."

Owen frowned. "So let me understand this. Ryan wanted a relationship with his cousin. Ryan is David Taylor's son, and the girl was Barry Kingsley's daughter?"

"Yep."

"Did they know? Seeing as David Taylor had changed his name?"

Eddy shrugged. "Look, I have no idea. Maybe they did, maybe not. You should ask Maggie."

"Maggie," they both said at once.

"Yes. She saw it more than I did. She should know what happened."

"We believed she may have been murdered," Brooke said.

"What? When? I only saw her last week."

"You saw her? Where is she? We need to talk to her today."

He wrote down the address. "It's the care home. Pinetrees."

"Okay, Eddy. Going back to the girl. Ryan liked his cousin. Who was she, or who is she?"

"A very strange young lady, as far as I can remember. They brought her in around 2015. A sad case."

"Sorry, Eddy. They brought her there? What do you mean?"

"To be honest, and I'm not sure of the correct terms, but she wasn't all there."

"You mean psychological problems?" Brooke looked at Owen. Both were thinking the same thing. The pieces of the puzzle were just waiting to be placed.

Brooke tilted her head. "So you and Ryan Thomas were working together, and no one thought to say anything about the relationship?"

Eddy blinked, then shrugged. "Wasn't exactly a tight-knit team. Half the people working there were either pissed or off their heads. Taylor was a creep, but no one wanted to get involved."

"Do you know where Ryan is now?" Owen asked.

Eddy shook his head. "Moved away years ago. Haven't seen him since. But like I said, ask Maggie. She was the kitchen girl at the time. Not long after. She was close to Taylor. Knew him better than most, and knew Ryan too."

Daniels scribbled in her notebook. "You know her full name?"

"Maggie Ross. She was from Croydon, I think. Bit of a temper, but a good worker. Tough girl. Took no shit."

"Thanks, Mr Brooke," Owen said. "We may be back in touch."

As they walked back to the car, Daniels glanced at Owen.

"That's two people now who've mentioned Maggie. And Thomas. This could be something."

Owen nodded. "Feels like loose threads are finally tying themselves together."

He started the engine.

"Let's find Maggie. And get eyes on Thomas. Before someone else disappears."

"Just one thing, Owen. Who was the dead girl found and believed to be Maggie, but listed as a Jane Doe?"

"Good question, Brooke. To be honest, I'm starting to think the dead girl might be Melanie. Or whatever her real name was. But if she was locked away, there'll be records. We should at least get some answers."

"Yes. But let's go and see Maggie first."

Chapter 44

Linda hadn't stopped crying.

She sat in the far corner of the small room, arms pulled tightly around her knees, trying to disappear into herself.

Her wrists were raw from the rope. Her ankle burned where the chain bit into her skin.

It wasn't just fear anymore.

It was shame. Rage. And something dangerously close to hopelessness.

The door opened.

Rosie stepped in. Linda didn't look up.

Behind her, Blue entered, his steps deliberate and unhurried.

He stopped, eyes on Linda. "Is she going to behave, Rosie?"

"I'm not sure, Blue," Rosie said. "Hard to get through to her."

Blue nodded. "Get her on the bed. I want her now."

"Okay, Blue. Just give me a minute, please."

Rosie moved towards Linda and crouched beside her. She reached for Linda's hand, but Linda jerked away, recoiling like she'd touched fire.

"Look, Linda," Rosie said softly. "Now is the time. He's going to take you anyway. Give yourself. It'll be worse if you fight."

Silence stretched between them.

Then Linda spoke, her voice hoarse. "Why are you helping him? Why do you even care?"

Rosie hesitated, then said, "I chose you."

Linda blinked. "What?"

"I'm sorry. I had to pick someone. And I picked you."

"You chose me?" Her voice cracked with disbelief and fury. "You fucking chose me?"

"I know how it sounds. But if I didn't, he would've punished me. He would've taken someone anyway."

"I don't care," Linda snapped. Her face twisted with rage and hurt. "You let it be me. You threw me to him to save yourself. You're worse than him. You pretend you're a victim too, but you're not. You chose this. You let him do this to me."

Rosie's face darkened. Her voice wavered. "I know what he's going to do to you. I know what he did to me. And I don't want it to happen again. But if you don't play this right, you'll die. Or wish you had."

Linda shook her head, tears spilling down her cheeks. "I won't be like you."

Rosie stood up, her expression hardening. "You think I wanted to be?"

She helped Linda to her feet. Linda resisted, then gave in, silent and shaking.

"You'll need your strength," Rosie said. "Save the anger for later."

Blue's voice came from the doorway. "Thank you, Rosie. Now go next door. We'll talk later."

"Okay, Blue. Enjoy yourself."

She left quietly and shut the door behind her.

Linda lay trembling on the bed as he approached, rage boiling in her chest. But maybe Rosie was right. Maybe the only way to survive was to give in.

Still, the fear was louder.

Out on the landing

Rosie stopped.

She realised something.

She wasn't chained.

Blue had let her walk unescorted for the first time since he had taken her. No leash. No hand on her shoulder. No threat.

It was a test.

She could run. Take the van. Get out. She knew it.

But her body didn't move.

Not yet.

Not now.

Not like this, her inner voice whispered.

She stood there, frozen, listening to Linda scream. She turned slowly and stepped into her room. Closed the door. Sat on the bed.

And smiled, just faintly.

Because she understood something now.

Her day was coming.

Another test passed.

Another mask worn.

Another inch closer to the moment she would make him bleed.

Chapter 45

The community centre smelled like cheap coffee and furniture polish. It was mid-morning, quiet except for a toddler group down the hall. Owen and Brooke stood outside Room 3, waiting for the organiser to bring Maggie through.

"She sounded jumpy on the phone," Daniels said. "Didn't want to come to the station. Said she doesn't trust anyone anymore."

"She's not the only one," Owen muttered.

The door opened, and Maggie stepped in slowly. Early sixties, tall and lean with short grey hair. Her eyes were sharp, but her hands trembled slightly, and her gaze flicked around the room like she was waiting for trouble.

Owen gestured to the seats. "Thanks for meeting us. I'm DI Owen. This is DC Daniels."

Maggie sat slowly, fidgeting with the strap of her handbag. "You said it was about...?"

"Pinetrees," Brooke said.

"We're looking into an incident that might connect to your time there," Owen added. "A man, possibly under a false name, worked at Pinetrees around 2015. We understand you were let go shortly after an altercation."

Maggie's expression tightened. "They said I was unstable. That I made things up. But I know what I saw. They wanted me to be a patient there, but I ran off."

Owen leaned forward. "Please, go on."

"There was this new carer. He called himself Ryan. Just a youngster. They used him to help out during lunchtimes, clean up, things like that. Left the specialist staff to look after the real patients. He was a nice-looking lad. Polite. Too polite. He had that fake calm, you know?" She paused. "I noticed he spent a lot of time around the younger girls. Not just the ones in care. Staff too."

Brooke glanced at Owen.

"I reported it to the manager. Said he gave me a bad feeling. A week later, David Taylor, the manager, was pushed down the stairs by Ryan. He was arrested, and they questioned me. They tried to say I was involved. I told them. I saw it happen. But they said I made it up. Wanted to do a psych evaluation on me."

"So what happened then, Maggie?" Brooke rested a hand on hers, gently.

"Well, I knew what that place was like, so I ran. Went miles away. Found somewhere to hide."

"Do you know what happened to Ryan?"

"It all went very quiet. He was involved with that girl."

"What girl, Maggie?"

"His cousin. She wasn't right in the head. Locked in there permanently. Completely broken, they said."

"Why?" Brooke asked.

"Look, I was older than Ryan and her. Worked in the kitchen. I can only tell you what I heard. Rumours. I did see, by chance, a couple of drawings she'd done."

"This is important, Maggie. Can you remember what they were like?" Owen asked.

"Remember them? I still have nightmares. Always done in black, blue, and gold. Drawings of men and women. Tied up in cellars. Dungeons. In the woods. People being taken. I remember one where a young woman was being grabbed by someone in black, and they were putting something in her neck."

"Maggie, is it alright if I show you a couple of photos? Just something the girl might've drawn."

She hesitated, then nodded.

Owen took out his phone and showed her a photo of the blue rose tattoo.

"Yes. She was always drawing a rose. A blue rose with up to ten petals. She'd do those nasty drawings on anything she could get. Walls, napkins, food trays."

"Did you ever hear why it was always ten petals?"

"Not really. Someone said it had to do with her name."

"Her name?"

"Shawnnessy. She hated it."

"What was she called there? We've seen different names."

"Well, I didn't deal with her directly. But someone once asked for a meal for Lesley."

"Thank you, Maggie. Just a couple more questions."

"That's okay. But first, can you show me that phone again? I saw something else there."

Owen looked at Brooke and raised an eyebrow.

"Of course." He scrolled and showed the next image.

"This one?" he asked.

"Yes," she replied, pointing to the gold triangle. "That was a pendant. A gold one. Given to her by her late mother. They took it off her. What happened to it, I've no idea."

"Is there anything you can tell us about David Taylor? We're led to believe you knew him."

"Well yes, I knew him. I wouldn't say well. And when he died, I thought he got what he deserved."

"Why's that?"

"He tried it on with me once. I was alone in the kitchen. Never been with a man before, and he starts touching me. Between the legs. Asking if I liked it. Said he wanted me. Was going to have me. Someone came in and he backed off. I didn't complain. He was the manager. But I know he was having sex with the patients. They were out of it. He could do what he wanted. Free sex, anytime he wanted it. No one cared. And if they did, they said nothing. When Ryan saw him trying it on with Shawnnessy, well, you already know the rest."

"One last question, Maggie. Do you know what happened to her?"

"I'd already run off. But someone who's passed away since told me later that Ryan took her out for a picnic in the woods nearby. He came back. She didn't. She couldn't stand him. He was like Taylor. Always after a bit."

"Thank you so much, Maggie. You've been very helpful. Here's our card. Please call if you remember anything else."

They stepped outside into the sunlight, the door clicking shut behind them.

"That wasn't just useful," Brooke said quietly. "That was the first crack."

Owen nodded. "And maybe the first person to see him for what he really is."

He looked out across the car park.

They were getting closer.

And he knew it.

Chapter 46

"Owen, it's getting late. I'm starving and could do with some rest. How about dinner at my place and a fresh start tomorrow?"

"You read my mind. I thought my stomach was going to interrupt Maggie."

Brooke laughed. "You know, it's nice to hear you laugh. We haven't had much call for it, I know. By the way, shall we go to my place tonight?"

"If you weren't driving, I'd thump you hard. My place, or you can drop me home," she said, turning with a smile.

"Well, okay. If you insist."

It took some time to reach Brooke's place, what with the weather and traffic.

"You, shower first, Brooke. I'll order a takeaway."

After a warm shower and a meal, they sat together, talking about the case.

"You know how much I hate bringing work home, Owen."

"Yes, you're right. But the main thing tomorrow is finding out about our Jane Doe. Clearly not Maggie. So, who? I think I know."

Brooke looked at him. "Shawnnessy."

"Yes. Maybe. Or another dead end."

"Come on," she said softly. "Let's get to bed."

He hesitated for a second, wondering if she truly meant just sleep. But he followed her anyway, heart pounding just a little too fast.

The room was dark, the only light filtering in from the streetlamp outside. They had fallen asleep tangled together, exhaustion from the long case finally claiming them. But sometime in the early hours, he stirred. He turned towards her, his arm instinctively reaching out to pull her close. Her back was to him, the curve of her spine a tempting invitation.

He pressed a soft kiss to the nape of her neck. She stirred in her sleep, a low murmur escaping her lips.

He kissed her again, this time lingering, his lips exploring the sensitive skin behind her ear.

"Owen," she whispered, her voice thick with drowsiness.

"Go back to sleep, love," he murmured, but he didn't release her. Instead, he brushed a stray strand of hair from her face, his fingers lingering on her cheekbone. He leaned down and kissed her again, this time on the lips. It was a gentle kiss, a sweet and tender invitation.

She responded without hesitation, her lips parting slightly, inviting him deeper. The kiss deepened, becoming more urgent, more demanding. Her hands found their way to his chest, her fingers tracing the contours of his muscles beneath his t-shirt.

He pulled back slightly, his eyes searching hers in the dim light. "Brooke," he breathed, his voice rough with desire, "are you sure?"

She didn't answer with words. Instead, she reached up, pulling him back down to her, her lips meeting his in a kiss that left no room for doubt.

He shifted, moving on top of her, careful not to put his full weight on her. He braced himself on his elbows, his gaze locked on hers.

"God, you're beautiful," he whispered, his voice husky with emotion.

"So are you," she whispered.

He could feel the beat of her heart, the quickening of her breath, as he moved over her body. He reached down and gently cupped her breast, his thumb brushing across her nipple.

She gasped, her body arching towards him.

"Owen," she moaned, her voice barely audible.

"I love you," she whispered.

He didn't hesitate. "I love you too," he murmured, and as his lips found hers again, his hands moved over her with reverence and care. No more words were needed. In the way he touched her, slow and certain, she felt everything he couldn't say.

There was nothing rushed, nothing demanded. Just the soft rhythm of skin and breath, tangled sheets and whispered names. In that moment, all the noise of the world fell away.

They drifted into sleep again, wrapped around each other, but dawn crept in far too soon.

Owen blinked at the pale gold light spilling across the ceiling. For a second, he forgot where he was. Then he felt her beside him. Her warmth. The soft curve of her hip under the sheet.

Brooke stirred, blinking up at him. Her hair was tousled, her voice low. "You're staring."

He smiled faintly. "Sorry. Just making sure last night wasn't a dream."

A silence passed between them. Soft. Loaded. Then:

"Brooke," he said quietly. "Did you mean it? What you said last night?"

She didn't look away. "I did. Did you?"

"Every word." He reached over, brushing his fingers down her arm. "It wasn't just the moment. I'm all in, if you are."

Her lips curved slightly. "Good. Because I'm tired of pretending I don't need you."

He leaned in, kissed her forehead, then her lips.

And then her phone buzzed.

She grabbed it, scanned the message, and swore under her breath. "They found a body. Female. Same MO. Behind Whitecroft canal."

Owen sat up fast. "Sarah."

He stared at the floor for a beat, his pulse suddenly thudding in his ears.

Brooke nodded, already throwing back the covers. "We need to move."

They dressed in silence, urgency cutting through the morning tenderness, but not replacing it. As they left, their eyes met again at the door.

The world was waiting. Ugly. Brutal. Loud.

But something between them had settled.

This time, they didn't just have each other's backs.

They had each other.

And that was everything.

Chapter 47

The rain had returned by the time DI Owen and DC Daniels reached the canal path behind Whitecroft. The area was cordoned off, blue tape fluttering in the morning wind. Uniforms moved about quietly, faces grim, boots sinking into the mud. A few early commuters had gathered behind the tape, craning their necks.

A patrol officer spotted them and waved them over.
"DI Owen, DC Daniels. She's down here."

"Who found her?" Daniels asked.

"Dog walker. Local lad, maybe eighteen. Name's Steven Shaw. Bit shaken, but he's giving a statement now."

Owen nodded.
"We'll speak to him after."

They followed the path down through a gap in the hedgerow. The air was heavy with the smell of wet earth and decay.

Then they saw her. Sitting beneath a tree near the lake's edge. The branches shielded the body from the rain, but the mud and moisture clung to everything around her.

Sarah Whitmore.

"This is different, Brooke," Owen muttered. "She's been dumped. Like garbage. Something went wrong with Sarah. Did she fight back? Upset him somehow?"

"No theatre this time," Brooke said quietly. "No white sheet. No propped-up pose. Just left here to rot."

She lay sprawled awkwardly, one arm twisted behind her, face turned toward the reeds. Mud clung to her bare legs, her hair soaked and tangled across her back. Her eyes were closed.

"Brooke, take a look at this."
Owen pointed toward the torn flesh in Sarah's chest, where blood still clung to broken skin.

Brooke crouched beside the body and studied the wound. Her voice was low but steady.

"This isn't a clean incision. Whatever he used wasn't surgical. It tore the skin apart. Could've been a blunt-edged weapon with weight behind it. Maybe a tyre iron or something similar. Could've even had jagged edges. But it's not just the wound. It's how deep it went."

She glanced toward the tree behind Sarah.
"She wasn't killed by it, but look at the angle of her body.

She was placed against it after death. Or maybe thrown nearby. There's force behind how she ended up here, but the tree wasn't the weapon."

Behind them, a voice called out.
"Good morning, you two. Hope you're not messing up my crime scene."

"Morning, Smithy," Owen replied. "We haven't touched anything. Just trying to get a head start. Forensics might help us understand what's changed here. Her death doesn't fit his usual MO, but she matches the description of a young woman snatched this week. Seen anything useful yet?"

"For God's sake, I've only just got here," Smithy said, walking over. "I know you're keen to stop him, but gathering evidence takes time."

Brooke stepped forward.
"We know, and I'm sorry. I'm DC Brooke Daniels. Please, call me Brooke."

Smithy gave Owen a tired look, then offered a nod.
"Nice to meet you, Brooke. Shame about the circumstances."

He crouched beside the body, squinting at the wound.

"You're right. That's not from a knife, at least not a standard one. If it was a blade, it was something crude and brutal, not clean or controlled. But more likely it was a blunt object. Look at the trauma. He hit her with real force. Could've been a tyre iron, pipe, something that could puncture and tear in one go."

Owen winced.
"She didn't stand a chance."

"No," Smithy agreed. "And if I had to guess, that kind of strike wasn't planned. It was rage. Something set him off."

He sat back on his heels.
"Livor mortis puts time of death somewhere around six to eight hours ago."

Owen scanned the surroundings.
"No drag marks. He carried her."

"He didn't stage her," Brooke added. "That's the biggest change. Every other victim—Rose, April, Terri, Alena—he made a scene. A statement. But this? He just wanted her gone."

"Smithy, sorry, but can you confirm any tattoos?"

Smithy nodded.
"Yeah, looks like it. Give me your phone."

He took a few quick photos and handed it back.
"Best I can do for now. I'll get more detailed shots once she's in the lab."

"Thanks, Smithy."
Brooke peered over Owen's shoulder as he zoomed in on

the image.

"Five tattoos."

Owen's brow furrowed.
"She was supposed to be number six. Does that mean Rosie's still alive?"

They both fell silent, the idea taking root.

"She could be," Owen said finally. "My mind's running through every possibility. Did Rosie escape? Did she die somewhere else, injured and alone? Did she kill Sarah?"

Brooke examined the tattoos more closely.
"Look at the first one. It's the letter N. That would make Sarah the fifth, not the sixth."

Owen blinked.
"What?"

"She wasn't meant to be next. Maybe she was a mistake."

"Or she disappointed him," Owen said. "Didn't perform. Didn't play along. Maybe she fought back in ways the others didn't."

Brooke's expression twisted, a mix of sadness, frustration, and fury behind her eyes.
"Owen, we have to stop this bastard. There can't be more. Just look at her."

"Or she saw something she wasn't meant to," he said. "And he panicked."

They stood in silence for a moment, the only sound the gentle rustle of wind through the reeds.

Smithy cleared his throat.
"Look, it's not much, and until we get back to the lab, I can't be sure."

"Understood," Owen said. "But what is it?"

"I don't know what the weapon was yet, but I can tell you this. It wasn't calculated. He didn't kill her like the others. This was messy. Angry. Maybe even rushed."

"Thanks, Smithy."

Owen turned to Brooke.
"This changes everything. Where's the planning? The control? The precision?"

Brooke nodded slowly.
"He's not in control anymore."

Owen's voice dropped, steady and commanding.
"I want everyone back to the office. Now."

Chapter 48

The house was quiet again.

Linda hadn't spoken in hours.

She sat opposite Rosie, legs tucked in tight, chin trembling slightly. She'd stopped crying at some point. Her eyes were puffy, red-rimmed, but dry now. The fear was still there, raw, simmering just beneath the surface, but Rosie recognised something else. The beginning of numbness.

That was how it started.

Rosie had hated him at first. Completely. Every second of every day filled with revulsion and rage. But she'd learned how to hide it. That was survival now, pretence. And she was good at it.

She knew Blue was always watching, always listening, even when he acted like he wasn't. Especially then.

She wished she could tell Linda. Just whisper across the room, "He sees everything. Don't trust anything." But she couldn't risk it. Linda was too fragile. Too raw. Rosie needed her to hold on, needed her calm. Needed her to play along, just like she had learned to.

The door creaked.

Rosie didn't flinch, but Linda twitched, recoiling automatically as he stepped inside. Blue.

He closed the door behind him, slow and casual, as if he had all the time in the world. He was wearing a clean shirt. Smelled faintly of smoke. The paint on his hands had faded, but Rosie could still see the flakes around his nails.

He smiled at them both like a man returning to his pets.

"Nice to see you getting along," he said.

Neither of them replied.

He walked over to Linda, crouched low, looked her in the eye. She didn't move, but Rosie saw the tiny shake in her fingers.

"Still not speaking?" he asked her. "That's okay. You will."

He stood and turned to Rosie. "How about you, my little rose? You've been quiet."

Rosie kept her tone neutral. "Just trying to make her feel safe."

Blue tilted his head, considering that. "That's sweet. Thoughtful. I like that."

He moved to the small cupboard in the corner, pulled out a bottle of water and a protein bar. He tossed them onto the mattress between the girls.

"This is for you, Linda, but you have to earn it."

Linda flinched. "Please..."

He snapped toward her. "No. Pleading doesn't work here. You're here because she," he pointed at Rosie, "chose you."

Linda turned to Rosie, eyes wide, furious and confused from what Rosie had already told her, and why.

Rosie swallowed. She had prepared for this, but it still hit hard. "I told you it was the only way. He was going to take someone either way."

Blue laughed. "See? Practical. That's what I like about her. Maybe you'll learn from her, Linda."

He stepped forward again, but this time Rosie moved. She stood, slow and calm, positioning herself slightly between him and Linda. Not in a challenge, not yet, but enough to make him pause.

Blue's smile faded.

"You're getting bolder," he said softly.

Rosie didn't drop her gaze. "I'm sorry, Blue. Really, I don't mean to overstep the line. But I know what you like: control, obedience... and someone who pretends not to be afraid. You said so."

He blinked. And for a brief moment, she saw something behind his eyes: confusion, curiosity... maybe even approval.

"Get her washed," he said, stepping back. "She stinks. And after that, we'll see if she's ready."

"Yes, Blue. I'll make sure she's ready for you."

"I know you will, my girl. But today will be different."

"Different how, Blue?"

"Well, I was watching a movie. These guys went into a bar and watched two lovely ladies put on an act for them. I don't have a bar. But I do have two lovely ladies."

"You want us to put on a lesbian show for you, Blue? No problem."

Blue walked up to Rosie, gently pulled her toward him, and kissed her on the lips. She responded, wrapping her arms around him, playing the part like a lover.

He left the room.

The silence returned.

Linda stared at Rosie, shaking her head slowly.

"I don't understand you. How can you kiss him like that? He's raped both of us."

Rosie knelt down, keeping her voice soft. "You don't have to understand. Just stay alive. And... to be honest, I'm beginning to like it. Blue really knows how to kiss.

And when he makes love to me, he makes me climax like no other."

"You're sick. You are fucking sick. And he wants us to do what?"

"We're going to put on a show. You and me, making love on the bed while he watches. When we're done, he'll take one of us, or both."

"You mean have sex in front of him? No fucking way. Don't touch me."

Rosie grabbed her by the throat and lifted her up.

"Get off me, bitch!"

"Now you fucking listen. If we don't, he'll punish us both. He may even kill one of us. We have to do it to survive."

"You mean he'll kill me. He won't hurt his little fuck pet, will he?"

"You stupid girl. Get in that bathroom now and wash, or I'll drag you in there and scrub you until you bleed."

Rosie watched Linda carefully as she walked into the bathroom. If only she knew... that everything said and done was watched by him. Every word. Every movement. Rosie wasn't looking forward to what was coming, but this wasn't about liking anything. It was survival.

And in this house, survival belonged to the fittest.

"How?" Linda asked from inside the bathroom. "You talk to him like you like him."

"It's not about liking," Rosie said through the door. "At first, it was just survival. But now... I don't know. You won't understand. I don't hate him anymore. He can be kind. Loving... when he wants to be."

"You're sick. And don't expect me to love him that way."

Rosie stopped in her tracks. Love? She hated him with every breath. Love was never in her mind. Never.

"Rosie... if we do this for him... will he be nice to me?"

"Linda, there is no if. We are going to put on a show."

Linda wanted to cry again, but she fought it down.

"Okay. So... when we do it... will he be nice to me?"

Rosie sighed. "Honestly? I don't know. I believe so. Just do your best."

"When he first took you and forced you... what did you think of?"

Rosie wanted to say the same thing she still thought of now: killing the bastard.

"Well... when I realised there was no way out, I stopped being angry. At first, I just lay there and let him do what he wanted. But then... he started making me feel good." She paused. "But to answer your question, I used to think about seeing my family again."

"Okay... thank you, Rosie. I'll try. And please... be gentle, when we... you know."

Linda stared at her. Rosie stared at the door. Footsteps.

The door opened.

"Hello again, ladies. Ah, much better, Linda. Thank you, Rosie, and thank you for the show."

Rosie, stomach sick with dread, took Linda by the hand and whispered, "Copy me."

She led Linda over to Blue. He was seated in a chair, watching. Rosie bent down and kissed him. She stood up and nodded toward Linda, who then bent and kissed him too, hesitant, lips trembling.

Rosie pulled Linda close, kissed her on the lips, held her. To her surprise, Linda kissed back, and it actually felt nice.

They moved to the bed. Rosie gently pushed Linda onto the mattress, then lay beside her, kissing her again. She touched her softly. Linda responded, a little slower. Rosie let out a low moan, fake, but convincing.

Blue smiled.

"Thank you, ladies. That was a lovely show."

"Thank you, Blue. We worked hard to get it right for you."

"Yes. And it was very satisfying. Now, Rosie, return to your room. Linda and I have some unfinished business."

"Of course, Blue. Enjoy yourselves."

Rosie looked at Linda, still lying on the bed, and kissed Blue once more.

"Blue... I want some later too, please."

"You won't be disappointed, Rosie. You'll be spending the night with me again."

She looked him in the eyes and smiled.

"I can't wait."

Rosie stepped quietly back into her own room, the door clicking shut behind her with that familiar, unnatural softness. She didn't bother turning on the light. She just stood there for a moment, letting the silence settle.

It was getting harder to walk out and leave Linda behind. Harder still to act like none of it affected her.

She sat on the edge of the bed, muscles tight, her breath coming in shallow pulls. The mask she wore, quiet, calm, cooperative, fit better now. Too well, maybe. But under it, everything still twisted.

She didn't feel strong. Not tonight.

She sat in silence, barely breathing, listening to the sounds that weren't there.

Sometimes that was worse, when it was quiet. When you couldn't hear the things he was doing, but your imagination filled in the gaps anyway.

Rosie stared at the floor. She didn't move. Just waited.

Because she knew what came next.

He was with Linda now. She could feel it like a shift in the air. It wasn't guessing anymore. It was a rhythm. A routine. And when he was done there, when he'd had enough of breaking the new girl down piece by piece, he'd come to her.

That was the deal.

She didn't cry. She hadn't in days. The tears stopped meaning anything a long time ago.

She lay back slowly, adjusting the blanket, covering herself even though it made no difference. He'd peel it off when he came in. Sometimes gently. Sometimes not.

But tonight, she hoped it would be quick. No talking. No questions. No soft hands pretending to care.

Just get it over with.

She glanced at the ceiling again, at the tiny lens hidden in the corner. And for a split second, she wanted to shout at it. Not from rage. From exhaustion.

But instead, she turned her face to the wall, closed her eyes, and waited for the sound of the door unlocking.

Chapter 49

The incident room buzzed with low chatter as Owen and Daniels stepped inside. It had the feeling of a storm gathering. Coffee cups sat half-drunk, eyes darted to screens, and chairs had been dragged closer to the centre table. Everyone was waiting for something.

"Right, everybody, listen up. I want to know what everyone's got, and no one goes home tonight until I'm happy. Is that clear?"

A few moans and groans echoed around the room, but they quickly stopped. All eyes turned to Owen, now joined by Brooke.

Smithy spotted them first and hurried over. "Owen. You're gonna want to hear this."

Owen nodded. "What have we got?"

"DNA match on the Jane Doe," Smithy said, holding up a tablet. "She's not a nobody. Her name's Shawnnessy Kingsley. Daughter of Barry Kingsley."

"The same Barry Kingsley from the 2015 abuse allegations?" Brooke asked.

Smithy nodded. "Yeah. But get this. She's also cousin to Ryan Kingsley."

Owen felt his stomach twist at the name. It was all tying back together. The old case. The family. The ones they'd let slip through the cracks.

"Thank you, Smithy, for confirming what we've been told," Owen said. "We spoke to a couple who knew David Taylor — who, incidentally, had changed his name. He's also the brother of Barry Kingsley."

Owen turned toward one of the team.

"Ross, I need you to check and confirm whether David Taylor and David Kingsley are the same person. Also confirm his death and the circumstances surrounding it."

"On it, boss."

"Now, from what we've gathered, Ryan was obsessed with Shawnnessy Kingsley — also known as Lesley and Melanie Chambers. There may be more aliases. Police were involved at the time, but it looks like they focused on the wrong person. In the end, the family told police she'd run off."

"Smithy, can you tell us more about Shawnnessy's body? How was she murdered? Where exactly was she found?"

"Sure thing, Brooke. Just bear in mind she'd been buried for some time. From what I can tell, she was killed with a rock or blunt object. Her skull was smashed into too many pieces to count. Whoever did this, I'd say they totally lost it. The grave was shallow. My guess is the rain washed the dirt away. I don't think this was planned."

Owen stepped forward. "What makes you say that, Smithy?"

"Well, I can't prove it. Maybe something will come up. But if I were planning a murder, I wouldn't use my hands to dig a grave."

A chill rolled down Owen's spine. "And now we find her buried like that."

Brooke crossed her arms, eyes locked on the screen. "That's motive. Obsession. Rejection. Rage. Then silence. It fits."

Smithy nodded. "Yeah. It fits all right."

"Thanks, Smithy. Great work. Right now, we need everything we can get on Ryan — who he really was, the type of person he was, any photos. Anything else, Brooke?"

"Yes," she said, stepping forward. "Ladies and gents, Sarah was found this morning."

"She was dumped in woodland," Owen added. "Not far from where April was found. Tattooed like the others. But this one was different. More force. Brutality. Smithy's working with the forensic team now, but we're assuming something went wrong. Sarah had only five tattoos, yet she was the sixth. Does that mean Rosie is still alive?"

"Up until now, he's had everything well thought out. Everything planned. So what went wrong?"

Gasps rippled across the room.

A heavy silence followed.

Brooke swallowed hard. Her voice came out quieter, more raw. "He lost control. Maybe Sarah fought back. Maybe something broke in his pattern. Either way, it wasn't supposed to happen like this."

She paused, then straightened, steel behind her eyes. "But if Rosie's still alive, then we still have a chance."

Owen scanned the faces in the room, letting that flicker of hope take hold.

"We've got a window. Whoever's doing this is keeping them alive for a reason. Rosie might still be out there. And if she is, we're not going to find her by sitting on our arses."

"Find him," Owen snapped. "Everything. His address. Known associates. Tech history. Every job he's worked in the last fifteen years. If he scratched a wall wrong, I want to know about it."

"Someone bring up Barry Kingsley from the holding cells, please," Brooke said, looking around the room.

No one moved.

"Barry Kingsley. Now," Brooke snapped.

A young officer raised his hand, hesitant. "Excuse me... Brooke. He was released a couple of hours ago."

"He was what?"

"Released. Sorry."

"Did you release him?"

"Yes. He'd been held overnight, so I thought—"

"You thought? Well, think about this. If he's not back here within two hours, the best thing that'll happen is you walking the beat."

The young officer bolted from the room, nearly falling over himself.

Owen looked around the room, voice firm. "So we push. We pull every thread, dig into Ryan Kingsley, and find where this bastard's hiding. Because if Rosie's alive, we don't let her become the next body."

The team snapped into action.

Owen turned to Brooke, voice lower now. "If we're right, this changes everything."

She nodded. "Then let's make sure we are."

Chapter 50

The morning light filtered through the cracks in the boarded-up windows, casting pale, broken lines across the floor, slicing through the gloom like prison bars.

Rosie sat on the edge of the mattress, still naked. She had remained that way since the beginning, a constant reminder that she had no control here. Her legs were folded beneath her, and her eyes were fixed on the table near the door. She wasn't moving. Not yet. Just watching.

The keys.

They had been left out again, carelessly, almost arrogantly.

She couldn't take them, not while he was still in the house, but she could study them. Every shape. Every detail.

She leaned forward slightly, pretending to scratch her ankle, her eyes locked on the bunch of keys hanging from a rusty nail.

A small gold object caught the light.

Her stomach clenched.

It was a necklace. Delicate. Childlike. A gold chain with a tiny heart pendant, etched with markings inside. Twisted tightly through the keyring was a thin red ribbon, frayed at the edges. It didn't belong. It was out of place, ornate, sentimental, and female.

Had it been around someone's neck once?

Rosie blinked, frozen. The heart pendant looked familiar, too familiar. Her thoughts twisted, trying to place it. A news image? A photo?

She hadn't seen that ribbon before. Not here. Somewhere else. But that necklace...

Her chest tightened.

It was wrong. That ribbon wasn't his. That necklace wasn't his. It belonged to someone else. Someone who hadn't made it out. Someone important.

Or someone he couldn't let go of.

Her heart started to race.

He walked in a moment later, towel around his neck, shirt undone. She looked away quickly, afraid he'd seen her watching.

But he didn't speak. He just grabbed something from the counter, humming softly under his breath. Still in control. Still the man who thought he owned them.

When he left, the lock clicked with brutal finality.

Linda lay curled on the floor, her arms wrapped tightly around her knees. She hadn't spoken much that morning. Barely touched the bread and water he'd left.

Rosie sat beside her, gently stroking a hand over her shoulder.

"You have to eat," she whispered. "You can't give up."

"I'm tired," Linda murmured, eyes vacant. "Every time I close my eyes, I see April."

"April? Who is April?"

"It was in the news. She was taken not long ago. Her body was found, beaten. Dumped in some layby."

"How do you know all this?"

"It was in the papers. On the news. I guess you haven't seen it. Maybe he'd already taken you."

Rosie nodded slowly. "Yeah... maybe I was another replacement. For this April."

Linda hesitated, then: "Rosie, can I ask you something?"

"Yeah, sure. What's on your mind?"

"How many times did he force you... before you got to like it?"

Rosie flinched. "Like it? What the fuck, Linda."

She took a breath, held it, then let it out slowly.

"Look, I lost count how many times he raped me before I gave myself to him. It wasn't that I got to like it. It just stopped mattering. That's different."

"Rosie... were you a virgin before this?"

"No. Why, were you?"

"Yes."

Linda's voice cracked, and she started sobbing, tears spilling down her cheeks. Rosie leaned forward and pulled her close.

"Shh... Linda. You're doing well, okay? Let's just keep going. One day at a time."

Linda clung to her, trembling.

"If you escape... you'll take me with you, won't you?"

Rosie hesitated, just a heartbeat, but it felt like an eternity. "Linda, there's no chance of escape. But yes. Of course I would."

She lied so easily. It scared her.

Rosie knew her time was getting closer. She could feel it in his eyes when he looked at her now. Her usefulness, her value, it was running out. And she doubted she'd be able to take Linda with her. But the thought of leaving her behind...

It made her throat close.

Linda's breath shuddered in and out. "He's going to kill us."

Rosie didn't answer. Not yet.

Her eyes drifted back toward the keys, toward the gold necklace.

That had meant something. She could feel it in her bones. That necklace, the red ribbon, it wasn't just a trophy. It was a memory. A wound.

A thread left dangling. One he couldn't cut.

"No," she said finally, steadying her voice. "Not today."

Chapter 51

At the station, Barry Kingsley wasn't walking this time. He was dragged into the interview room, arms cuffed, one eye already bruised. His expensive coat was torn at the shoulder. He looked less like a respected businessman and more like a man losing everything.

Owen stood just inside the doorway, arms crossed, watching him squirm.
"You've got a bloody nerve," Barry growled, yanking at the cuffs. "This is harassment. You had no right."
"We had every right," Owen cut in coldly. "You lied to

us. You protected a predator. And now we know your daughter, Shawnnessy, didn't run away."

Barry paled, just slightly, but enough.
Owen leaned in, eyes fixed on him. "She's dead. Buried. Head caved in. Want to guess who was obsessed with her? Want to guess who kept her necklace?"

Barry's lips parted, but no sound came out.

Brooke stepped into view, calm but sharp. "You're going to tell us everything about Ryan. Every conversation. Every cover-up. Every disgusting little secret your twisted family buried. Because someone else is out there with him right now. And we are not going to let her die too."

Barry opened his mouth, hesitated, then shut it again. Owen watched him carefully.

He knows something. The bastard knows something. And they were going to tear it out of him.

Barry slouched in the interview chair, lips tight, the smugness slowly draining from his face. Owen had seen it before, the moment when arrogance gave way to dread.

Brooke pressed the recorder.
"Interview commenced at 11:42 a.m. Present are DI David Owen, DC Brooke Daniels, and the interviewee, Barry Alan Kingsley."

Owen folded his arms. "Let's start with the basics. When did you last see your daughter, Shawnnessy?"
Barry looked up slowly. "Not since she was fifteen."
"Fifteen," Brooke echoed. "You mean when she disappeared and you told the police she'd run away?"
"She did run away," Barry said stiffly.
"No, Barry," Owen snapped. "She didn't. She was murdered. Buried in a shallow grave, likely not long after she vanished. So, try again."

Barry shifted, throat working.
Owen leaned in closer. "We have a man, Ryan Kingsley, your nephew, who was obsessed with her. Who lived in your house. Who had full access to that girl. And no one was watching him."
"She wasn't that young," Barry muttered.

Owen started to rise, but Brooke slammed her hand on the desk.
"She was your daughter!"
The words hung in the air. Barry didn't flinch, but he didn't meet her eyes either.

"She had problems, didn't she?" Brooke pressed. "You knew she wasn't well. That she had mental health issues."
Barry stared down at the desk.

"Look," Brooke said, voice sharpening, "if you don't talk, I'll turn that camera off and leave you in here with Owen. Do you understand me?"
Barry scoffed. "What's this, good cop, bad cop? You wouldn't dare. I want my solicitor, so fuck off."

Brooke turned wordlessly and walked to the socket on the wall, flipping it off.
"Don't make too much of a mess, Owen."

Barry panicked. "No, no! Wait! Okay, okay, I'll talk. Just don't do anything, alright? What do you want to know?"
Owen stepped forward. "What happened when Ryan stayed with you and your daughter?"

Barry's voice dropped. "He was worse than she was. At first, I thought it was just him. Then I saw them together. I even caught them at it one night."
"At it, Barry?" Brooke asked, eyes hard.
"She was in his bed. You can figure it out. I told them to stop. At first, they did. Then they just told me to fuck off."
"So, you let two fifteen-year-olds sleep together under your roof?" Owen asked.

Barry bristled. "When you put it like that, yeah. I guess I did. But I never touched her. Never. Do you hear me? Never. But."
"But what?"
"Ryan was working late one night. And his father, David, popped in. I wasn't home. I was running late. When I got back… he was with her."

Owen's voice dropped into something deadly. "This is your brother. You walked in, and you didn't stop it. You did nothing."
He leaned closer, eyes burning.
"You're sick, Barry. Sick. You sure you didn't join in?"

"Fuck you, copper," Barry snapped, face flushed. "I was a bad father, yeah. But I didn't touch her. Never. Not once."
Brooke placed a steady hand on his arm. Her voice was quieter, but no less cutting.
"Okay, Barry. What happened next?"

Barry exhaled, gaze distant.
"Ryan found out. I remember, he was furious. Proper mad. He hit her a couple of times, and I threw him out."
"And then?"
"It was only a couple of days later... David got pushed down the stairs."
"Who pushed him?" Owen asked.
"David, my brother. They said Ryan did it. But no one they believed came forward. I think they just wanted to cover it up."

Owen's jaw clenched. "What was David like, really? We've been told he was after every woman in that house."
"I'm not surprised. Him and Ryan, neither could keep it in their pants."

The silence was thick.
Brooke leaned in again. "Tell us about David changing his name. After the abuse allegations."
Barry looked at the camera, then back to them.
"He didn't want the past catching up with him. He wanted to start over."
"And after David died, where did Ryan go?"
"He stayed with me. For a while. But he got weird. Shut off. Wouldn't talk. He started drawing all the time.

Strange stuff."
"Like what?" Brooke asked.

"Women. Tattooed. Bound. Crying. He'd rip the pages up and burn them. Wouldn't let me see most of it."
Brooke's voice cooled. "You said your daughter used to draw strange things too, roses, dark places?"
Barry nodded. "Yeah. She did. They locked her up. Said she wasn't right in the head."

Owen's stomach twisted. "And you never reported Ryan? Never warned anyone?"
Barry scoffed. "What was I supposed to say? 'My freak nephew's drawing tits and roses, better lock him up'? I didn't know he was dangerous."
"You knew," Brooke said. "You just didn't care."

Barry looked away.
"Barry," Owen said, "how did your daughter escape? We've seen records that she got out. Someone helped her."
"Yeah, sounds about right. I reckon it was Ryan."
"Did you see her after that? Did you see them together?"

"All I remember is Ryan coming home late that same day. I thought she'd run off with him. Or maybe he'd just helped her get away."
Owen stepped closer. "He didn't help her. He killed her. Do you have any idea why he would do that, to someone he said he loved?"

Barry hesitated. "This is just guesswork… but she wasn't the same after David had sex with her. She shut down.

Wouldn't talk to anyone. Before they locked her up, she was seeing someone, getting help. She used different names to hide who she was."

Brooke's voice softened, but only slightly. "We know. One more thing, Barry, the gold necklace. Tell us about it."

"The necklace?" Barry blinked. "That was her mum's. She gave it to Shawnnessy before she died. It was the only thing she had from her. She must've been about nine, ten, no older. Why? Have you found it? She never went anywhere without it."

Owen didn't answer. He stepped back, eyes hard.
"You protected him because you thought he was all you had left. But your daughter died. And you covered it up. And now more girls are dying, because you said nothing."

Barry's jaw trembled.
"I didn't kill her," he whispered.
"No," Owen said, cold and final. "But you let the man who did keep walking."

Chapter 52

Rosie hadn't told Linda about the necklace.
She hadn't told her about the red ribbon or the way it had been twisted through the keyring like a trophy. Or how it had glinted in the light, mocking her.
She kept it all inside.
Every second she spent pretending was fuel.

Blue. Ryan. He was playing a part. The careful captor. The false protector. The master of his own world. But he wasn't invincible.
He'd made a mistake.

The ribbon had belonged to someone. Maybe Sarah. Maybe one of the others.
That was the weakness. The sentiment. The thing he couldn't throw away.

Rosie sat by the wall, arms wrapped around her knees, listening as he moved about the house. She could tell by the rhythm of his steps where he was. Kitchen. Hallway. Then upstairs again. Restless. Twitchy.

Linda was asleep or pretending to be. Curled under the scratchy blanket, one hand clenched as if she were still holding someone else's.
Rosie couldn't risk sharing hope.
Hope got people killed in this place.

She stood and crept to the door. It was unlocked.
She turned back. Linda was still chained by the ankle.

Rosie opened the door quietly and padded down the hall to his room. She stopped, listening.

He was crying.

She stood there a moment. Should she knock? Or go back?
She knocked.

Silence.
Then footsteps. Slow. The handle turned. The door creaked. It had never done that before.
"Yes, Rosie?"
"Sorry, Blue… I was lonely. I wanted you. Are you okay? You look… sad. I've never seen you like this."
"Come in, Rosie. You know you shouldn't leave your room."
"I know, but Linda's still chained. I didn't go anywhere else."
He nodded slightly. "Take a seat."

She stepped inside, cautious. Something about him felt unsteady. Off.
Then she saw it. The ribbon. Twisted through the keyring. The gold charm she'd seen before, dangling in the light.
"What's that, Blue? It looks… nice."

He snatched it up into his fist.

Rosie froze.
Is he about to hit me? Or worse? Did I just ruin everything?

He looked at the ribbon, then slowly turned toward her.
He stood still. Then walked toward her.

Her breath caught. Her chest tightened. This is it. This is my last night.

But then… he stopped. And handed it to her.
"This is beautiful, Blue. It looks very old. Does it belong to someone special?"
She watched him carefully.

The door was open. She could run.
But how far? No shoes. No clothes. Nothing but bare skin and desperation.

"It used to," he said. "She was my first love. I think her mother gave it to her. It's all I have left of her, apart from the memories."

Rosie stood and gently gave it back. Then she wrapped her arms around him and held him close.

He rested his head on her shoulder and cried.
She didn't know what to do. She just held him.

This wasn't what I expected. It scared me. I thought I was getting to him. But this? This is something else.
"Rosie… you remind me a little of her."

He lifted his head and kissed her gently on the crown. Then he sat on the edge of the bed. Rosie joined him.

"What happened to her, Blue?"
"She didn't want me. She teased me. Pretended she loved me so I'd help her escape from the home she was in."
Rosie didn't ask what kind of home. She didn't want to

know.
"She wanted someone else. So I made sure she couldn't have him."
"Oh, Blue… I'm so sorry. Really, I am."

And strangely, she meant it. Some part of her pitied him. That frightened her more than anything.
"I got her out. I thought we'd be together. But she laughed at me. Told me I was pathetic. Said she was going off alone. I held her. Tried to kiss her. She spat in my face."

He paused, trembling.
"She was the first. I killed her. I didn't want to, Rosie. She made me. You understand, don't you?"
"Yes, Blue. I understand. She treated you terribly. And you did everything for her. You must have really loved her."
"I did. And you… you've become special to me, Rosie. You know that, right?"
"Yes, Blue. I know. And thank you. I never thought I'd feel this way since you took me… but I care about you. I want you. I don't want anyone else. Just you."

She felt sick as she said it.
But she had to say it.

Blue gently pulled her down onto the bed. She braced herself, but he didn't force her. He didn't touch her the way she expected.
He just kissed her and lay beside her.

She lay still, watching him. Watching his chest rise and fall.
He's getting sloppy, she thought. Overconfident.

The keys were always on him or close by. But twice now, she'd seen them left out. Carelessly. Close enough to notice.
Not yet close enough to grab.
But that would change.
She just had to wait. No rushing. No mistakes.

Just like he had patterns, so did she.

When morning came, she felt his hand on her waist. She must've fallen asleep.
"Good morning, Rosie. You look wonderful in the morning."
She turned to him, smiled, and kissed him softly.
"I want you, Blue. Take me. Take me now."

They spent the next hour making love, talking, laughing.

"Rosie," he whispered, stroking her hair, "I think you're finally starting to understand what this is. Why you're here. You were meant to be mine."
She met his eyes. Unflinching.
"Then show me," she whispered. "Teach me."

He stared at her, pleased. Moved closer. Reached to touch her cheek. She didn't pull away.
She let him think he'd won.

Inside, she was building her escape, brick by brick, lie by lie.
And he wouldn't see it coming.

Chapter 53

It had been another long day.
They headed back to Brooke's flat, much against her usual rules, to carry on working.

"You know, Owen, you're a bad influence," she said, tossing her keys onto the counter. "In all my years on the force, I've never worked from home. Not once. Until I met you."
"Ah, but Brooke, would you have it any other way?"

She gave him a look, half stern, half amused. She knew exactly what he meant.

With two hot coffees, they sat at the kitchen table and fired up her laptop. Moments later, it pinged. A new email.
"Anything interesting?" Owen asked.

Brooke clicked it open. "Lab results. From forensics. Oh… yeah. This is good."

Several high-res images loaded on the screen. Tattoo scans. Enhanced, cleaned up, and side by side.
"The lab's mapped out every tattoo from all five confirmed victims. Including Sarah."
"Great," Owen said, leaning in. "Anything useful?"

Brooke nodded. "Listen to this. Sharon, the escapee, had only one tattoo. Gold ink. The image was faint, but enhanced, it clearly showed a rose. Small, basic. No letter."
"Right. I remember. She got out early."
"Next: Rose. Technically the first victim found. One tattoo, a blue rose with a single petal. Still no letter."
"Okay."
"Terri, victim two, had two tattoos. First was the letter S, second a blue rose with two petals."
"Letter one," Owen said, ticking it off.
"Alena, victim three, three tattoos. First was an H, second gold, third a rose with three petals."
"Letter two. Got it."
"April, victim four, had four tattoos. First: A, second: gold, third: R, fourth: blue rose, four petals."
"Letters three and four," Owen said. "A and R."
Brooke nodded. "And now Sarah. Victim five. Five tattoos. First was W, second gold, third Y, fourth a heart, fifth a blue rose with five petals."

Owen paused, frowning. "So Sarah's the fifth in order, but only the fourth with a letter."

"Exactly," Brooke said. "Rose had no letter. The sequence starts with Terri."

Owen stood, grabbing a notepad. "Okay. Let's line it up. Terri gave us S. Alena, H. April, A and R. Sarah, W and Y."
"So far we've got S H A W," Brooke said quietly. "And then Y. Possibly the start of Ryan. But the name Shawnnessy fits the victim count better."
"Ten letters," Owen said, writing it down. "S H A W N N E S S Y. We've got the first four now. S H A W."
Brooke nodded slowly. "If the pattern continues, and Rosie's next, she'd be number six. That would mean the next letter is N."

Owen's expression hardened. "He's spelling out her name. Tattoo by tattoo. Victim by victim."
Brooke stared at the screen. "It's not random. It's deliberate. Personal. He's branding them with her name."
"And maybe his too," Owen said. "R Y could be his signature. Ryan. The final two."

Brooke tapped the screen. "But Sharon throws the count off. If she wasn't part of the name, then maybe she was a trial. A mistake. Or even a test."
Owen nodded. "Which would still leave ten. Ten victims, ten letters. And Rosie's number six."

Brooke said it quietly. "He's halfway through."
They stared at each other in silence, both knowing what that meant.
If they didn't find her soon, she'd be marked.

Permanently.
And if she wasn't the end, someone else would follow.

Owen paced slowly, staring at the whiteboard, lost in thought.
"Assuming she's still alive…"
Brooke looked up at him. "She is."
He nodded, then spoke again, quieter. "If she is, then the question becomes… is she still fighting him?"
Brooke's eyes narrowed. "Or has he turned her?"
"You mean Stockholm syndrome?"
She nodded. "It happens. People start identifying with their captors. Especially when there's trauma. Isolation. He's grooming her, Owen. That much is clear."
"She's smart," he said. "Too smart to fall for him."
"Maybe," Brooke replied. "But even smart people break. And if he's treating her differently, if he sees her as special, he might be manipulating her without her even knowing."
Owen sat down, hands clenched. "Either she's playing him… or he's got full control."
Brooke met his eyes. "And if it's the second one, we may not get her back. Not fully."

They sat in silence, the weight of it pressing in around them.

Meanwhile...

In the cold, dim room, Linda stirred beneath the scratchy blanket. Her ankle throbbed where the chain rubbed raw. Her mouth was dry. Her stomach ached.
She blinked slowly, trying to adjust to the murky light.

Rosie wasn't there.
Again.

The panic crept in before she could stop it. Where is she?

Rosie had changed. She moved differently now. Spoke less. Her eyes had gone quiet. Too quiet.

Linda rolled onto her side, glancing toward the door. It was ajar. Had Rosie gone to him again? Was she still playing the game?
Or had it stopped being a game?

At first, Rosie had been her comfort. Her anchor. The one thing keeping her from falling apart. But lately...
She didn't share as much. Didn't explain where she was going. Didn't even flinch when Blue came into the room anymore.

Is she still pretending? Or is she starting to like him?

That thought made Linda's stomach turn.

Had Rosie decided she was better off staying on his good side? Had she decided to survive alone?
Would she leave me behind?

She didn't want to think it, but she'd seen the shift. The way Blue looked at Rosie now. Like she was his. Like he trusted her.
And Rosie… Rosie let him.

Linda squeezed her eyes shut. She didn't want to be suspicious. But she was terrified. Not just of him, but of being truly alone in this place. Forgotten. Left behind.

If Rosie was planning something — an escape, a manipulation — she hadn't said a word.
Maybe she was smart. Maybe she was brave.
But maybe she was dangerous too.

Linda curled tighter beneath the blanket, the cold creeping into her bones.
She didn't know who to trust anymore.
Not even the girl who once promised they'd survive together.

Chapter 54

Rosie was losing herself.
She could feel it, like slipping through her own fingers. The performance that once felt calculated and necessary now clung to her like a second skin. She couldn't tell where the pretending stopped and the surviving began.

She lay curled on the bed, the warmth of Blue's body still lingering beside her. He'd fallen asleep quickly, breathing soft and deep. She stared at the ceiling.

She'd kissed him first tonight.
She'd whispered that she loved him.
And he believed her.

The worst part wasn't the lie.
It was how easy it had become to say it.

Her throat tightened. Her mind screamed.
Don't forget who he is. What he's done. What he'll do again.

She slid out from under the covers and crept back into the other room. Linda stirred when she entered, eyes blinking in the low light. The chain at her ankle clinked faintly. "You were gone a long time," Linda murmured, voice thin and brittle.

Rosie didn't answer. She sat in the corner, knees drawn up, arms wrapped tight.

Linda watched her. "Did he hurt you?"
Rosie shook her head. "No."
"Then why do you look like that?"
Silence.
"You said we'd get through this together."
"We will."
"You sure?" Linda asked sharply. "Because it doesn't feel like you're on my side anymore."

Rosie looked up, face pale and drawn. "I'm trying to keep us alive."
"Are you? Or just yourself?"

The words cut deeper than Rosie expected. She flinched.

"I'm doing what I have to," she said quietly. "He trusts me now. That gives us time. A chance."
Linda's gaze didn't soften. "And what does that trust cost?"
Rosie looked at her, then toward the door. "You have to go along with what he wants."
Linda sat up, wincing. "What's the point if he's just going to kill me anyway?"

She moved closer, and Rosie did too — cautious, slow. Linda shifted back slightly. Just enough for Rosie to feel the rejection.

"Linda, listen — and keep your voice down. Before you, there was another girl. Sarah. She didn't do well with him. She fought back. She wouldn't play along. I was there when he killed her. I saw what happens when he loses control."

Linda's face twisted. "And you didn't do anything?"

"Maybe I could've," Rosie admitted. "But then I'd be dead too."

She hesitated.

And maybe... he killed Sarah for me. To keep me safe. To prove something.

The thought made her feel sick.

No. Don't go there. Don't believe that.

"Do you want my help or not?" she said instead.

Linda hesitated. "I guess I do. But I don't know how much I can trust you."

Rosie took a breath. "I've been where you are. When he comes to you, when he wants... things — he expects submission. But more than that, he expects you to play along. To want it."

Linda looked away.

"I know how it sounds," Rosie said. "But if you just lie there, he sees it as rejection. That's when he gets dangerous."

"I don't even know how," Linda whispered. "I've never had to pretend like this before. Not like this. I've never... faked it."

Rosie nodded. "I'm sorry. I forgot."

She lowered her voice. "When he wants oral — don't just do the bare minimum. Try to act like you want to. Use your hands, your mouth. Make him think it matters."
Linda swallowed hard. "You make it sound like it's supposed to be fun."
"No," Rosie said sharply. "It's not. But if he thinks it is, he doesn't lash out. It's the only control you get."
Linda was quiet a moment. "And when he… when he has sex?"
"Don't go limp. React. Move with him. Let him think you're enjoying it. Like you would if it was real."
"Why would that matter?"
"Because he needs to believe he's wanted. That's what this is all about. Control. Worship. If you give him that, he eases up."

Linda stared at her. "You're good at it."

Rosie looked away.

"You don't fake it anymore, do you?" Linda said quietly. "I think you actually want him now."

Rosie didn't answer.
She couldn't.

Later, when Blue called for her again, she went without hesitation. Not because she wanted to. Not because she didn't fear him anymore.
But because she feared losing control.
Because deep down, she wasn't sure where the performance ended.
Was Linda right?

He sat on the edge of the bed, half-dressed, stroking the red ribbon through his fingers.
"She used to wear it in her hair," he said. "Told me it made her feel like a princess."
Rosie knelt beside him. "It's beautiful, Blue."

His eyes were distant, fragile. "Do you think I'm a monster?"
"Blue… can I be honest?"
He nodded.
"The first time you took me — yes. I thought you were a monster. But now? I don't know. I think you're just… broken."

He closed his eyes.
"You miss her," Rosie said softly. "And sometimes, when you're hurting, it's hard to know what to do with the pain."
He nodded slowly. "It helps. When I'm with you. You make it quieter."
Then he touched her cheek. "But Linda… she doesn't understand. She still fights."

Rosie hesitated. Then the words came.
"Maybe… maybe you should remind her."

Blue tilted his head.
"She needs to learn," Rosie said. "Like I did."

He stared at her. Then nodded.

When he left the room, Rosie stayed kneeling by the bed, her stomach twisting.

She didn't follow.
She didn't watch.
But she heard everything.

Linda's muffled cry. The sound of chains shifting. The low, deliberate commands. Then silence.

Rosie covered her ears.
You did that.
You made that happen.
You said those words.
You handed her over.
Because it bought you time.
Because it made him trust you more.
Because he believed you loved him.
Because maybe…
just maybe…
a part of you started to wonder
if you could.

When he returned, Blue passed Rosie on the landing.
He didn't stop.
He just leaned in and whispered, voice low and pleased,
"She was better. You're teaching her well."
Then, with a small nod,
"Go and see her. Then come to me."

He walked away, and Rosie stood frozen.
She didn't answer.
Didn't breathe.
She just stood there, heart pounding in her throat.

Chapter 55

Linda didn't scream anymore.
Not when it hurt.
Not when it ended.
Not even when he whispered in her ear and left her on the bed, body shaking, the chain biting into her ankle again.

She just lay still.
Her face was turned to the wall. One arm stretched above her head, the other tucked beneath her chest, like she was trying to disappear into herself.
Her mouth was open, but no sound came out.
The room was silent again.
She didn't cry.
Not yet.
She couldn't — not while he might still be listening.

It was only after the door closed, and she heard the soft click of the lock, that her throat finally tightened. The first sob cracked out like it had been torn from her lungs. The rest followed like rain.

Rosie didn't come in right away.
And when she did, she didn't speak.
She just stood in the doorway, watching.

Linda turned her face, her eyes swollen and red.
"Why?"

Rosie looked like she'd been crying too — but quieter. Deeper.
"I didn't want to," she whispered.
"Then why?"
"Because if I hadn't said anything… he would've come for me instead."

Linda pulled her knees tighter to her chest. Her whole body trembled.
"So, you chose me."
Rosie didn't answer.

Linda let out a laugh — a dry, hollow sound.
"I trusted you."
"I'm trying to survive," Rosie said. "I'm trying to keep us both alive."
"Then why does it feel like I'm the only one dying?"

Rosie moved closer, kneeling.
"Linda, listen to me. He told me you were better this time. I think he… enjoyed it. You must've done what I said. That's what kept you alive."

Linda stared at her.

"I know you hate me," Rosie added. "But you'd do the same in my position."
"No," Linda said coldly. "I wouldn't. I couldn't put someone else through this just to save myself."

Rosie sank to the floor, back against the wall. Her hands were trembling, fists clenched in her lap.

She couldn't look at Linda now. Not yet.
Not after what she'd done.

Linda was right.
Maybe she was becoming him.

Elsewhere, Blue stood in the hallway, staring at the closed door.
His breathing was steady. Calm. Controlled.
But his thoughts weren't.
They spun in circles. Not in chaos, but in obsession.

Rosie.
She understood.
She saw the pain.
She didn't flinch anymore.
She didn't lie.
She loved him, he could see it now.

Or if she didn't yet, she would.
Because love wasn't something people just had.
It was something you earned.
Something you taught.

He walked to his room and sat on the edge of the bed.
The ribbon was still there. He picked it up, ran it through his fingers. Then opened the drawer and took out the necklace.
The gold caught the light. The charm sparkled softly.

Shawnnessy.
Her name echoed through him like a prayer.
Like a promise.

He didn't want to hurt Rosie. Not the way he'd hurt the others.
Not the way he'd had to hurt Linda.

Rosie was different.
She was his second chance.

But Linda… Linda wasn't learning. She was a shadow. A failure. A threat to Rosie's focus.

He'd almost gotten rid of her.
Almost.
But Rosie had stopped him.

He was going to let her keep Linda, for now.
Rosie could train her. Mould her.

If Linda failed… they'd both die.

He smiled.
That was real love, making the hard choices. Putting herself first, for once. Understanding what had to be done.

She was getting stronger.
She was becoming what he needed.
And when the name was complete, when the pattern was perfect, Rosie would be the one left standing.

The survivor.
The reward.
The rose that never wilted.

Chapter 57

Brooke's flat was quiet, save for the soft ticking of the wall clock and the occasional creak from the radiator. The chaos of the case felt far away for once, almost like a different life.

Owen leaned against the kitchen counter, sipping from a chipped mug.
Brooke, barefoot in a cardigan and jeans, sorted through photos.. and notes laid out across the coffee table.

He watched her in silence for a moment.
"Brooke."
She looked up. "Yeah?"
"Thanks. For not letting this bury me."
She gave a soft smile. "It nearly buried both of us."

He stepped closer, then reached out and gently tucked a loose strand of hair behind her ear.
"Have I ever told you how sexy you look in an old pair of jeans and a T-shirt?"
"No, but thank you."

Brooke turned and kissed him on the cheek, running the palm of her hand over his chest.
"Later, Owen. We've got work to do."

Owen moved back to the kitchen sink, rubbing his eyes.
"Tell me something, Brooke. Why hasn't he killed Rosie? Do you really think it could be Stockholm syndrome, in such a short time?"
"I've studied this," she said, sitting on the edge of the sofa. "It depends on the person, the situation, the threat to their survival. It can develop in days or weeks. From

what I understand, the stronger the threat, the quicker the bond."

She picked up one of the photos and held it loosely.
"Take Rosie, for example. If she saw him kill Sarah, and she believes she's next, then yes — there's a good chance it's happening. The longer he keeps her, the more she becomes part of his world."

She looked up at Owen.
"Did you know that back in 1973, during a bank robbery, the hostages started sympathising with their captors?"
"No. Where was that?" he asked.
"Guess."
"Stockholm?"
"Yes. That's where the term comes from."

She leaned forward.
"Maybe if we talk to her family again — and her close friends — we'll get a better sense of what makes her tick. How she might respond under pressure."

Just then, Owen's phone rang. He answered it quickly.
"What? You sure?" A pause. "Brooke and I will meet you there in forty minutes."

He hung up and turned to her, eyes wide.
"You're not going to believe this. Guess who rented out the garage where we think April was held?"
Brooke stood, already grabbing her jacket.
"No idea. Let's not waste time, tell me."
"Remember where Sarah worked? That estate agents?"
Her expression darkened.

"No way."
"Oh yes. Let's get dressed and go have another word with that fucker. I told you there was something off about him."

Chapter 58

The estate agent's office looked exactly the same: clean glass windows, polished metal handles, tidy property brochures in neat rows. But this time, Owen wasn't in the mood for polite smiles or fake apologies.

He pushed the door open, Brooke close behind him. A bell chimed overhead.

From behind Mia's desk, Rohan Vyas looked up from his office. Mid-thirties, smart shirt, watch too expensive for the postcode. His confident expression flickered the moment he saw Owen.

"Morning," Owen said flatly. "Mr. Vyas?"
"Yes, uh... yes. Detective Inspector, wasn't it?" He stood and held out his hand. Then glanced at Brooke and forced a smile. "And DC Daniels. Is something wrong?"

"We've got a few follow-up questions," Owen said, already walking past him. "You might want to sit down."

Brooke made a point of slamming the door closed.

Vyas hesitated, then sat back down, fidgeting with some papers on his desk.

"We've been going over rental records connected to a lock-up garage in Holloway," Brooke said, setting her notepad down in front of him. "You know the one. April Weaver was likely held there."

Vyas blinked, lips parting. "Right... I saw something about that in the news. I thought you were here regarding our poor Sarah?"

"You rented it," Owen said bluntly. "Under your business account."

Vyas froze.

"That garage," Owen continued, stepping closer, "was registered to this office six months ago. Listed under a generic company sublet. But the payment trail leads back to you personally."

"I manage a lot of properties," Vyas stammered. "I don't always check every individual—"

"Oh, come off it," Brooke snapped. "You're a small office. You knew what you were signing."

Owen lowered his voice. "Who were you renting it to?"

"No one specific. It was a guy who'd rented from me before, someone I knew through another client. He needed short-term space. Cash-in-hand arrangement."

"What was the name?"

Vyas hesitated too long.

"I think it was... Smith. Something like that. Yes, a Mr. T. Smith. That's what he told me. I didn't press."

Brooke and Owen locked eyes.

"You're telling us you rented a property to someone called Smith on a cash-in-hand basis," Brooke said flatly.

"Yes," he replied quickly. "That was the name he gave me."

"Did you meet him in person?" she asked.

"A couple of times. Quiet guy. Polite. Paid on time. I didn't ask questions. Wasn't really my business."

"It is now," Owen said coldly. "Do you have any CCTV on-site? Emails? Texts?"

"No CCTV. This isn't a bank. And the whole deal was informal."

"So no paper trail," Brooke muttered. "Convenient."

Vyas licked his lips. "Look, I didn't know anything about that girl. If I'd known—"

"You didn't know because you didn't want to," Owen interrupted. "You leased space to someone off the books and never questioned what he was doing in it."

"I didn't do anything illegal!"

"No, just stupid," Owen said. "And now a girl's dead because of it. Another one might be next."

Brooke stood, arms crossed. "Maybe we should have a word with Inland Revenue. Unregistered income. Possible fraud. I'm sure they'd be very interested."

Vyas paled.

"Here's what's going to happen," Owen said. "You're going to give us every scrap of contact you've had with this man. Phone numbers, emails, any name he gave, any messages. You're going to go through your records with us, right now. Because if we find out you're hiding anything—"

"I'm not," Vyas said quickly. "I'll help. I will. I just... need time. Some of it's at my home office."

"You'd better be quick, Vyas. Very quick. Someone will go with you to help."

Vyas wiped sweat from his brow as a patrol car pulled up outside to escort him.

It wasn't enough to name Blue.
But it was something.
A link. A face. A trail to follow.
Maybe even a number.
And maybe, just maybe,
It would lead them to Rosie.

Chapter 59

The Osbourne home sat on a quiet cul-de-sac, a small semi with cream brickwork and a front garden that had seen better days. The grass was overgrown in patches, the hedge uneven, but the windows were spotless, as if someone had cleaned them just that morning.

Brooke parked the car at the kerb and glanced across at Owen.

"We've never spoken to them properly, have we?"

"No," Owen said, unbuckling his seat belt. "It's overdue. We need to understand who Rosie is, how she might react if she's still with him."

"If," Brooke repeated softly.

"She's alive," Owen said, almost too quickly. "She has to be."

Brooke gave him a small nod, then got out of the car.

The front door opened before they reached it. A woman in her late forties stood there, thin-framed but with squared shoulders. Her eyes, ringed with tired shadows, darted between them.

"Mrs Osbourne?" Brooke asked.

"Yes. That's me."

"I'm DC Daniels. This is DI Owen," Brooke said. "We're leading the investigation into Rosie's case. May we come in?"

"No... please don't tell me she's dead. Please, no."

"No, Mrs Osbourne. We're not here to tell you that."

Mrs Osbourne's face softened for a moment. She stepped aside and let them in.

The hallway was narrow but clean, smelling faintly of lavender polish. Family photos lined the wall. Rosie as a smiling child. A school portrait. One of her in a blue dress at what looked like a family wedding.

"Please," Mrs Osbourne said, gesturing to the lounge. "Sit. Do you want tea? I've been making too much tea lately."

"Tea would be nice," Brooke said gently.

While Mrs Osbourne went to the kitchen, Owen looked around the lounge. More photos. A stack of unopened mail on the sideboard. The quiet hum of a clock on the wall.

Brooke sat forward, flipping open her notebook.

"We'll take this slow," she murmured. "She's been through enough."

Mrs Osbourne returned with tea and sat across from them, hands wrapped around her mug like it was the only warm thing she had left.

"Thank you. Mrs Osbourne, are there any other family members?"

"Please call me Shirley. Yes, my son, her brother, is upstairs. He's taken this really badly. He idolises his sister. You've never seen a bond like theirs."

"That's lovely to hear, Shirley. Would it be okay if we spoke to him before we go?"

"I think that'll be alright. So, how can I help? Have you any news about my Rosie?"

"Sorry, Shirley. I wish we had something to tell you. We're hoping you could tell us more about her," Brooke said, now sitting beside her.

"I don't know what else I can say," she replied. "I've given the police everything I could think of."

"We're not here to go over old ground," Owen said. "We want to understand Rosie. What she's like. What makes her strong. It could help us find her."

Shirley blinked, her eyes shining.

"You still think she's alive?"

"Yes," Owen said firmly. "We do."

"She's stronger than people think," Shirley said, her voice catching. "She's quiet, but determined. When her dad died, she was only fourteen. I thought it would break her, but she got through it. She doesn't give up easily."

Brooke leaned in slightly.

"How does she cope under pressure? Does she fight, or...?"

"She doesn't like conflict," Shirley said. "She'll avoid it if she can. But if someone else is in trouble, she'll step in. Always has."

"Protective," Owen said.

"Yes."

"What about her friends?" Brooke asked. "Has anyone mentioned anything unusual in the days before she went missing?"

Shirley shook her head.

"She kept things to herself. If she was struggling, she wouldn't show it. But she wrote things down. Always had a notebook."

"A diary?" Owen asked.

"I suppose. I don't know what's in it. She never let anyone read it."

"Do you still have it?" Brooke asked.

Shirley hesitated. "There might be one in her room. I can look."

Before she could move, a voice came from the doorway.

"Are you going to find her?"

A boy stood there, sixteen or so, tall but thin, his hair messy, his face pale. He had Rosie's eyes.

"Jamie," Shirley said softly.

Brooke turned.

"Hi, Jamie. We're doing everything we can."

"Promise?" he asked, his voice small but direct.

"I promise," Brooke said.

Jamie gave a slow nod, but his gaze lingered on Owen, as if silently asking for something more.

Owen met his stare.

"We'll bring her home. Maybe you could tell us a little about your sister while your mum looks for something?"

Jamie sat next to Owen.

"You a policeman?"

"Yes, Jamie. We both are. And we're trying really hard to find your sister."

They watched as Shirley, reassured, left the room and headed upstairs.

"I really miss her," Jamie said. "She was my friend too."

"Tell me, Jamie. Did she look out for you?"

"We didn't really have problems, but once, when I had a fight at school, Rosie came straight down. She wasn't having any of it."

"Sounds like a very special person."

Jamie didn't answer. He leaned against Owen and cried.

Owen leaned forward, elbows on his knees.

"She's a survivor, Brooke. You can feel it in this house."

Brooke nodded.

"She's holding on. We just need to reach her before that changes."

A minute later, Shirley returned. She held a small, spiral-bound notebook in one hand. It was worn, slightly curled at the edges, and a pen was still tucked into the spine.

"This was under her bed," she said. "She always hid things. I haven't read it."

Owen took it gently.

"We won't share anything we don't have to."

Brooke flipped through the pages carefully. Most of it was ordinary. Lists. Dates. A few scrawled poems. A sketch of a window looking out onto trees. Then, near the middle, she stopped.

"What is it?" Owen asked.

She turned the notebook so he could read.

Sometimes I feel like I disappear in pieces. A different version of me in every room. The happy one for Mum. The strong one for Jamie. The calm one for work. The real one stays hidden.

But I think that version would survive anything.

Even if she was terrified.

Even if no one came for her right away.

Brooke stared at it for a long time.

"That was written three weeks before she went missing, according to the date," Shirley whispered. Then she broke. "She never showed that side to us."

Owen took a deep breath. This was going to be harder than he'd expected.

"She knew how to endure. Even back then."

Brooke gently closed the notebook and looked at Shirley.

"We'll hold onto this, if that's okay. It might help us understand her mindset."

"Of course," Shirley said quietly. "Just bring her back."

Outside, the rain had started again. Light and cold.

As Owen got into the passenger seat, he looked down at the notebook resting on Brooke's lap. That single page had told him more than anything else.

"She's still fighting," he said.

Brooke nodded.

"But we're running out of time."

She started the engine.

And somewhere far away, behind locked doors and thick walls, Rosie Osbourne was waiting.

Somewhere else...

Rosie sat in the dark, knees pulled up, arms wrapped tightly around them. The walls were the same. Grey. Damp. Lifeless. But something felt different. Not in the room. In her.

She couldn't explain it. A flicker. Like the tiniest pulse of warmth through her chest. Like someone had said her name from very far away.

She tilted her head, listening, even though she knew no sound would come.

Blue hadn't been back in hours. Maybe longer. Time didn't mean anything anymore. Not really.

But something had shifted.

Her fingers closed around the edge of the blanket, gripping it tightly.

They were looking for her.

She didn't know how she knew. She just did.

And if they were close, if they were really coming, then she had to hold on a little longer. Stay smart. Stay alive.

No matter what.

Chapter 60

The next day started as usual. Rosie could hear him moving around, humming, sounding almost cheerful. She glanced over at Linda, who spent most mornings pretending to be asleep. Or maybe she really couldn't face Rosie anymore.

Moments later, the door creaked open, letting a shaft of sunlight into the room.

"Good morning, ladies. Come on, Linda, you know the routine."

She did. They both did. Once he was done with them, they sat side by side on the bed, not speaking, just watching as he pulled his trousers back up.

"So, Rosie," he said, brushing his hair back. "I've been thinking... maybe it's time we got another friend to play with. You picked well last time. Let's dig out my notes."

"You're sounding cheerful this morning, Blue. What's brought that on? The idea of a third girl?" Rosie kept her voice light.

"Well, you know, I might get bored with one of you. Might need a change."

Rosie forced a small laugh. "Come on, Blue. You don't mean that... do you?"

He didn't answer. He just stared at her.

Linda pulled her knees up to her chest, shrinking into herself.

"Blue," Rosie said carefully, "since Linda's still here and improving, maybe she could help us pick the next one. From your notes?"

"No, Rosie, please," Linda whispered, panicked. "I couldn't. Please don't make me. I can't."

"Well, Linda," Rosie said coolly, "if Blue says you help, then you help. Unless, of course, you want to be replaced."

"Now, now, ladies," Blue chuckled. "There's enough of old Blue to go around. And yes, I like the idea. Let's have a look."

He walked over and handed the notes to Linda, who took them with trembling hands. She spread the creased pages across the bed.

Rosie scanned them quickly. No mention of Brooke.

"Well, Linda?" Blue asked. "What do you think I'd like?"

"I... I can't decide," she stammered. "Maybe one of these two. Tracey, nineteen, slim, works at Tesco. Or Jane, twenty-one, slim, dresses smart, works for a solicitor."

Blue turned to Rosie. "What about you? What do you think?"

She knew this was a test. A trap.

"Jane," Rosie said smoothly. "I think she'd look beautiful on our bed. Don't you?"

Blue's eyes lit up. "You're getting naughty, Rosie. Wanting to see her naked already. I love that."

He chuckled, then nodded. "It'll take a couple of days to arrange. I need to check a few things."

"Can't wait," Rosie said, smiling sweetly. "Looking forward to meeting our new playmate."

Blue walked over and kissed her, slow and deliberate. She kissed him back, just as deeply, feeding the lie. When he finally left the room, he didn't lock the door.

Linda sat frozen.

"I'm sorry," she whispered. "I didn't realise you were telling the truth."

Rosie walked over and hugged her. "It's OK, Linda. No one could make sense of this place, not really. And Linda—"

She pressed a finger to her lips. "Quiet. He hears everything."

Linda pulled her tighter, whispering into her hair. "Rosie, I know you're planning something. If you can take me, I'd be grateful. But if you can't, go. Don't look back. Save yourself."

"But Linda, what if he—?"

"I'll take my chances. Maybe it'll save Jane."

They held each other, crying softly. Rosie still didn't fully trust Linda, but she needed her now.

"Later," Rosie whispered. "When he takes us to his room again, I want you to try something."

Linda gave her a wary look. "Like what?"

"If he does the usual... you know, has us both, I want you to give him everything. And afterwards, stay close to him. In the bed. Instead of me."

Linda blinked. "And what will you do?"

"Honestly?" Rosie said. "I don't know yet. But I'm scared. For both of us. If anything goes wrong..."

Linda nodded slowly. "Rosie... I trust you."

Rosie blinked back tears. "Thank you."

They held each other until the door handle turned.

Blue stepped in. "Everything OK, girls? You looked upset when I was watching you."

"No, we're good, Blue," Rosie said quickly. "Linda was saying she understands now. How hard it was for me when I picked her."

"Ah. Friends now, are we?" He smirked and walked to Linda.

"Rosie," he said casually, "could you pop downstairs and grab some bottled water? Just outside the back door."

"Sure, Blue. Won't be a minute."

She walked out, heart racing, and glanced back. Blue was already leaning over Linda. Linda caught Rosie's eye and gave the faintest nod.

This was a test.

Rosie rushed to the kitchen and opened the back door. There were crates of bottled water. She grabbed three and paused.

The van was parked just beyond the shed.

Every time he left and returned; he turned it around.

One way in. One way out.

She closed the door quietly and turned.

"Jesus!" She gasped.

Blue was standing there.

"Oh—Blue! You made me jump. Everything alright?"

"It is now, my Rosie."

She smiled faintly and followed him back upstairs. Another test passed, she told herself. You bastard.

Back in the bedroom, Blue returned to Linda, then called Rosie over.

She walked past the cabinet, eyes flicking to the van keys.

There. Right there.

She kept walking to the bed.

"Come on, Linda," she said sweetly. "Make room. We can share him."

Chapter 61

Rosie lay on the edge of the bed for a long time, waiting for him to fall asleep. His breathing deepened. Slowed.

She waited longer.

Then, carefully and silently, she eased off the mattress.

She crept around to check on Linda.

One arm was wrapped tightly around Blue, her body curled into him. She didn't stir, but her lips moved.

Good luck.

Rosie's stomach clenched. Her legs felt weak, but she forced herself to move.

She stepped toward the cabinet, knowing exactly which floorboards creaked and avoiding them. Her legs ached. Her feet were tender from the cold wooden floor.

No shoes. No clothes. Not even a blanket.

She reached the keys. Just inches away now.

She glanced at Blue. He hadn't moved. His face was still, peaceful, almost innocent.

It made her want to scream.

She lowered both hands over the keys, smothering them in her palms to muffle any sound. Slowly, she lifted them.

No noise.

They were cold against her skin. The red ribbon was still threaded through the fob. The gold necklace hung from it like a charm — delicate, mocking.

She stared at it for a second.

His trophy.

Her fingers tightened around it.

She had them.

The door was open a crack from earlier. Inch by inch, she eased it open, just enough to slip through. She paused in the doorway, heart racing, sweat prickling across her skin.

She looked back once.

Linda. Still chained. Still in danger.

A big part of Rosie wanted to turn back. Grab her. Try to make a run for it together.

But it was impossible. And if she failed now, it might cost them both.

Sarah flashed in her mind. Blood on the floor. Lifeless eyes.

She wouldn't end like that.

There were twelve steps to the bottom. Rosie took them one at a time, barefoot, her toes curled tight for balance. The wood was cold and rough. A splinter caught her heel and she bit back a gasp.

Blue had grown careless. Or maybe just cocky.

He thought he'd broken her. Thought she was his. That she wouldn't run.

And maybe he wasn't entirely wrong.

But tonight, she was going to prove him wrong.

At the bottom of the stairs, she paused. Her heart hammered in her chest. Her breath came fast and shallow.

She crept to the front door.

Hands trembling, she tried the first key.

Didn't fit.

Second. No.

Third.

Click.

The bolt slid open.

She let out a gasp. Too loud. But the house stayed silent.

She turned and looked back again. Just once.

Linda.

What would he do to her? Would he kill her?

Would it be Rosie's fault?

Her hand lingered on the door.

Take her.

Her chest tightened. Her knees wobbled.

But she couldn't.

Not yet.

She pushed the door open and slipped outside.

The night air hit her like a slap. Cold, sharp, glorious. The grass was slick with dew. Her bare feet sank into the earth and the mud squelched between her toes.

She didn't care.

She walked toward the van, every step a battle against fear.

Her mind raced.

Is this a trap? What if this is where it all goes wrong?

She saw the van.

Her stomach dropped.

What if there's an alarm? What if it doesn't start?

But there was no going back now.

She didn't know how far they were from help. From a town. A road. Another person.

She just knew she had to move.

Behind her, the house was dark.

But that wouldn't last.

When Blue woke.

When he found the door open.

When he saw she was gone.

He'd come.

And if he caught her, he wouldn't take his time. He wouldn't lecture her. He'd kill her. Quick. Brutal. No second chances.

She opened the van door carefully. Didn't shut it fully. Just pulled it close enough that the interior light blinked off.

She slid into the driver's seat, legs shaking, heart slamming against her ribs. Found the key. Slipped it into the ignition.

Clutch down. Gear in place.

Please. Please. Please.

The engine coughed, then roared to life.

She shut the door and moved off, flipping on the headlights as she rolled away from the house.

She didn't look back.

She wasn't thinking anymore.

She was surviving.

She was free.

For now.

Chapter 62

Rosie just kept driving. A quick glance showed she had half a tank of fuel. She pressed harder on the accelerator, the van picking up speed, faster and faster, until she spun almost out of control on a sharp bend.

"God, where am I?" she muttered. "Now I'm free, I don't want to get killed driving this thing."

The roads were dark and narrow, country lanes with no street lights. Somewhere, there had to be help. But then a thought struck her. A bad one.

How far had Blue gone when he went shopping? Did anyone know this van? What if they recognised it — recognised her?

Her stomach clenched. She was naked. She couldn't just walk into the last shop he'd been to.

She slowed, checked her mirrors. Nothing behind.

Deep breath. Drive as normal as you can.

But everything in her was screaming.

Every white van looked like his now. Every reflection in a shop window made her flinch. She could see him pulling up behind her, one hand on the wheel, the other holding that goddamn chain.

She was getting frustrated. No signs. No lights. Just black roads and bends that seemed to twist back on themselves. She was terrified the next turn would take her straight back to the house, that he'd be there, waiting.

Then, finally, she saw them.

Lights, faint at first, growing brighter. And then... a sign.

A3. Cobham.

She veered onto the road, relief flooding her, but fear still rode shotgun. It wasn't over. Not until she was safe. Not until she saw a real face. A kind one.

The next sign gave her a jolt of hope.

M25. Services. People. Crowds. Help.

She followed the slip road off the M25 into the Cobham services. It was busy. Good. But she couldn't stop shaking. What if someone looked too closely? What if the wrong person saw her?

She didn't want to get out. Not yet.

She waited, scanning the car park.

Then, a car pulled in. A family. Man, woman, two kids. Rosie moved the van closer, heart pounding. The man glanced her way, frowning. He looked uncertain.

Then he closed his car door and turned toward her fully.

Panic gripped her.

What if they thought she was the kidnapper?

What if they didn't believe her?

What if they recognised the van and called him?

She stopped the van.

Her arms were trembling. Every bump in the road had sent fresh shocks of pain through her thighs. She gripped the door handle. Her hand slipped once, slick with sweat and blood.

Then she opened it.

And fell.

She landed at the man's feet, trembling, bruised, filthy, naked. Her chest heaved with shallow, panicked breaths. Her eyes locked on his.

"D... D.I. Owen," she rasped, the name she'd whispered in her head for days.

Then — darkness.

And somewhere, not far away, Owen's phone began to ring.

.

Chapter 63

Owen was halfway through a stale sandwich when his phone rang. The number wasn't familiar, but something in his chest tightened as he answered.

"DI Owen."

"Control here, sir. St. Peter's Hospital just took in a female matching the description of your active case. Early twenties, no clothes, severe bruising. She was found at Cobham Services by a family. Paramedics say she collapsed at their feet and said your name."

Owen shot to his feet, his chair screeching back.

"She gave my name?"

"Yes, sir. Just that. 'DI Owen,' and then passed out. Ambulance took her straight in. She's been treated for hypothermia and dehydration. Hospital staff are securing the area. Sounds like it could be Rosie Osbourne."

Across the desk, Brooke looked up, instantly alert.

"Send a car to Cobham Services. I want statements from the family and a full canvas of the car park."

"Already dispatched, sir."

"Good. We're heading to the hospital now. Make sure no one goes near her unless they're police or medical staff.

And I want an armed response unit outside her room until further notice."

"Understood."

Owen hung up. Brooke was already pulling on her jacket.

"Rosie?" she asked.

He nodded once. She could see the hope in his eyes.

"Alive. Cobham Services. She asked for me."

They didn't speak again until they were in the car, blue lights flashing. Owen drove like the city was on fire.

He picked up the radio. "DO 1 to Control."

"Go ahead, DO 1."

"We're en route to St. Peter's. Any updates on scene?"

"No change reported, DO 1. ARU is already on site. Witnesses at Cobham are being interviewed."

Brooke looked over at him. "If it is Rosie, do you really think he'd come for her? In public?"

"I don't know. But I wouldn't put anything past him. It has to be her, Brooke. It just has to be."

"Owen, slow down. Having a go at me won't help."

He exhaled hard. "I'm sorry. It's just... this case, what he's done, what he's capable of. I'm scared we won't stop him in time."

Brooke reached across, resting her hand on his arm. "We will. We will."

The corridors of St. Peter's were lit with that cold, too-bright hospital light. Everything smelled of antiseptic and urgency.

Two armed officers stood outside a side room.

A nurse met them as they arrived.

"She's stable," she said quietly. "Scared. Barely speaking, but she's alert. We've cleaned her up, started fluids. She's been through hell. The doctor said she can speak with you briefly, but not for long."

"Thank you," Owen said.

The nurse hesitated. "Inspector... she was raped. Multiple times. With force. She has bruised ribs and lacerations. When she arrived, she was completely naked. That's how she escaped. She keeps mentioning someone named Linda. And... she asked for you."

Owen's jaw tightened, but he just nodded.

He paused outside the door, but Brooke touched his arm.

"Let me go first."

"Yeah. Good idea. Just... tell her I'm here."

Brooke stepped quietly into the room.

Rosie lay on her side, cocooned in blankets. An IV trailed from one arm. Her face was pale and bruised, but her eyes fluttered open as Brooke approached.

"Rosie?" Brooke said gently.

Rosie looked at her. She didn't speak.

"You're safe now. My name's Brooke. I work with DI Owen. You said his name when they found you."

A flicker of recognition passed over Rosie's face.

"You're real," she whispered.

"Yes. And so is Owen. We've been searching for you."

A tear slid down Rosie's cheek. Her lips moved as if to speak, but no words came. Then she reached up. Brooke leaned forward, and Rosie managed to pull her close, clinging to her as she broke down sobbing. Brooke held her tightly, her own eyes wet.

"You don't have to talk yet," Brooke said softly. "You've been through hell. But if there's anything you can tell us, it might help us find him."

Rosie swallowed. Her voice was thin, broken.

"You have to save Linda. He has her. I don't know if he'll kill her now. Please... please, it's my fault."

"No. It's not. But we need your help. Do you know where he's keeping her?"

"He said I belonged to him. That I was his. He made us do things. He'd... drop his trousers... and made us take turns."

Brooke clenched her teeth, keeping her voice calm. "But you escaped, Rosie. You did that. Not him."

Owen stepped into the room. Rosie saw him and stiffened slightly.

"Are you DI Owen?" she asked.

"I am. And I can't tell you how relieved I am to see you alive. We've been looking for you for weeks."

"Linda... you have to find her. She told me to ask for you. She read your name in the papers. She's not in a good way, and if he blames her—"

Brooke leaned in. "Rosie, do you remember where he was holding you?"

"I don't know exactly. It was a big house. Middle of nowhere. When I took the van, there was only one road in and out."

The door opened and the doctor stepped in.

"Officers, I'm sorry. She needs to rest."

"No," Rosie said, forcing herself upright. "I need to tell them. They have to save Linda."

The doctor frowned but stepped back. "Fine. Five minutes."

Rosie nodded faintly. "There was someone else. Another girl. Sarah. He... he killed her. Right in front of me. I couldn't stop it."

Brooke softened her voice. "We know about Sarah. We found her body. If you'd tried to intervene, he would have killed you too."

"He moved us," Rosie whispered. "Different place. But in the last house... he let me look out the windows. All I could see were green fields. When I escaped, it was dark. Narrow roads. I nearly crashed on a bend. Then I saw lights and followed them."

Owen stepped forward. "Rosie, this is important. Do you remember any road signs?"

"Yes. A3. Cobham. Then the M25."

"That's very helpful. Thank you."

Rosie turned to Brooke; eyes wide. "Please, find him. Find Linda. She trusted me. She could've told him, but she didn't."

"We will," Brooke said, fierce with emotion.

Owen's phone rang. He stepped aside.

"DI Owen. Yes. Okay. Escort them up."

He returned to the room.

"Rosie, your family is here. They're coming up now. Also, from now on, you'll have armed protection, wherever you go."

"Thank you, Owen."

Just then, cries rang out in the corridor. Rosie's mother burst in, ran to her daughter, and almost collapsed onto the bed as she embraced her.

Brooke signalled to Owen and stepped out.

In the hallway, she wiped her eyes.

"Well," she said softly, "that makes this job worth it. Let's do the same for Linda."

Chapter 65

He dragged Linda downstairs. She could hardly walk, her feet scraping along behind her. He stopped at the kitchen door, taking a good look around—just in case the police had already arrived. Then he pulled a set of keys from his pocket.

Once outside, he continued dragging her toward a locked garage. Inside was a **blue Nissan Qashqai**. He opened the boot and tossed Linda in, then wrapped more duct tape around her legs and torso, binding her tightly in a fetal position.

Her ribs screamed with every movement. Her wrists throbbed.
This was it.
She had no idea if she'd ever see daylight again.

The car bounced once as Blue pulled onto the narrow road.

The engine rattled, tyres crunching over loose gravel, but the Qashqai held steady.

Linda was in the boot—bound, silent, bruised, and out of sight.

He hadn't spoken since they left the house.

He switched on the radio. Smooth Radio was playing. It was five minutes to the hour—news time.

He'd need to stop for supplies. There hadn't been time to prepare the next hideout.

But he didn't stop at his usual shop.

The police were bound to be canvassing by now.

He reached across the seat, picked up the envelope, and traced a finger over the name he'd written:

DC Brooke Daniels.

Was this too risky?
He shook it off.
No. This needed to be done.

He drove for about an hour before coming across a Tesco. Parking in a side street, he made sure there were no CCTV cameras nearby, then walked the few hundred metres toward the main car park.

He looked around and spotted a young guy in a high-vis jacket. As he approached, he scanned the area without drawing attention to himself.

"Morning, my friend."

The startled young man pulled out his headphones. "Morning. What's up, guv?"

"Look, I found this envelope. It's for some copper. Here's a tenner—take it to that copper over there drinking coffee."

"Why can't you do it?"

"I had a run-in with them a few years back. They still give me the shits."

The young man laughed. "Yeah, I get it, Gov. No worries—consider it done."

Blue handed over the envelope and stepped away, watching as the kid headed toward two uniformed officers on their break.

He turned and walked quickly back to the car.

Before getting in, he paused a few metres away, checking behind him.

No one was following.

Right, he thought. *Now for safety.*

The engine turned over.

He pulled away, leaving the envelope—and the message—behind.

The game had changed.
And this time, it was personal.

Chapter 64

Brooke stood frozen in the corridor outside Rosie's room, her back to the wall, arms crossed tight.
She'd been there for nearly an hour, waiting while the doctor checked Rosie over, then while her mother had time alone with her. She hadn't wanted to intrude.

Owen had gone in just a few minutes earlier.

Her heart was still racing. She could still feel Rosie's grip around her neck. The raw need in her voice.

She had asked for Owen. Had held onto his name like it was oxygen.

Now Owen stepped out. He didn't speak, just looked at Brooke. Nodded once. Then turned and walked down the corridor.

Brooke followed him.

In the car park, the air was cool. Owen reached into his coat pocket, pulled out a cigarette, and paused. His fingers were shaking. He stared at it, caught off guard. Then muttered to himself and flicked it into the bin, still unlit.

He'd given up smoking after meeting Brooke. A week, maybe less. He couldn't remember. Time was not a friend. It figured now would be the moment his old habits came clawing back.

"She knew me," he said quietly.

Brooke nodded.

"She said my name. After everything she's been through…"

"She's not the same, Owen. But she's strong."

"She's stronger than we ever imagined."

They both stood silently for a moment.

Then Owen spoke again, more to himself than her.

"He'll know she got out. He'll know she told us something."

Brooke folded her arms. "Then he'll run."

"No," Owen said, eyes narrowing. "He'll react."

Back at the house

The door stood open.

The chain was on the floor.

The keys were gone.

Blue stood motionless in the bedroom, staring at the empty space where she'd lain.

Linda hadn't spoken. Hadn't moved. She was curled up, her breathing shallow. She knew better than to make a sound.

Blue slowly walked to the cabinet. Reached for the place he always left them.

Gone.

The keyring. The ribbon. The necklace. All of it.

His hand hovered there for a second, then curled into a trembling fist.

"She took it," he whispered.

His voice cracked.

He stood still. Not angry. Not yet. Just hollow.

She had lied to him. Kissed him. Slept beside him. Pretended.

And then stolen from him.

From her.

He turned and walked out into the hallway. His bag was already packed. He had always known someone might get away, but didn't expect it to be Rosie. Always known he'd need to disappear fast.

But this wasn't just running.

She had taken something sacred.

He opened a side drawer, found one of her drawings. The blue rose. Ten petals. Soft ink strokes. Slightly smudged where she'd shaded it with her thumb.

He stared at it for a moment.

Then, with no warning, he screamed and flipped the table across the room. The crash was deafening. Linda let out a gasp but didn't move.

Blue stormed down the hallway. Kicked the doorframe. Grabbed a chair and smashed it against the wall.

He stood panting.

Then turned back to the bedroom.

Linda.

He walked slowly toward her, breathing heavily through his nose.

She didn't cry. Not this time.

Linda was trying to make herself into a ball and as far away from him as possible, but there was nowhere to go.

It came so fast she didn't see his hand slap her hard, and again. She begged him, trying to pretend she didn't know what was going on.

"Please, Blue, please, what have I done wrong, please don't kill me, I'm sorry whatever it is."

He stopped and knelt beside her, hand closing around her wrist.

"You didn't stop her," he whispered. "You let her leave me."

Linda didn't respond. Her eyes were vacant.

He pulled a zip tie from his pocket and looped it around her wrist, and then to the metal headboard, and repeated it with the other hand. Then gagged her tight with the grey duct tape.

He went back to the cabinet and took out an old Polaroid camera and took a photo of Linda.

He waited until it developed in his hand. Then showed it to Linda.

"What do you think, Linda, shall I make you a copy?" Unable to answer, Linda—her eyes wide—just shook her head.

"You're going to remind her what happens when you steal from me."

Back at St. Peter's

Rosie sat up straighter in the hospital bed. Her mother had finally gone home. A kind nurse had helped her clean up again. She was still sore, still raw, but more present now.

Brooke came back into the room and pulled up a chair, leaving Owen standing in the doorway.

"Rosie," she said gently, "I need to ask you one more thing. Did he ever mention anyone else? Another name? Something unusual?"

Rosie frowned. Thought about it.

Then nodded.

"He called me Rosie most of the time. But once... he said, 'Shawnnessy would've liked you.'"

Brooke froze.

"What did you say?"

Rosie repeated it.

Brooke's mouth went dry. "Are you sure that's what he said?"

Rosie nodded.

Brooke stood up. "Thank you. You've just given us something huge."

She turned to leave.

"Brooke," Rosie said suddenly. "Your full name—what is it?"

Brooke turned back. "Daniels. Brooke Daniels."

Rosie's breath caught.

Her eyes widened. "It's you."

Brooke stopped. "What?"

"You're the other name."

Brooke stepped forward, slowly. "What do you mean?"

"He showed me a list. I had to pick a replacement after he killed Sarah. There were some names crossed off. I remember seeing mine, Sarah's, and Linda's, but there was one written in blue."

Brooke whispered, "Mine."

Rosie nodded.

"I didn't know. I didn't make the connection. Not until now."

Brooke stood very still, heart thudding, her knees starting to give way. Owen caught her just in time.

"He wants you. He said you were the last. And special."

Rosie's voice was barely a whisper.

Brooke turned without speaking and walked into the hallway.

She didn't even realise she was holding her breath.

Owen pulled up a chair.

"Brooke, sit down a minute."

"He has my name. My name. Why? She said that he told her I was going to be last. And special."

"Brooke, it's going to be fine. I promise. He won't get near you. He is a sick bastard, and we will stop him."

Brooke stood up, gave Owen a hug, and walked away.

Chapter 66

Brooke sat down at her desk with a nasty cup of coffee. It wasn't good, but it was better than nothing. Then she saw it.

There was an envelope sitting on her desk.

White. Plain. Unmarked, except for her name.

DC Brooke Daniels.

Her heart skipped as she stared at the handwriting, blocky, confident.

It felt like it was watching her back.

"Brooke," someone called from across the incident room. "That came in earlier, passed through uniform. Some guy handed it over outside a Tesco."

She didn't answer straight away. She was already reaching for gloves.

Something felt wrong.

Owen had been gone for over two hours now. No message. No call. Not even a text.

She'd tried not to panic, told herself he was just taking a walk, clearing his head. But that excuse wore thin fast.

It wasn't like him to go silent. Not anymore. Not with everything going on.

And if Blue had somehow gotten to him…

Carefully, she ran her gloved hand over both sides of the envelope. She couldn't feel any wires, just what seemed like a single sheet of paper. Or maybe a photo.

She slipped the envelope open and pulled out the contents.

Her breath caught.

Linda.

Tied to a bed. Mouth sealed shut with grey tape. Wrists bound in front of her. Bruises across her face.

Brooke felt sick.

Bound. Beaten. Helpless.

And this was meant for me.

She turned the photo over.

There was writing on the back, done in blue whiteboard pen.

She read it silently:

Hi Brooke. I asked her to smile for you, but I guess she couldn't. I expect Rosie's with you now. That bitch took something from me. And I'll be wanting it back soon.

Her fingers clenched the edges of the picture until they creased. She took out her phone and snapped photos of both sides.

Where the hell was Owen?

The office buzzed with activity again. Smithy came over but paused when he saw her face.

"You okay, Brooke?"

She nodded too quickly. "Fine. Where's Owen?"

Smithy shrugged. "Said he needed a break. Think he went to the gun range."

"The what?"

Smithy blinked. "You didn't know?"

Brooke stood abruptly, nearly knocking over her chair.

"No. Take this. Excuse me."

She shoved the photo into his hands and stormed off.

She wasn't just worried now. She was pissed.

She found Owen outside, just walking in from the car park, still carrying a kit bag.

"Owen!"

He stopped.

Brooke marched right up to him, barely managing to keep her voice level. She shoved him hard, making him drop the bag. Then she started hitting his chest with both hands.

He grabbed her and held her tightly, refusing to let go. He could see the tears running down her cheeks.

Then she clung to him, her voice cracking.

"You've been gone two hours. You didn't say a word."

"I needed to clear my head. I went to the range."

She pushed him back. "You could've told me."

"I didn't think," he paused, reading her expression. "I'm sorry, Brooke. I just... I needed time. That list. Your name. It rattled me."

Her voice softened, but only slightly. "You don't get to vanish when things get hard. Not now."

He nodded. "You're right."

"I got a photo," she added quietly.

Owen's eyes locked onto hers.

"Linda?"

Brooke nodded. "Alive. For now."

She held out her phone and showed him the image, front and back. He studied it, his mouth tightening.

"God, I'm sorry, Brooke. You're not leaving my sight now."

"What did Rosie take from him?" Owen asked.

"I think it's the one thing that sends him over the edge. He can't be without it. The van keys Rosie escaped with had a red ribbon attached to a gold necklace. Now he wants it back. And I guess he's going to ask me for it."

Before they could say more, Brooke's phone buzzed.

She checked the screen. "It's the estate agent."

She answered on speaker. "Daniels."

A nervous voice crackled through. "You asked if we'd rented that property? I've just gone through our archive. We did. Two years ago. I found the ID. You're going to want to see it."

Owen leaned in. "Who rented it?"

"Name used was Mr. Taylor. Same as the one who viewed 23 Duncan Street. But this one, he actually took the property. Large house just outside Guildford. Six-month lease."

"Send us the address now. And thank you," Brooke said.

She ended the call and looked at Owen, who was already on his phone.

Forty-five minutes later, they arrived at the house. An armed response unit was already there, waiting for Owen to give the go-ahead.

Just minutes later, the ARU sergeant called out:

"All clear!"

Owen and Brooke gloved up. He gave orders for the rest of the team to search the surrounding grounds. No one was to disturb the interior. Strict orders: look, don't touch.

The front door creaked open.

The smell hit first. Old blood, sweat, bleach, and something worse.

As they moved from room to room, the reality of what Rosie and the others had endured came into focus.

Rags soaked in blood. Torn clothing. A mattress stained and rotting. Evidence of restraint. Horror in every corner.

"Owen, this is something right out of a horror movie."

"This is as real as it gets. I feel for Linda right now. Let's hope there's something here that helps."

Owen noticed Brooke standing still, staring at the bed and the mess around it.

"Brooke? You okay?"

"No," she whispered. "Not really. Owen… has he got all this planned for me?"

He stepped closer. "He won't get the chance. I promise you that."

Brooke didn't reply.

She just kept staring at the bed.

At what might've been hers.

Chapter 67

The house smelled of bleach and blood.
It was a quiet kind of horror, the kind that soaked into the walls. Every footstep felt too loud. Every room too still.

Owen stood just inside the doorway as the forensic team moved through the scene like shadows. Gloved hands. Evidence bags. Flashing cameras. A low murmur of radio traffic filled the background.

Brooke stood silent beside him; arms folded tightly across her chest. She'd seen many horrors in her career, but this one felt personal. Too personal. She knew what Owen had promised, but couldn't stop imagining someone finding her own beaten body, discarded like Sarah's.

They both knew what this place was.
A hunting ground.

A prison.
A grave that hadn't yet been filled.

Smithy approached from the hallway.
"We've started cataloguing. It's bad."

He handed over a clear evidence bag. Inside was a bundle of red cloth, stiff with blood.

"Found under a loose floorboard," Smithy said. "Looks like it was hidden in a rush."

Brooke glanced at it.
"That could be Sarah's."

Owen nodded.
"Or someone before her."

"I don't think so. From what Rosie said, this place was about her, Sarah, and Linda."

"Well, you may be right. Only time will tell."

"Yes, Owen, but I don't have time. I mean... Linda doesn't have time."

He caught the slip. He was going to have to do more to keep her safe, and he knew it.

Brooke looked at Smithy.
"Any sign of their clothes? Rosie's or Linda's?"

He shook his head.
"Nothing but that. Looks like he took everything with him—or burned it."

"Figures," Owen muttered. "He wouldn't leave anything that personal behind."

They moved down the corridor together, past a small bathroom and into what could only be described as a holding room. A large space with bars across the windows. A steel-framed bed bolted to the floor. A rusted chain locked to one of the legs.

"Jesus," Owen muttered. "All they could do was walk to the bathroom and back."

A voice called from the next room.
"Boss!"

They hurried in.

The room was similar—two single beds, both bolted down. One had a piece of the frame missing.

Forensics had uncovered a scorched tin box, half melted at one corner. It had been shoved inside a small cavity behind a kitchen cabinet panel, along with a bent metal bar.

Brooke stared at the bar.
"That's the weapon," she said, her voice tight. "The one he used on Sarah."

Owen was beginning to worry about the pressure she was under.

"Brooke, I'm not sure you should be here."

"Owen, I'm okay. And I'm not going anywhere unless you order me to."

He saw the look in her eyes and thought better of it. But the worry didn't leave.

Inside, they found:

- A charred sheet of paper, its edges burned black
- A disposable phone with a cracked screen
- Two Polaroids—burned, but still visible enough to show faces

The tech handed over the page with tweezers.

Only a few names remained readable, the rest eaten away by smoke and fire. But one name at the bottom was still perfectly intact.

Brooke Daniels
Written in the same blue pen.

She stared at it, her breath catching.
"It's real. He wrote it down."

"We'll get it scanned," the tech said. "Might lift more detail."

Owen bagged the phone.
"Check the call history, texts—anything that's left, we want it."

Another officer leaned over the banister.
"Owen—we found a crawl space. More photos. And something else."

They climbed quickly.

In the cramped attic, under a plastic sheet, they found three driver's licenses. Fake names—but the same face.

The man who took Rosie.
The man who posed as Mr Taylor.
The man who rented this house.

Brooke stared at the image.
"It's him. He's been planning this for years."

"Three aliases," Owen said. "At least."

She turned toward the hatch and looked back down the narrow hallway.

This wasn't just a crime scene.
It was a map.
Of everything he was.

"We need a profile update," Owen said. "We're not dealing with someone impulsive anymore. He's controlled. Methodical. Every step pre-planned."

Brooke nodded, her voice flat.
"And now he's improvising."

She glanced at the list again, folded neatly in a sealed bag.
Only one name remained.

Later, back at the station, they found that Rosie had been released from hospital.

Rosie sat in the family room with her mother. Her skin was pale, her expression tired—but her eyes were sharp.

"Hello, Rosie. How are you feeling now? We didn't expect to see you out of hospital yet."

"Thanks for asking. I'm just so worried about Linda. Is she still alive? What's he done with her?"

"Rosie, are you up for us showing you something? Mrs Osbourne, this may be very upsetting."

Rosie looked at her mother, who seemed older and more exhausted than when they'd first met.

"Go ahead, Owen."

Brooke sat beside Rosie for support. Owen passed her an A4 photo, and Brooke handed it over.

Rosie broke down the second she saw it. The crying went on for some time—raw and uncontrollable. No one said a word. No one could blame her.

When it stopped, the room fell deathly silent. The tension was heavy, like smoke.

"Rosie," Owen said gently. "I'm sorry, but can you confirm—is that Linda?"

She nodded, unable to speak.

Owen stepped out briefly and returned with bottles of water. A soft knock at the door—Smithy entered quietly.

"Sorry to disturb, but Brooke, can I take that?"

He gestured toward the evidence bag, and as Brooke turned to grab it, Smithy glanced at Owen, then at her, and mouthed silently: **I've done it.**

Brooke didn't notice—her attention was on Rosie—but Owen caught it.

Brooke handed over the bag, her voice low.
"Sorry."

Owen turned back to Rosie.
"It's real. We found it behind a false panel. Your name was there. So was Sarah's. April. Linda. Jane. But one name was left untouched."

Rosie stared at it.
"Blue kept it. Even after I ran. But… why not take it with him?"

Brooke spoke gently.
"He's not thinking straight anymore. You changed that."

She hesitated, then added,
"And Rosie—you just called him Blue. You haven't said that before."

Rosie's voice was quiet but firm.
"He told me I could call him that. When he thought he was winning me over. Like a lot of things… I went along with it. I had to."

Rosie's voice trembled.
"Then stop him before he gets to her. Before he gets to you."

Owen stepped forward.
"We've already found Jane and Tracy. They're under full police protection. And you and your family are being moved to a safe house."

"Do you think he'll come for me?"

"Rosie… I don't know. But if Blue does, we'll be waiting."

She looked between them.
"No. You have to get him first. Together."

Brooke reached for her hand.
"We're not going to let him take anyone else."

Owen looked down at the list.

This had to stop.
And it had to stop now.

"We're ending this."

Chapter 68

Brooke stood in the locker room; her reflection blurred in the metal of the cabinet door.
She hadn't moved in five minutes. She wasn't sure she'd even blinked.

She kept thinking about the evidence bag, the scorched list.
She couldn't get it out of her mind. It felt like it was still there.
Breathing.

Brooke Daniels.
The last name.
The only one not crossed out.
Written in blue. Special. He had said so.

She jumped slightly as the door creaked open. Owen stepped in, quiet, watching her.

"You alright?" he asked gently.

She didn't answer at first. Just nodded, then shook her head.

"I keep going over it," she said. "The way he planned everything. The house. The list. The photo. And now, me."

She turned, leaning her back against the locker.

"Do you know how many women we've interviewed? Victims. Survivors. Families. And I always said the same thing. We're going to catch him.'"

"We still are," Owen said.

"But now it's me, Owen. He chose me."

Her voice cracked, but she pushed past it.

"I've always tried to understand people like him. I've sat through lectures, case studies, training modules, 'this is how killers think,' 'this is what they want.'
But now I don't have to imagine it. I don't have to guess."

She pointed at the list.

"He wrote my name. He's thinking about me. Not as a detective. Not as a person. Just... the next."

Her fingers trembled slightly as she wiped her face. Not enough to look weak. Just human.

Owen stepped forward, but she held up a hand.

"I need to say this. Please."

He stopped, hands at his sides.

Brooke took a breath.

"He won't stop until he gets what he wants. Not with Linda. Not with me. This isn't about a list anymore, it's personal."

She lowered her voice.

"What if we gave him what he wants?"

Owen frowned. "What are you saying?"

"We know he wants the necklace. He wants me. So maybe... maybe we stop chasing. Maybe we let him come to me."

Owen's expression hardened. "No."

"Just hear me out."

"No, Brooke. You're not bait."

"I already am," she snapped.
"Every time I step outside, I feel him watching. Every knock on the door, every unknown number, it's him in my head."

He stepped closer now, close enough to touch her, but didn't.

"I get it," he said quietly. "I really do. But I'm not putting you in front of him. Not like that."

He wished he believed that. But the idea of losing her, now, after everything—that fear was real.

There was a long silence between them. Her eyes flicked toward the floor. When she spoke again, her voice was softer.

"I hate feeling helpless."

"You're not."

"But I feel it."

He reached forward, finally touching her hand.

"Then we do this together. We take him down, but not like this."

Brooke looked up at him, eyes shining with something between fear and fire.

"I'm scared, Owen."

Her fingers trembled again.

He nodded. "Me too."

They stood there quietly, while the world outside kept turning.

But something between them had shifted.
And it wouldn't shift back.

Back in the office. Owen was keeping a close eye on Brooke. He hadn't known her long, but this, this was new for him. All of it.

"Jesus, Owen," Brooke said, not looking up from her desk. "I can feel your eyes on me."

"Sorry," he muttered. "I just... I can't lose another love. Not now."

Brooke turned to him slowly. She could see it in his face—sadness, years deep.

"You've never really spoken about your loss."

"Well," he said, rubbing his hands together, "short version: we were together a while. Not married. We wanted kids. And she died in childbirth. I sold up after that. Moved into that lovely flat of mine."

For the first time in a while, Brooke let out a soft laugh.

"I'm sorry, Owen. I don't mean to laugh—and I'm sorry for your loss—but that flat... we'll talk about that another time."

Owen smiled. He hadn't meant to make her laugh. But he was glad he did.

"When this is over," she added, "I'm dragging you to IKEA."

He looked at her. "Are you offering to decorate?"

"No," she said, cracking a small smile. "I'm offering to fix your taste."

Chapter 69

They arrived at the next hideout, but this one wasn't rented or borrowed. This was his. Every last brick.

It sat quietly on the outskirts of Addlestone, near Chertsey. There were other houses nearby, but far enough away. As he turned into the long drive, he pressed a button on his keyring. The automatic garage door opened.

No one saw him drive inside. The door closed quietly behind him as the lights flicked on.

He stepped inside, drew every curtain closed, and locked the doors. Then he went back to the car and opened the boot.

Linda hadn't moved. The duct tape had done its job.

He carried her upstairs and into a bedroom. He chained her to the bathroom pipes and laid her across the bed. She looked up at him through wide, scared eyes. This wasn't the Blue she'd tried to survive. This one was colder.

"Right, Linda. Listen real good, and I'm only going to say this once." His voice was low but firm. "This is my home. Nothing's changed between us. I'm going to remove the tape. Then you're going to shower and clean yourself up. Blink if you understand."

Linda blinked rapidly.

He wasn't gentle. He pulled the tape away, dragging her body with it. She winced and whimpered but said nothing. When it was done, she tried to stand, but her legs were numb from being tied.

"I'm going to wait right here," he said. "Leave the bathroom door open."

"Yes, Blue."

She felt a different kind of fear now—sharper, more personal. The distance between them was gone. No cellar, no barrier. Just her and him.

As she crossed the room, she noticed how normal it all looked. Clean carpet. Fresh sheets. A room that smelled of laundry detergent and air freshener.

Everything smelled clean—except her.

She didn't want to upset him. She didn't want to test how far this version of Blue would go. She showered quickly and felt the smallest relief. When she stepped back into the bedroom, he was standing there with his trousers around his ankles.

She didn't wait to be told.

She dropped to her knees and made him happy.

"Thank you, Linda," he said when it was over. "I needed that."

He pulled up his trousers and began pacing.

"Now, rules. You wear this at all times when we're downstairs. If someone knocks on the door, you say nothing. If you scream, if you try to warn them, they die first. You'll be chained to the bed at night, and to the pipes during the day. When I go out, you'll be gagged and locked in the cellar. Understand?"

She nodded.

"Good. Let's go downstairs. I'll make us something to eat."

Linda sat near the radiator; her chain wrapped around the pipe. They ate in silence. The food was warm, but she barely tasted it.

Afterward, he just sat at the table, staring at the wood grain.

The red ribbon was gone.
The necklace, her necklace, was gone.
Rosie had taken it.

He slammed the table with both fists.

"She took it from me."

His voice was quiet, but sharp, grinding through clenched teeth like gravel.

Linda watched him, fiddling with the plastic spoon he'd given her. Her face was bruised. One eye nearly swollen shut. Her ribs ached beneath a long, plain dress.

She hadn't spoken much since they arrived. He hadn't wanted her dead. Not yet. But she was close, and she knew it.

One wrong word and she'd be next.

Slowly, she stood, crossed to him, and rubbed his shoulders gently. Then she sat again. He didn't react. He wasn't here anymore. Not really.

He rose and began pacing from window to window, twitching the curtain aside just enough to peek out. Every few minutes, over and over. It was a ritual now.

The paranoia hadn't started yesterday.

It had started years ago.

But it had grown teeth in the last twenty-four hours.

Rosie had escaped.
Now everyone was looking.
They'd find the house.
They'd find the list.
They'd know who was next.

He returned to the table and stared again at the blank surface.

The missing necklace haunted him.

She'd worn it every day.
Shawnnessy.

He could still see her in it. Still hear her voice. Still remember the last thing she said before—

He stopped the thought before it finished.

He pulled a burner phone from the drawer. Flipped it open. New SIM. No trace.

He typed a single word into the message bar:
Brooke

Then paused.

It was too soon.
But not by much.

He looked over at Linda. She was watching him, her face tight with pain. He walked over, lifted her chin. She flinched.

"Please..." she whispered.

He walked away, opened the fridge, took out an ice pack, and handed it to her.

"Here. This'll help your eye."

"Thank you, Blue. Is there anything I can do to help?" Her voice was soft, hesitant.

He didn't answer right away.

"I'm thinking," he said calmly.

She flinched anyway.

Then he reached into his pocket and pulled out a small notepad and pen.

"I'm going to write her a letter," he murmured. "A real one. From me to her."

Linda whimpered.

Blue smiled.

"I think she'll appreciate the personal touch."

Chapter 70

The whiteboard in the incident room was covered in scribbles, photos, arrows. Victims. Locations. Blue roses. But no clear shot of his face.

Two names stood out. Ryan Kingsley and Blue.
No trace of where he was now.

Owen stood staring at the board, arms folded, expression tight. Brooke sat a few feet away at her desk, absently scrolling through crime scene reports, though her mind was elsewhere. Her gaze kept drifting back to the envelope, the one with her name on it, written in that thick, deliberate scrawl.

"I don't like it," Owen said suddenly. "Even if we find him… what then? He's smart. He plans everything. If we hit the wrong place at the wrong time, we could lose Linda. Or worse."

"What do you mean, or worse? Me?"

"No. Brooke, I mean we lose Linda, and he gets away." He paused. "Brooke, are you sure you're okay to be here?"

Brooke ignored the comment.

"We need to think ahead," she said instead. "Plan for when, not if, we find him."

Owen glanced over. "We might need armed backup. Tactical support. We can't go in like we did at Duncan Street."

"You're right," Brooke said quietly. "We can't afford another mistake. And if he's watching us… if he knows I'm the last name..." She trailed off.

Owen turned toward her. "Don't even think about going off alone."

She gave a quick smile. "I'm not stupid."

But she didn't say she wouldn't.
She was already thinking ahead.
What she'd do if it came to that.
What she might risk, if no one else could stop him.

"Owen, has the sketch artist seen Rosie yet?"

"No, but, Brooke."

Before Owen could press her further, Patterson's voice cut across the room.
"DI Owen. DC Daniels. My office."

They exchanged a look. Owen sighed. "Here we go."

Patterson stood by the window in his office, arms crossed. He didn't sit. He looked like he hadn't slept, not just tired, but weighed down.

"I've reviewed everything. The letter. The photo. The pattern. And the fact that the killer directly addressed Daniels." He turned to face them.

"This, changes things. Daniels, you're no longer just a detective on this case. You're a target."

Brooke remained steady. "Sir, I understand the risk."

"I'm not sure you do. If this man has fixated on you, then we're walking a tightrope. This isn't just about finding him anymore. It's about preventing another abduction, or worse."

"Sir, as I said, I understand the risk. Owen's not letting me out of his sight. I'm not just another woman walking home at night. I'm a goddamned cop."

Patterson said nothing, but his look said it all.

Owen stepped forward. "With respect, sir, if you pull us now, you risk setting everything back. No one knows this case like we do. We've been living it."

Brooke added, "And if I am the target, pulling me out won't make him stop. He'll just change tactics. We need to be in this, so we can see him coming."

Patterson studied them both for a long moment. The silence stretched.

Then he moved back to his desk, eyes never leaving theirs.
"You stay on. For now. But if either of you push too far, or if it gets even a fraction more dangerous, I pull you both. End of story."

"Understood," Owen said.

Brooke gave a single nod. "Thank you, sir."

"And Brooke," Patterson added, "you may be a goddamned cop, and a bloody good one, but I don't want to see your body on a slab in the morgue. Now get out of here."

Outside the office, as they walked back toward their desks, Owen leaned in.
"Whatever you're thinking, don't."

Brooke's smile didn't reach her eyes. "Just planning. Same as you."

Owen turned and looked back at the board, then over his shoulder.
Yes, Brooke. But what are you planning?

Chapter 71

The new place was quieter.
Cleaner.
Less like a prison, more like a home, but only on the surface.

Linda had remained at the table. He hadn't spoken to her much since the move. Just pointed where to sit. Where to go. What not to touch.

After the meal he prepared, he cleared the plates, washed them, and left them to drain.

Blue moved through the kitchen with far calmer than before. No slamming fists. No snapping orders. He seemed in a world of his own, humming and unpacking with quiet purpose.

The shopping bags sat half-empty on the kitchen counter. Bread, tinned food, bottled water, bleach.

In the lounge, the curtains had already been drawn tight. Locks checked. No windows could be opened more than an inch.

No way out.
Not without him noticing.

There was something different about this place.
More settled.
Permanent.

She could feel it in the way he moved—the calm precision, the lack of urgency. Even when he told her what to do, it wasn't like a threat anymore.

It was worse. Soft, almost caring. Like she was meant to thank him for it.

He looked at her, still holding the ice pack against her bruised eye.
"How's the eye now?"

"Starting to feel much better, Blue. Thank you. Can I ask you something?"

"I guess."

"Well... you were very upset earlier. About a necklace. And you said... Shawnnessy. I was just wondering about it, that's all."

"Nothing for you to worry about."

He'd stopped pretending.

Brooke was seated in the office, going through the CCTV footage from the petrol station again and again. Nothing but a shadow passing the envelope.

Owen had stepped out for air.

But her mind wasn't in it.

She picked up the envelope and started toward the door just as Owen returned.

"Feel better?" she asked. "Bit of fresh air to clear the mind? I'm just going to log this. I don't want it sitting there, reminding me."

"Yeah, okay. Want company?"

"Owen, I'm okay. I'm not even leaving the building. Please stop."

Owen stood back and raised his hands like he was surrendering.

She moved quickly. Logged the envelope into the large evidence box with all the other items.

Then she saw what she'd really come for.

The necklace.
Gold chain. Small heart pendant. Red ribbon tied to the clasp.

Her fingers brushed the ribbon, and for a second, she hesitated. It felt warm, like it didn't belong in a box. Like it still carried weight. Like it was watching her.

A quick glance around the room. No one watching.

She slipped it into her pocket. Took a deep breath.

Then returned to her desk.

She'd seen it before.
She just hadn't realised the weight of it—back when Rosie described the keys she'd taken from the van.

Shawnnessy's.
His first love.
His first kill.
His first possession.

Brooke was remembering Rosie's words.
Rosie had taken it.
And now he wanted it back. Desperately.

It would hurt him.
And it might be the only thing powerful enough to draw him in again.

She knew it was madness.
She knew what it would mean.

But the idea was growing roots.

Trade me for Linda.

She could offer him what he wanted. The necklace. The final girl. The full circle.

She could put an end to this.

Owen would never agree.
No one would.

That's why she couldn't tell them.
Not yet.

Her only hope, if she even made it out alive, was that he'd come for her…
and they'd be ready.

Back at the house, Blue sat in the hallway, crouched over something. A small travel case.

From it, he pulled a bundle of items wrapped in cloth.
Keepsakes, each one carefully chosen.

April's.
A piece of her hair.
Sarah's locket.
A broken heel from a red shoe.
A scrap of faded pyjama cotton.

One by one, he laid them out.

Then, last of all, an empty slot.

The necklace.
Gone.

He stared at the space a moment longer than the rest.
Then slowly zipped the case shut.

He'd get it back.
And this time…
There would be no more running.

Chapter 72

Owen watched Brooke from across the room.
She was quieter than usual. Still working, still efficient, but something had shifted. Her eyes lingered too long on certain files. She looked over her shoulder more than once. And twice, he caught her with her hand in her coat pocket, fingers brushing against something she never showed him.

"All right?" he asked casually.

She looked up and nodded. "Fine."

But it was too quick. Too smooth.

He wanted to press, but the last time he'd questioned her like that, she'd shut down completely. So he let it go for now.

Still, something in his gut twisted.

She wasn't shutting him out like before.
She was disappearing, inch by inch, and he didn't know how to stop it.

An hour later, back in the incident room, Smithy burst through the door holding a sealed evidence bag and a sheet of lab results.

"You're going to want to see this."

He handed it to Owen. Brooke stood beside him as he scanned the contents.

"The debris recovered from the fire—burned photo fragments, partial documents. Lab ran a chemical test. Traces of DNA on what's left of the singed photo. Female."

"Who?" Owen asked.

"Unclear. Too degraded. But they also found something else. Bits of plastic and paper fused together. ID cards. Multiple. Some fake, some stolen. Two of the names match missing persons cases going back over a decade."

Brooke's eyes narrowed. "So, he kept trophies. Documents. Maybe even another list."

"We're working on reconstruction," Smithy said. "But it's clear now. That place in Ashford wasn't just a dump site. It was part of the whole system. A drop zone. A disposal pit. He's been doing this longer than we thought."

Owen stared at the charred evidence photo again, the fragments of IDs, the names partially burned away.

And in his mind, a face returned. A woman from three years ago, mid-thirties, vanished walking home from a train station. A file that never went anywhere. No press. No family pushing. Just gone.

Now he knew where she ended up.
And one more space on that list.
Brooke's.

He closed the file.

"Double the shift rota. We need eyes on every station, road camera, and traffic camera between Addlestone and Godalming. He's circling back. I can feel it."

He noticed Brooke on her phone, speaking quietly. Then he watched her get up and head into the ladies', still on the call.

"OK, I can talk now," she whispered.

"Hello, Brooke. So nice to finally talk to you."

"Hello, Ryan. Or should I call you Blue?"

"I like Blue. For now. I was going to write to you, actually. Something more personal. But this works too. Where's the boyfriend?"

"Outside in the office. I'm in the ladies. What do you want?"

"You know what I want, Brooke. You and the necklace."

"And what do I get?"

"Why, Linda, of course. She's lovely, but she's not you."

His voice was calm. Almost polite. That's what made it worse.

"And Brooke," he added, almost playfully, "that green coat you wore yesterday… very flattering. You always look good in green."

She froze.
That coat had never left the building.

She tried not to imagine what he'd do if it all went wrong.

"OK, Blue. But first, I want proof of life."

"Hmm. Do you now?"

She heard what sounded like a woman in the background. A scream. Then muffled crying.

"Now, Linda, tell Brooke who you are. And that you're OK."

More muffled sounds. Then:

"Ah… hmm… it's me. It's Linda. I'm OK. Please, he."

"There you are, Brooke. Happy?"

"Yes. I guess. When and where?"

"I shall ring you in the morning, Brooke. Sleep well."

Sleep well, you bastard, she thought.
Tomorrow, then.

She hung up and leaned against the sink, her knuckles white.

If this goes wrong, he'll kill me.
Quickly if I'm lucky. Slowly if I'm not.

But if it got Linda out… if it ended this…

Then maybe it was worth it.

Brooke returned to her desk.

"Brooke," Owen said. She nearly jumped.

"Yes, Owen?"

"Fancy stopping off for dinner on the way home?"

"Thanks, Owen. But not tonight. I want to spend some time on my own."

He didn't like it. Not with a killer still out there and her name on the list.
But she was already standing, already moving.
And he had placed the tracker in her coat the day before.
Just in case.

Rosie had been asked to return to the hospital for further checks. She was happy to do so—it had been nice visiting the police station, but most of all, it was the freedom.

She knew armed police were just outside, yet part of her was still worried.
He was still out there.

Rosie curled up beneath two blankets, like she was trying to hide.

She hadn't said much. Not since the last round of questioning.

The doctors said she was healing. Physically, at least. But the bruises were deep.
Not just on her skin.

When the nurse offered her a mirror earlier, she refused. When someone knocked too hard on a door down the corridor, she flinched and didn't stop shaking for nearly a minute.

But something in her had hardened too.
She wasn't done.

She'd escaped, yes, but not finished.

Rosie was tired. Nothing seemed to send her to sleep.

Then, a soft knock at the door.

From under the covers, she peeked out.
"Brooke? This is a surprise. Please, come in."

"Thank you, Rosie. I was surprised to hear you were back in hospital."

"To be honest, I just couldn't take all the fuss. Mum wouldn't leave me alone for a minute. Then her phone wouldn't stop. Press found her number. I just needed to escape. Again."

"Apart from that, how are you feeling?"

"Every time I shut my eyes, he's there. I wait for him to call me. To… to pleasure him. Please tell me there's good news. Have you found Linda?"

"Sadly, no. But that's why I'm here."

Rosie looked at her with a puzzled expression.

"Rosie, I need you to do something for me. And keep this between you and me."

"Hmm. OK…"

"I've had that feeling all day. He's close. I can feel it. He wants me. And this."

Brooke took out the gold necklace, still attached to the red ribbon.

Rosie shuddered just looking at it.

"Why do you have that, Brooke? What's going on?"

"Look… he wants me. And this. I think he'll offer up Linda in exchange."

She didn't say it was already arranged for the morning.

"What? Are you crazy?"

"Shh, Rosie. I know what I'm doing."

"Do you? You have no idea what he's capable of. One minute, he's sweet. Almost gentle. Then he beats you. Or rapes you. And acts like it never happened."

"Well… thank you. That's what I'm here for. To find out what he's really like."

"Brooke, trust me. He's not as stupid as he acts. He gets stronger somehow. When he was taking turns with me and Linda—he could just keep going. Like he didn't run out of energy."

"That helps, Rosie. Is there anything else you can tell me?"

"Yes. He'll make you think you're in control. You won't be. Don't give him the chance."

"Thank you, Rosie. Hopefully we'll have news on Linda soon. You rest up."

Brooke turned and left the room without looking back.

And if Brooke was going to walk into the lion's den… She'd play his game. Just long enough to win it.

Chapter 72 – Final Version (All Edits Applied)

Owen watched Brooke from across the room.
She was quieter than usual. Still working, still efficient, but something had shifted. Her eyes lingered too long on certain files. She looked over her shoulder more than once. And twice, he caught her with her hand in her coat pocket, fingers brushing against something she never showed him.

"All right?" he asked casually.

She looked up and nodded. "Fine."

But it was too quick. Too smooth.

He wanted to press, but the last time he'd questioned her like that, she'd shut down completely. So he let it go for now.

Still, something in his gut twisted.

She wasn't shutting him out like before.
She was disappearing, inch by inch, and he didn't know how to stop it.

An hour later, back in the incident room, Smithy burst through the door holding a sealed evidence bag and a sheet of lab results.

"You're going to want to see this."

He handed it to Owen. Brooke stood beside him as he scanned the contents.

"The debris recovered from the fire—burned photo fragments, partial documents. Lab ran a chemical test. Traces of DNA on what's left of the singed photo. Female."

"Who?" Owen asked.

"Unclear. Too degraded. But they also found something else. Bits of plastic and paper fused together. ID cards. Multiple. Some fake, some stolen. Two of the names match missing persons cases going back over a decade."

Brooke's eyes narrowed. "So he kept trophies. Documents. Maybe even another list."

"We're working on reconstruction," Smithy said. "But it's clear now. That place in Ashford wasn't just a dump site. It was part of the whole system. A drop zone. A disposal pit. He's been doing this longer than we thought."

Owen stared at the charred evidence photo again, the fragments of IDs, the names partially burned away.

And in his mind, a face returned. A woman from three years ago, mid-thirties, vanished walking home from a train station. A file that never went anywhere. No press. No family pushing. Just gone.

Now he knew where she ended up.
And one more space on that list.
Brooke's.

He closed the file.

"Double the shift rota. We need eyes on every station, road camera, and traffic camera between Addlestone and Godalming. He's circling back. I can feel it."

He noticed Brooke on her phone, speaking quietly. Then he watched her get up and head into the ladies', still on the call.

"OK, I can talk now," she whispered.

"Hello, Brooke. So nice to finally talk to you."

"Hello, Ryan. Or should I call you Blue?"

"I like Blue. For now. I was going to write to you, actually. Something more personal. But this works too. Where's the boyfriend?"

"Outside in the office. I'm in the ladies'. What do you want?"

"You know what I want, Brooke. You and the necklace."

"And what do I get?"

"Why, Linda, of course. She's lovely, but she's not you."

His voice was calm. Almost polite. That's what made it worse.

"And Brooke," he added, almost playfully, "that green coat you wore yesterday… very flattering. You always look good in green."

She froze.
That coat had never left the building.

She tried not to imagine what he'd do if it all went wrong.

"OK, Blue. But first—I want proof of life."

"Hmm. Do you now?"

She heard what sounded like a woman in the background. A scream. Then muffled crying.

"Now, Linda, tell Brooke who you are. And that you're OK."

More muffled sounds. Then:

"Ah… hmm… it's me. It's Linda. I'm OK. Please, he—"

"There you are, Brooke. Happy?"

"Yes. I guess. When and where?"

"I shall ring you in the morning, Brooke. Sleep well."

Sleep well, you bastard, she thought.
Tomorrow, then.

She hung up and leaned against the sink, her knuckles white.

If this goes wrong, he'll kill me.
Quickly if I'm lucky. Slowly if I'm not.

But if it got Linda out… if it ended this…

Then maybe it was worth it.

Brooke returned to her desk.

"Brooke," Owen said. She nearly jumped.

"Yes, Owen?"

"Fancy stopping off for dinner on the way home?"

"Thanks, Owen. But not tonight. I want to spend some time on my own."

He didn't like it. Not with a killer still out there and her name on the list.
But she was already standing, already moving.
And he had placed the tracker in her coat the day before. Just in case.

Rosie had been asked to return to the hospital for further checks. She was happy to do so—it had been nice visiting the police station, but most of all, it was the freedom.

She knew armed police were just outside, yet part of her was still worried.
He was still out there.

Rosie curled up beneath two blankets, like she was trying to hide.

She hadn't said much. Not since the last round of questioning.

The doctors said she was healing. Physically, at least. But the bruises were deep.
Not just on her skin.

When the nurse offered her a mirror earlier, she refused. When someone knocked too hard on a door down the corridor, she flinched and didn't stop shaking for nearly a minute.

But something in her had hardened too.
She wasn't done.

She'd escaped, yes, but not finished.

Rosie was tired. Nothing seemed to send her to sleep.

Then—a soft knock at the door.

From under the covers, she peeked out.
"Brooke? This is a surprise. Please, come in."

"Thank you, Rosie. I was surprised to hear you were back in hospital."

"To be honest, I just couldn't take all the fuss. Mum wouldn't leave me alone for a minute. Then her phone wouldn't stop. Press found her number. I just needed to escape. Again."

"Apart from that, how are you feeling?"

"Every time I shut my eyes, he's there. I wait for him to call me. To… to pleasure him. Please tell me there's good news. Have you found Linda?"

"Sadly, no. But that's why I'm here."

Rosie looked at her with a puzzled expression.

"Rosie, I need you to do something for me. And keep this between you and me."

"Hmm. OK…"

"I've had that feeling all day. He's close. I can feel it. He wants me. And this."

Brooke took out the gold necklace, still attached to the red ribbon.

Rosie shuddered just looking at it.

"Why do you have that, Brooke? What's going on?"

"Look… he wants me. And this. I think he'll offer up Linda in exchange."

She didn't say it was already arranged for the morning.

"What? Are you crazy?"

"Shh, Rosie. I know what I'm doing."

"Do you? You have no idea what he's capable of. One minute, he's sweet. Almost gentle. Then he beats you. Or rapes you. And acts like it never happened."

"Well… thank you. That's what I'm here for. To find out what he's really like."

"Brooke, trust me. He's not as stupid as he acts. He gets stronger somehow. When he was taking turns with me and Linda—he could just keep going. Like he didn't run out of energy."

"That helps, Rosie. Is there anything else you can tell me?"

"Yes. He'll make you think you're in control. You won't be. Don't give him the chance."

"Thank you, Rosie. Hopefully we'll have news on Linda soon. You rest up."

Brooke turned and left the room without looking back.

And if Brooke was going to walk into the lion's den… She'd play his game. Just long enough to win it.

Chapter 74

The morning air in the station felt thick, the kind of tension that brewed quietly before something snapped.

Owen poured himself a bitter coffee and made his way to the desks. Brooke was already there, typing. She gave him a small nod, eyes tired.

"How are you feeling?" he asked.

"Fine. Tired. You?"

"Same."

There was an awkward pause. He watched her for a beat too long.

"You sure everything's alright?"

Brooke hesitated. "Yeah. Just nerves, I guess."

Owen nodded, but didn't believe it.

A few minutes later, Brooke stood. "I'm heading to the ladies."

Owen checked his watch. "Alright. Don't be long."

She walked briskly down the corridor. Her phone buzzed in her coat pocket.

She glanced around before answering. "Yes?"

"Brooke," Blue said, his voice soft and composed. "It's time."

Her pulse spiked. "Where?"

"I'll text you the location. Be there in one hour. And come alone."

"Is Linda still alive?"

"For now. Let's keep it that way."

Then he hung up.

Brooke stopped outside the ladies', gripping the phone tightly. A second later, the address came through. A disused office complex, not far from Chertsey.

She slipped the phone back into her coat, walked into the toilets, and sat quietly in the stall.

Her fingers found the necklace in her pocket. This was it. Her choice. Her risk.

She stood, fixed her hair in the mirror, then slipped quietly out of the station—without another word to anyone.

Ten minutes passed. Then fifteen.

Owen looked at his watch again.

Something didn't feel right.

He walked over to her desk. Her scarf still lay draped across the back of her chair. Her coffee was half full.

He pulled out his phone and dialled her number.

It rang. Once. Twice.

Then straight to voicemail.

"Brooke, call me the second you get this."

He hung up. Something was wrong.

He opened the tracking app.

Her signal was moving, heading southwest, toward Addlestone and Chertsey.

"Damn it, Brooke," he muttered. "Why couldn't you just listen?"

Without hesitation, he grabbed his coat and his Glock, strapping it to his belt as he bolted down the corridor.

He didn't knock, he burst straight into Patterson's office.

"Sir, I believe Brooke's gone to meet him. I'm going after her. Smithy has her tracker. I need armed officers there now—and I need authorisation. I'm carrying."

Patterson stood, alarmed. "Owen, wait—"

But Owen was already out the door.

"Damn it, you two," Patterson muttered. "Just don't get yourselves killed."

"Pardon, sir?" one officer asked nearby.

"Nothing. Carry on."

Patterson turned, marched back into his office, and snatched up the phone.

Brooke pulled up outside the disused office complex. Derelict. Quiet. The wind moved broken leaves across the tarmac.

She scanned the area, twice. Nothing.

She double-checked the address, then waited, standing by the car with her hand in her coat pocket.

Her phone rang again.

"Hello, Brooke," Blue said smoothly. "You're looking nice in that brown jacket."

She didn't flinch. "Well, Blue, I'm here. Where are you?"

"Nearby. Now, just go around the barrier on your left and keep walking. And remember—I'm watching your every move."

"I gathered that," she said coolly. "I brought your necklace. Look."

She held it up, letting it glint in the light.

"Now, Brooke," his voice turned harder, "you be very careful with that."

"Don't worry," she said. "I didn't come this far to drop it now."

"Keep walking. Slowly."

Each step felt like a mile. Her eyes darted left and right—searching for any shadow, any glint of movement.

Owen pulled up just around the corner.

He could see her car—but not Brooke.

He pressed the radio.

"Control, this is DO2, reporting on scene."

"Copy, DO2. You are received. Be advised: firearms team en route. Do not engage until—"

"Sorry, control, you're breaking up."

He ended the call.

Checked his gun.

A Glock 17—9mm semi-automatic. Reliable. Cleaned that morning.

He was a good shot.

But he'd never fired it at a person.

Not yet.

And especially not to save someone he couldn't afford to lose.

Chapter 75

The building smelled of damp plaster and old dust.

Every step Brooke took echoed faintly, her boots soft against the broken concrete. Somewhere overhead, a bird flapped in the rafters. Her hand stayed near her coat pocket, fingers brushing the edge of the necklace.

She passed rusted lockers, old office chairs tipped over, file cabinets without drawers. She kept walking.

"Good girl," came Blue's voice again—this time from a speaker hidden somewhere nearby.

"You always did follow instructions well."

"I came alone," she said firmly. "Just like you asked."

"That's one of the many things I admire about you, Brooke. You're loyal. Smart. Brave. You remind me of someone I used to know."

Her eyes scanned the ceiling. "Shawnnessy?"

A pause.

Then a low, thoughtful hum.

"So, you do know. Officer Bailey's been busy."

Brooke frowned. How did he know that name?

"She was locked away. Alone. Forgotten. She didn't belong in that place."

A pause followed, heavier this time.

"Your father put her there. You… you are his legacy."

Brooke's breath caught in her throat. Her father? The idea twisted inside her like broken glass. He had been strict, yes. Distant. But this? Could it be true? Or just another one of Blue's manipulations?

"She was ill," she said quietly. "She needed help."

"She needed understanding."

His voice dropped an octave. "I loved her."

"She was your cousin. And she never loved you—she loved your uncle, David. That's why you killed him."

"Shut up. Just shut up. He deserved to die. He took her from me. He had all the others, why did he want her?"

"So, tell me. Why the tattoos? I know you were going to spell out her name."

"Her. She has a name."

"Fine. Shawnnessy. Why the blue rose?"

"Why? Because she loved them."

Brooke clenched the necklace in her hand. "You killed her."

"That wasn't love, was it?"

Silence.

Then, another voice. Weak. Trembling.

"Brooke…"

Brooke froze.

She turned sharply toward the sound and spotted a shape in the shadows—one hand chained to a radiator. Eyes wide. Pale. Weak.

"Linda," she whispered.

Linda nodded, just barely. Her mouth was gagged, but the relief in her eyes was unmistakable.

"I kept her alive just for you," Blue said. "A gift. One last exchange before we begin."

Brooke raised the necklace. "I brought it. Like you wanted."

There was a soft click from behind one of the doors. Then footsteps. Measured. Calm.

Blue stepped out.

His hair was tied back neatly. His face calm, eyes bright. He wore black, everything fitted like he'd planned the look.

In his hand was a knife. Nothing fancy. Just practical.

"I'm glad you came," he said softly.

"I didn't come for you," Brooke said. "I came for her."

He glanced at Linda, then back at Brooke. "You always did have a hero streak."

Owen was just outside.

He moved through the side entrance, careful not to make noise. The GPS signal had narrowed it down to this wing. He heard faint voices. Female. Then male.

He pulled the gun from his holster. His hands were steady. His heartbeat wasn't.

Inside, Blue stepped closer to Brooke.

"You know why I chose you now, don't you?"

"Because of my father."

"Yes... and no. You were the last piece. The right kind of smart. The right kind of loyal. You understand pain, don't you? Not like the others. You would've made a good partner. Better than Linda. Better than April. Even better than Rosie."

Brooke could feel sweat running down her face. "You don't know anything about me."

"I know what you dream about. I've been in your flat. I've watched you sleep."

She didn't flinch. "And that's why you're going to die."

His smile widened.

"You sound so sure."

"I am."

Behind him, a faint sound, a scuff of movement. Blue turned slightly, eyes narrowing.

Owen was there.

"Let her go," Owen said, gun raised. "Now."

Chapter 76

The room was silent, except for the steady hum of the generator outside and the faint rasp of Blue's breathing. A single bare bulb swung slightly above, casting long shadows across the concrete walls.

Brooke stood still. Her palms were damp, her heart thudding too loud in her ears.

Across from her, Blue held the knife low, not lunging. Not yet.

Behind him, Linda lay slumped against the radiator, breathing, barely conscious. But alive. Her eyes flicked between Blue and Brooke, full of fear.

Owen was close now. Gun raised. Steady.

"Let her go," Owen said, voice low and lethal.

Blue laughed under his breath. "You're always so direct, Inspector. But she doesn't want to leave. Not really. Not now that she knows."

Brooke frowned. "Knows what?"

Blue's smile twitched. It wasn't gloating. It was bitter. Poisonous.

"Your father," he said. "You ever wonder why he spent so much time at Pinetrees? All those visits. All those smiles. You thought he was helping her?"

Brooke's stomach flipped.

"You're lying."

"I was there, Brooke. I saw them. He used to sit in the staff room with her. Touch her hair. Make promises. He didn't protect her. He groomed her. Like the others. Like my uncle. Like Kingsley. He was one of them."

"No." Her voice cracked. Her knees felt weak. Her father? She tried to hold the thought together, but it shattered instantly. This couldn't be true. He wasn't like them. He couldn't be.

"He loved her, didn't he? Just like I did. But he had power. A badge. So no one questioned it. And when she told him to stop, he threatened to have her transferred. To a far worse place."

Brooke's throat went dry. Her legs trembled, barely keeping her upright.

Owen stepped closer. "That's enough."

But Blue was watching Brooke now, feeding off the break in her expression. He moved toward Linda, who tried to shrink away.

"Now, Brooke. Come closer. Untie her. And take her place."

Brooke shook her head, but her hands trembled.

She saw it. How Blue shifted the blade, fingers tightening.

Owen saw it too.

Brooke took a step forward. Then another.

She didn't look back at Owen, just kept her eyes on Blue.

When she reached Linda, she froze.

"Now, Brooke. Take off your jacket. Throw it over there. I want to be sure you're not armed, like your boyfriend."

She slowly removed it, avoiding any sudden movements, trying to figure out how this was going to go.

"Good girl. Now untie her."

Brooke bent down, still not taking her eyes off him, until she was level with Linda. Without saying a word, she quickly released the hand that held Linda prisoner.

Before she had the chance to move, he grabbed her, yanking her upright and pulling her close. The blade pressed against her throat.

"Back off, Inspector, or I'll cut her open right here."

He kissed Brooke on the cheek.

"She does taste good."

"Blue, I'm warning you. Put the knife down. Let's talk."

"Talk about what?" Blue hissed.

"You got what you wanted. Brooke. Brooke got Linda back. You've even got the necklace. It's over."

Owen was watching his every move. He couldn't get a clean shot, not without risking Brooke.

"Blue, please. Put the knife down."

Blue just laughed and moved the blade slightly, showing Owen exactly what he could do to her.

Crack.

The shot exploded like thunder.

Blue jerked sideways, the knife clattering from his hand as blood bloomed from his upper arm. He snarled and lunged forward, grabbing Brooke again, trying to pull her in front of him as a shield.

"Get off me," she screamed, struggling hard as he reached for the fallen knife.

She broke free.

But he didn't see her.

Linda.

She had dragged herself across the floor, one hand clutching her side, the other stretched toward the knife.

Just as his fingers wrapped around the handle—

Linda struck.

She plunged it into his chest.

His whole body jerked.

His eyes found hers, wide, stunned, almost childlike for a second.

He staggered back, choking on his breath, crimson bubbling from his mouth.

"You..." he whispered.

Linda didn't say a word.

Blue dropped to his knees, then crumpled face-down to the floor.

Silence.

Only Linda's broken breathing and Brooke's gasp as Owen pulled her into his arms.

"It's over," Owen said, barely believing it himself.

Linda slumped back, the last of her strength gone. Brooke rushed to her, catching her before she hit the floor.

"It's okay," Brooke whispered. "You did it. You're safe now."

Linda nodded weakly, tears tracking down her dirt-streaked face.

"Shawnnessy," she murmured. "For her."

Owen lowered his gun.

Brooke looked at the body.

Still. Silent.

After everything, it ended like this.

The monster was dead.

But the scars he'd carved, on them all, would take far longer to fade.

Chapter 77

Blue's body lay motionless, face-down in a pool of blood.

The silence that followed wasn't peaceful. It was hollow, echoing, like a bell after a funeral.

Owen knelt beside Linda, checking her pulse. Weak, but there.

Brooke crouched with them; her hands blood-stained but steady as she pressed gauze from Blue's own kit against Linda's wound. It wasn't deep, thankfully. Just a gash, probably from the rough treatment he'd put her through. From what Brooke could tell, he must have thrown her against the radiator. A sharp edge, maybe a bracket, had caught her side.

Sirens wailed in the distance, growing louder.

Then: tyres screeched. Doors slammed. Boots pounded the ground.

"Armed Police!" someone shouted.

Seconds later, officers swept into the room, weapons raised and scanning.

"Clear! Suspect down!" a voice called.

"Two females, injured. One officer on scene."

Owen stood, lifting his hands.

"I'm DI Owen. Weapon discharged. Suspect is deceased. These women need medical attention, now."

A paramedic team pushed through, dropping immediately to Linda. Another gently guided Brooke aside.

"You're hurt too," one said, examining her quickly.

"I'm fine," she murmured, though her eyes were glazed and distant.

An officer stepped up to Owen.

"Sir, we'll need your firearm."

Owen nodded silently. He unholstered the weapon, ejected the magazine, cleared the chamber, and handed it over grip-first.

"One shot fired," he said.

"Thank you, sir. You understand the shots fired protocol, you'll be debriefed later," the officer replied, bagging the weapon.

Owen barely nodded. His eyes were locked on Brooke, who stood nearby, her jacket abandoned on the floor. One hand was still clenched around the necklace.

She hadn't let it go.

Brooke looked at him, tears sliding silently down her cheeks.

Owen crossed to her and pulled her into a gentle hug.

"It's over," he whispered.

Brooke paused, then gently pulled back, her expression tight but clear.

She reached into her trouser pocket.

"Here, Owen," she said softly. "You can give these back to Smithy."

She dropped two small tracking devices into his open palm.

Owen blinked. "You knew?"

A small smile tugged at her lips.

"Owen, I was counting on it."

Later – St Peter's Hospital

The corridors were quiet, the fluorescent lights humming faintly overhead.

Brooke sat beside Rosie's bed. She looked stronger than before, still bruised, still thin—but there was life in her now. Her eyes met Brooke's, both haunted and clear.

"She really killed him?" Rosie asked softly.

Brooke nodded. "Linda did it. Right at the end."

Rosie looked down at the hospital blanket, fingers twisting the edge. "Good."

A nurse poked her head in. "She's awake. Would you like to come through now?"

Brooke stood. "Come on," she said to Rosie.

They walked together down the corridor. The room was bright, sterile, filled with the soft beeping of monitors.

Linda was sitting up slightly, bandaged, pale, but conscious.

When Rosie stepped into the room, Linda's face crumpled.

"Rosie?"

Tears flooded Rosie's eyes. "Linda."

No words after that, just Rosie rushing forward, careful not to hurt her as she folded into her arms.

They held each other like sisters pulled from a nightmare.

Brooke stood back; her throat tight. Owen moved to her side.

"They made it," she whispered.

Owen nodded slowly. "Because of you."

Brooke didn't answer. She wasn't sure if that was true.

But for now, the monster was dead.

And two of his victims were alive.

Chapter 78

Two days later, the meeting room was small, windowless, and smelled of old paper and cold coffee.

Patterson sat behind the table, arms crossed, face unreadable. Two internal affairs officers flanked him, though they said little.

Brooke sat to the left of Owen, her hands folded tightly in her lap. She hadn't spoken much since the hospital.

"You're both lucky," Patterson said at last. "This could've gone very differently."

"Yes, sir," Owen replied.

"You broke protocol. Both of you. You kept this off the books. You didn't involve tactical. Daniels, you used yourself as bait without authorisation."

Brooke didn't flinch.

"But…" Patterson's gaze softened, just slightly, "…you stopped him. And because of you, both women are alive."

He paused, then added, "That matters."

The two internal affairs officers exchanged a glance, then nodded at Patterson. They said nothing.

No reprimand came. No commendation either. Just a nod, and a tired dismissal.

"Now, both of you, get out of here. You've got a week's leave. And Brooke, if you need more, say so. Oh, and one more thing: you'll both be expected to attend counselling before returning to full duty. No arguments."

"Thank you, sir," Owen said. No questions. No argument.

"Thank you, sir. I'll let you know," Brooke added.

As they passed Patterson and headed for the door, he spoke again—softer this time.

"Well done. Both of you."

Outside, the early evening light had turned golden. The kind of light that made things look cleaner than they were.

"You okay to get home?" Owen asked.

Brooke hesitated, then nodded. "Yeah. I'm fine. But… aren't you coming?"

"There's no place I'd rather be than with you."

He smiled, but didn't move.

Instead, he said, "There's someone I want to speak to. Someone who might know about your dad."

Brooke blinked. "What do you mean?"

"Officer Bailey did some more digging," Owen explained. "She found someone who remembers your father well."

"She remembers Pinetrees? Shawnnessy?"

"Yes. She worked there, back then. A cleaner. She's retired now, living in a care home. She might remember names. Patterns. I didn't want to mention it until…"

"Until it was over," Brooke finished.

He nodded. "She's willing to talk. Would you want to come?"

Brooke was quiet for a moment. Then: "No. I think I need to do this on my own."

"I understand," Owen said gently. "But I'm still driving you. No argument."

Brooke managed a small smile. "Okay. No argument."

The engine hummed softly as they pulled out of the station car park.

For a while, neither of them spoke. The silence between them wasn't awkward, just heavy. Full of everything that had happened, and everything still left unsaid.

Streetlights flickered across the windscreen, their glow casting brief golden lines across Owen's tired face. One hand rested loosely on the wheel, but his knuckles were pale from the grip.

Brooke stared out the window, watching the world blur by.

Her other hand sat in her lap, fingers curled protectively around something small and metallic.

Owen glanced over.

"You've still got it?" he asked softly.

She looked down, then opened her hand slightly, the necklace glinting faintly in the light.

"Yeah," she said. "I'm not sure why. I keep thinking I'll hand it in. Or give it to someone. But…"

"But you haven't," Owen said, not accusing, just observing.

Brooke nodded. "It's like… I can't let it go. Not yet. Not until I know for sure what it meant. Who he really was."

Owen's voice lowered. "Your dad."

She nodded again, eyes fixed on the pendant.

"I just… I need to know who he really was. The man I thought he was—it feels like he's gone. And if Blue was telling the truth…"

"You don't have to carry that alone," Owen said. "And Blue wasn't interested in the truth. He just wanted to break you."

Brooke was quiet for a moment, then said, "Maybe. But part of me still needs to know. For my own peace."

Owen nodded. "Then we find out. One piece at a time."

Brooke hesitated. "Owen… how did Blue even know about Officer Bailey?"

He exhaled. "Tech's looking into it now, but we think he might've bugged the station—or tapped the phones. He said he watched you sleep. We don't know how long he was listening."

She shivered. "Jesus."

He looked over at her. "Whatever's left, we'll clean it up. I promise."

For the first time all day, she looked at him properly, eyes tired but clear.

"Thank you," she said softly.

He gave a small nod, returning his focus to the road.

The rest of the journey passed in silence, but this time, it was a quieter, calmer kind of silence.

One that didn't feel like the end.

They arrived at the care home just after five.

Owen followed Brooke inside but stopped at reception.

"Brooke, the woman you're looking for is Margaret Smyth," he said gently.

Brooke nodded, her face pale. She felt sick, not like she had facing Blue, but sick with uncertainty.

What if it was true?

What would that mean for everything she believed about her father?

She approached the front desk, and a staff member greeted her with a wary look. Brooke flashed her badge. The tone changed immediately.

The care home smelled of lavender polish and warm toast. Peaceful. Almost too peaceful.

Near the window sat a woman in her seventies, her grey hair pinned up, her eyes sharp behind thick lenses.

Brooke walked over.

The woman looked up and smiled wide. "I know who you are. You're old Pete Daniels's daughter. I can see it in your face, those eyes. It's almost like looking at him."

Brooke froze. Her breath caught. Tears welled before she could stop them.

She leaned forward and hugged the older woman.

"Are you all right, my love? You look very upset."

"Yes, Margaret. But I need to ask you some questions. About my father—and about Shawnnessy."

Margaret's eyes softened, her smile fading.

"Wow. That's a name I haven't heard in a long, long time. What can I help you with?"

Brooke sat beside her and told her everything.

What Blue had said. What she feared.

When she finished, Margaret was quiet. Her hands shook slightly in her lap.

"No, no, dear. You've got it all wrong. I don't know who told you that, but it's not true," she said firmly. "Your father was a good man."

Brooke stared at her.

"He used to visit Shawnnessy. And a few of the others. He'd sit with them for hours, bring them things—small gifts he paid for himself. He cared."

"Was Shawnnessy confused?" Brooke asked gently.

Margaret nodded. "Yes. She had her struggles. But she was beautiful. And there were others who took advantage of that. The manager, David, somebody, and a young man named Ryan. A nasty little bugger. Killed David, you know. Knocked him down the stairs. All hushed up."

Brooke's pulse quickened. "What did my father have to do with that?"

"Well… before any of that happened, he told me Shawnnessy was being forced to sleep with David. She didn't want to. And your dad, being the man he was, confronted him."

"And what happened?"

"The management got involved. Your dad reported it to his sergeant. But when they questioned Shawnnessy, she denied everything. Wouldn't say a word. After that, Pete was banned from coming here. Just like that."

When Brooke returned to the car, her face was unreadable.

Owen stood up. "Did she say anything?" he asked gently.

Brooke looked away, toward the fading sun bleeding across the sky.

"She remembered him," she said. "Said he was always kind. Polite. Brought the girls gifts. One time, she saw him arguing with a supervisor about Shawnnessy. He wasn't hurting her. He was trying to protect her."

Owen stepped closer. "So Blue lied?"

Brooke turned to him, eyes shining. "I think… Blue believed what he wanted to believe. He saw my father sitting with her. Talking. Laughing. And in his twisted mind, he made it something ugly."

"Maybe he was guilty of being too kind," she added. "Of trying to help someone when the system wouldn't."

They stood in silence for a long moment.

Then Brooke took a deep breath, the kind that cleared more than just lungs.

Owen reached out, concerned. "You, okay? Need a hug?"

With tears finally spilling down her cheeks, she stepped forward, into his arms.

"Owen… I have something to tell you."

He froze, heart skipping.

"What's that, Brooke?"

"I love you."

Owen exhaled slowly, relief flooding him.

"I love you too."

They kissed. Slow, deep, real.

And when they held each other this time, they didn't let go.

One Week Later

Linda and Rosie were recovering. Slowly. Together.

They would need help, counselling, time. But they had each other.

The press had their story. The town had its relief.

The name Blue Rose Killer would fade from the headlines in time.

But not from their lives. Not fully.

Some things never go away.

But healing had begun.

And sometimes, survival was the quietest form of victory.

Printed in Dunstable, United Kingdom